MARIETTA'S
GIFT

Marietta's Gift

Published by The Conrad Press Ltd. in the United Kingdom 2022

Tel: +44(0)1227 472 874
www.theconradpress.com
info@theconradpress.com

ISBN 978-1-915494-07-8

Printed and bound in Great Britain by Clays Ltd, Elcograf S.p.A

Typesetting and cover design by The Book Typesetters
www.thebooktypesetters.com

The Conrad Press logo was designed by Maria Priestley

Author photograph by Joe Calo

The image for Book Two (p. 119), 'Vis en schelp in het water' by Leo Gestel (1891–1941), is reproduced courtesy of Rijks Museum (www.rijksmuseum.nl).

Marietta's Gift

PHILIP PLATTS

For my mother, Gladys, who inspired
my language journey.

And for Yvonne Bezerra de Mello, who saved the lives of
so many children from the Candelária Massacre in Rio de
Janeiro on 23rd July 1993.

If thou art rich, thou'rt poor;
For, like an ass whose back with ingots bows,
Thou bear'st thy riches but a journey,
And death unloads thee. Friend hast thou none.

William Shakespeare, Duke Vicentio, from
Measure for Measure

While with an eye made quiet by the power
Of harmony, and the deep power of joy,
We see into the life of things.

William Wordsworth, from *Tintern Abbey*

BOOK ONE

1

Monday had begun with a funeral and had continued to go downhill all day.

Hugo Whiting leaned forward and rubbed a viewing hole in the mist on the window. They had come to another halt behind a kaleidoscope of red tail lamps and, as the taxi crawled along, he peered out at the watery figures battling to hold on to umbrellas or covering their heads with newspapers or briefcases.

When the taxi passed under a bridge, Hugo caught his reflection in the window. He'd always had rugged features, with what someone had once intriguingly called 'boarding school hair', thick and sandy, even if it was now being gradually taken over by streaks of grey. Lately, though, he was developing bags under his eyes which he thought looked like soggy pasta shells. He shook his head and dropped back into his seat.

With his eyes closed it didn't take long for the images to return. White faces, rendered stark against dark coats and hats, lined up in an undulating row along the edge of the grave. Hugo's gaze had been drawn time and again to the small woman around whom the family had huddled.

Dressed in a long black coat which fitted tightly around her and which sported two vertical rows of gold-coloured buttons, she'd reminded him of a military general. What was not in doubt was that it had been at her direction that the man inside the coffin being lowered into the ground would spend his eternity four hundred miles north of the matrimonial home.

Had he not died, the woman's husband might well have found himself in trouble, because two days earlier he'd collapsed in a heap on the marble floor of a West End jeweller, just as he was about to spend a great deal of money on a necklace. Inconveniently, and not only for the jewellers, since the woman for whom he was buying the necklace and who was at his side at the time was not the one he was married to.

Hugo had once read something about people not being like snow or autumn leaves: they do not look beautiful when they fall. He thought his now-former client, a strategist who was probably still working out how to deal with being dead, would probably have appreciated that irony.

Since the tradition of the family's faith demanded that the deceased be laid to rest with all possible haste, Hugo had dutifully travelled to Scotland at short notice. And as he'd stood shivering on the rutted clumps of icy soil, his thoughts had drifted back to the last time he'd been at a funeral. Five years ago, or was it yesterday?

The rain had given way to hail, which sounded like buckets of gravel being tipped on the roof. Glancing at his watch,

Hugo groaned. Almost five-thirty. The crowd from the office would already be over at the wine bar. That's if they hadn't been there all afternoon, given they'd just learned the amount of their year-end bonuses.

Not for the first time, he knew he'd be glad of their company.

The elderly man rested a finger on Hugo's arm as he waved an empty wine bottle at the waiter serving a nearby table. When the waiter finished unloading his tray, he walked away without troubling to look over.

Edwin Trevelyan, Hugo's Eton-educated partner, thumped the bottle back down. 'Damn the man!' He stabbed a finger at the waiter's retreating form. 'Do you know what they'll put on that fellow's gravestone when he dies?' With his finger and thumb, he drew an imaginary epitaph in the air. 'God... finally... caught... his... eye.' Shaking his head, he turned back to Hugo. 'That reminds me, tell me about the funeral. How did it go?'

Hugo took a deep breath, exhaling as he spoke. 'Painful. I just kept thinking about Sarah.'

Trevelyan tightened his lips and nodded slowly. 'That's understandable. Remind me, old fellow, how long has it been now?'

'Just over five years.'

'And there's been no one since then?'

Hugo shook his head. 'Nothing that's lasted long.'

Trevelyan pulled a face. 'I have to say I don't really understand that. You're very popular with people in the office and I'd go so far as to say you're the proverbial life-

and-soul at dinner parties. Look at you; tall, in good shape, plenty of money. You'd be a good catch for some lucky woman.'

Hugo smiled. 'Well, the short answer to that is I haven't met anyone yet who'll put up with me long enough to find out, Ed. And I certainly don't feel like the life-and-soul of anyone's party right now.'

Trevelyan tutted. 'Dear boy, you've just come back from a funeral, you'll soon be back to your usual chirpy self. You know, though, in all these years I've never asked, so forgive me, was it a conscious decision you and Sarah made, not to have children?'

'No, Ed, just the opposite.' Hugo sighed. 'Both of us would have loved to have had kids. But Sarah had two miscarriages and after that it just never happened.'

'That's very sad, I didn't know that.'

'No, they happened very early on, before we'd even told anyone she was pregnant.'

Trevelyan frowned. 'But you're hardly very old, Hugo. Not compared to me anyway, and I've still got plenty of lead in my pencil. Maybe you need to start doing something about it, get yourself out a bit more.' He tapped Hugo on the knee and pointed. 'Ah, look, our friend has finally condescended to serve us. Got time for another bottle?'

Hugo shook his head. 'Thanks, but I need to get back to the office. I've got a conference to attend in the States this weekend and I've a pile of stuff to do before then, my big charity clients have a whole deputation going. Which reminds me, I'm planning to take an extra few days afterwards. I'm going to explore the Napa Valley and watch them bring in the wine harvest.'

'Oh, what fun!' Trevelyan exclaimed. He knitted his bushy eyebrows. 'But do think about what I've said, Hugo. You're far too young to be put out to pasture.'

Hugo gestured at the noisy group of young hopefuls on the far side of the table. 'Right now I feel positively ancient, Ed.' He stood and pulled his coat from the hook on the wall. 'See you in a couple of weeks.'

Hugo had removed his jacket and was spreading his arms in silent appeal when he heard the tinkling of china.

'Now don't start stressing, it's not as bad as it looks.' Laura Evans, Hugo's assistant, set the cup and saucer in front of him.

He sat down. 'I've got a stack of receipts. I think expenses must be the only situation in the world where you're forced to lend someone else your money, then told you can't have it back till you produce all the paperwork and fill in a load of forms.'

Laura smiled and shook her head.

'You have mentioned that once or twice before. I'll sort it all out while you're away.' She pointed to a folder on his desk. 'Everything's in there. Airline tickets, conference summary, hotel reservation.'

'Thanks.' Hugo sipped at the tea. 'I have to say, it feels a bit weird going to this conference.'

Laura cocked her head to one side. 'Why's that?'

'Well, it's just that those people are doing the exact opposite of what I do. Giving up their lives for others.

15

Most of them work for next to nothing.'

She shrugged. 'Even charities need someone to look after their money.'

Hugo grinned. 'And here I am to do it, the knight in shining armour. Forsaking all the comforts of life to bring prosperity to my poor clients. Did you book me first class or business?'

Laura chuckled and stood up, nodding at the folder in front of him. 'Just don't forget that, or you won't be going any class. And Hugo, do try and enjoy it. You're actually going to be in the same room as an Oscar-winning movie star. You might even get to meet her.'

2

The dark-haired woman was perched behind an enormous crescent-shaped reception desk. She was wearing a starched white blouse and a blue jacket, one lapel of which sported a bright green and turquoise peacock brooch, while a badge on the other announced her as 'Nancy'. There was something written in smaller letters underneath, though given where the badge was pinned Hugo decided he'd avoid looking too closely.

'Welcome to San Francisco, sir.' Nancy smiled and tapped a few keys on her keyboard. The smile quickly disappeared. 'Ah, yes, Mr Whiting.'

As she swivelled back, she kept her eyes on the screen at the side of her for as long as she could, before looking directly at him over the top of her horn-rimmed spectacles. 'Sir, I just need to clarify something with you? Can I please understand a little more about your dietary concerns?'

Hugo gave a quick shake of his head. 'I'm sorry. I don't know what you mean. I haven't got any dietary concerns.'

Nancy's attempt to suppress a sigh wasn't completely successful. She rotated her computer monitor towards him and, with the eraser end of her pencil, tapped on the screen.

'It says here,' she began reading each word with what Hugo thought was excessive precision, 'you're, quote, "semi-vegetarian – doesn't eat animals that eat other animals"?' She looked up at him. 'Could you please help me with that? What precisely is it you won't eat?'

Hugo knitted his eyebrows together. 'Oh dear, that was just a little joke with one of my HR people when he was filling out the booking. I didn't think he'd take it seriously.' He allowed himself a smile, but Nancy was clearly in no mood for it. She rested the pencil she'd been brandishing on the desk and replaced it with a scowl.

'Mr Whiting, I wonder if you're aware? There are over a thousand people attending this conference? We're trying to reach out to everyone's different requirements? It really isn't helpful if you populate your personal profile with misleading information.'

Hugo sensed that with the disappearance of the question mark on the final sentence, matters were getting serious.

Nancy rubbed the back of her neck and gave a look of despair, before sweeping her gaze across the expansive surface of her desk in search of his conference pack. She slid it towards him with the tips of her elegantly manicured fingernails.

'Now, would you like me to update your preferences?'

As she cocked her head to one side, her brooch caught the light and the peacock winked at him.

The army of red-jacketed servers had disappeared through the doors at the side of the vast ballroom as quickly as they'd appeared an hour and a half earlier, like a vaporised genie sucked back into its brass lantern. Some of them were now holding doors open, just enough to peek through.

As the woman spoke, Hugo began to realize just how little attention he'd paid to the conference blurb and to Laura's excitement. This was no minor celebrity. This was Hollywood A list.

'UNICEF estimates there are now a hundred million people under eighteen living on the streets of various countries around the world. As you can imagine, it's not long before many of these kids fall into the hands of people traffickers. As you'd expect, "thrown away children"' – Hugo felt himself shudder at her words – 'almost always come from poor families and are subject to all kinds of abuse and exploitation. And folks, could I ask you to remember that one of the worst problems is in Brazil, the country the sporting authorities generously handed the biggest soccer competition on earth *and* the Olympic Games for good measure, just a few years back? Are those people *serious*?' She gave an exasperated shake of her head. 'I visited Brazil myself recently, and what I'd like to share with you this evening is what the conditions are *actually* like for those kids…'

Though no big follower of new movies, preferring to watch his old favourites over and over again, Hugo realized he'd seen this woman's face in the newspaper not long ago. He had a vague memory of her being described as some sort of ambassador for a well-known charity, but dismissing it as being nothing more than another famous person's pet cause in the name of publicity.

The lights in the huge room began to dim. The woman swept her gaze across the rows of expectant faces, flickering black and white in the light reflected from the screen behind the podium. 'If what I'm going to show you upsets you, I can only apologise in advance, and perhaps ask you to understand: it upset me just a little too.'

Across the width of the screen, the lives of strangers from another world began to present themselves. Here we go, Hugo thought, other people's misery for the voyeurs. If they start playing Erik Satie, I swear I'll get up and leave...

But there was no music. No smiling children crowded around a celebrity dressed in combat drill, watched over by well-tailored dignitaries and security guards. Instead, there were streets, cars, shops, bars, restaurants, tower blocks. Grainy, vertical pictures with greyed-out panels down each side, taken with a mobile phone from a moving vehicle which was now drawing past a busy intersection.

And here they were, the young members of the world's new generation. Emaciated kids, some leaning against walls, others squabbling as they scavenged through the contents of a torn rubbish sack, searching for anything to eat, drink, smoke or sell. Squatted on pavements, surrounded by sheets of cardboard. The lucky ones on tattered blankets, the less fortunate lying on bare paving stones. A building site further along, where plush new apartments were already poking their heads above the tops of corrugated hoardings, while human draught excluders filled in the gaps at the bottom. Children lying on each other in bundles of tiny, tangled, thin legs and bare feet. The camera was zooming in on a boy, who couldn't be ten years old, clutching a plastic bottle of what? Glue, meths? Further along, a child of indeterminate sex, with wide, round eyes, holding out a hand towards the blackened windows of an SUV.

A flicker. Different footage now, night-time. A girl no more than eight or nine, dressed in a tight, mesh top and short skirt, one leg bent at the knee, foot resting up behind her on a street lamp.

Bathed in her own, personal, sodium spotlight.

It had happened without Hugo noticing. The room had fallen completely silent.

The images had disappeared from the screen, but the movie star's words broke into his thoughts.

'… for obvious reasons it's hard to get solid proof, but there were multiple reports of the police setting up squads to "clean up"' – she scratched the air with her fingers – 'before the fans started arriving in the cities where the soccer games took place. They call them death squads.'

She opened her arms wide. 'Everywhere you look, there are people of all ages at risk, in all kinds of ways. The young, the old. Babies, parents, grandparents. The sick. At risk from civil war, from famine, from droughts, from earthquakes, from epidemics. All those words of course are just politicians' euphemisms for poverty. Does anyone in this room personally know somebody who's died from a drought or a famine?'

As her words cut through the darkened stillness, the actress lowered her head and coughed into her hand, permitting herself the tiniest of smiles. 'You know, folks, I was brought up a Catholic, for my sins. I go to confession now and then. That's also for my sins.' Scattered laughter eased the tension. 'But here's a thing: a while back a girlfriend of mine said to me, "I'm a Catholic too, but I don't go to confession anymore." And I'm like, "Oh really, why's that?" "Well," she says, "I don't know what to say to the guy. I mean, I don't commit adultery or covet things or sleep with my neighbour's husband, I didn't murder anyone. What am I supposed to confess?"' The actress dropped her voice an octave. 'Okay, she's a good girl. I think some of what she said might even be true.'

She waited for the laughs to fade. 'Guys, let me tell you this. When half the world is starving and when all of us are complaining about not being able to get the latest iPhone because Amazon has sold out... well, isn't that something we might consider just a teeny bit sinful? If those emaciated street kids were lying on the sidewalk in front of your local Walmart, would you just ignore them as you push your overloaded shopping cart out of the store?' She smiled. 'I think you already know the answer: of course you wouldn't, because you're good people. But because we don't actually see those children right there in front of us, sometimes we forget about them. And other times we look away from the TV, tell ourselves we're such caring, sensitive people, like, *Oh my God, it's too much to bear, seeing those images*. Ring any bells?'

She took a sip of water, and Hugo thought he'd never in his life experienced a hush so absolute.

'I apologise to you if the reality stings. We all do it. But we have to get the message out there. All of us have to do

22

more. We need to make a lot more noise about what's going on in those places, tell our own politicians as loudly as we can, so they have no choice but to tell other people – the ones who run those countries, countries that depend on the western world. You know, folks, it isn't a sin to live a comfortable life. It's only a sin when we don't give a flying… fig if others don't have any kind of life at all. I hope every one of you…' she nodded, 'yeah, well, you look like respectable people, that was the toned-down version… I hope all of you will do your bit for those kids. And we're going to help with that. Over the next few weeks, we'll be sending out details of our new *Light a Candle* initiative. The Candle bit in the title comes from *Candelária*, and that'll all be explained when the stuff comes out to you, and also why it's more important than ever that all of us play our part now. Because, dear friends, we're the ones who will make the difference. If we don't, we might just find – to borrow a line from one of my favourite songs – what was over there is over here.'

She pressed the palms of her hands together in a *namaste* gesture. 'Thank you so much for letting me come and talk to you tonight. Do please have a great evening and enjoy the conference.'

As she sat down, the noise inside the room rose up. Hugo gazed around at the lights from dozens of mobile phones being held up in the air and people surging towards the top table clutching menu cards and uncapped pens. He shook his head, wondering if people had even remotely understood the message the woman had just delivered.

He made a decision, and turned to shake hands with the

people next to him, telling them he was feeling jet-lagged and had an early start in the morning. With a shrug and an apologetic wave to the guests on the opposite side of the table, to whom he'd hardly spoken during the evening, he headed for the exit.

The back of the room was clearly where the less-privileged guests had been consigned and Hugo realized the escape route he'd chosen meant he'd have to wriggle between the backs of chairs. He squeezed behind a woman sitting bolt upright, glaring at the man next to her, her face flushed, and caught the slightest drift of her perfume. He didn't know the unfortunate man, but he thought he'd seen the woman somewhere.

But so many faces were beginning to look like so many others. He'd catch up with the people he knew when the conference began tomorrow. Right now he was exhausted.

3

The twelve members of the charity's so-called Investment Oversight Committee had gathered to listen to Hugo's annual report and ethics were once again at the top of their agenda.

Opposite Hugo, a youngish woman with beads and braids sat rotating from side to side in her swivel chair, like a child let loose in a toy shop. She'd made it her business to raise at least one question in response to almost every point Hugo had made, and he had made lots of them. He could feel a headache coming on. He looked down at the papers in front of him, pretending to rest his chin on the thumbs of each hand, so that he could massage his temples with his middle fingers without making it obvious.

Now the woman stared at him. '*Oh-my-God!*' Each word lasted precisely two beats on the same note. 'Have we been putting our money into entities that do *that*?'

Hugo raised his gaze to her. 'That's what we agreed last year.'

The woman's face lengthened. 'Well, don't we have a duty to get into the swim lane with these people? We have to insist on transparency. As stakeholders, surely we command enough goodwill to help them calibrate our expectations?' She tapped a fingernail on the table. 'Any investments we make have to be sustainable and those people have to buy into that ideology.'

Hugo contemplated asking if she'd let him have a few moments to google some of those expressions before replying, but resisted the temptation. He shrugged. 'It's part of their established DNA.' He hoped that might appeal to the woman's own vocabulary and it seemed to work, because she blew out her cheeks and allowed herself to fall back into her seat.

The committee's chairman, a small, neat man with a white pointed beard and a beautiful claret-coloured waistcoat, grunted and held up a finger. He turned to speak in a low voice to the two people on either side of him and, after a moment, looked over at Hugo. 'Thank you very much for your clear explanations, Mr Whiting. May I suggest we adjourn for coffee, then we'll hear your revised proposals after the break.'

The committee members were in obvious agreement. Chairs clattered on the polished wooden floor and a babble of conversation gathered momentum around the room.

Hugo skipped the queue for stewed coffee, opting to buy himself a mocha from the machine in the hotel's reception. Spotting an unoccupied bench opposite the entrance, he crossed the driveway towards it. The bench nestled underneath a gnarled old cypress tree and, as its scaley leaves swished around in the gentle breeze, they began to emit a faint perfume of lemon. Hugo peered up at the branches and imagined the architects grumbling at being told they had to work round this tree, an ancient relic surviving amid the modern world sprouting up on all sides. He rested his hand on the ragged bark, feeling like a kindred spirit, and the tree seemed to be reciprocating. As though celebrating its reprieve from the march of commercialism, the branches swayed again, allowing pale sunlight to break through and dapple the ground around his feet, so that for one brief moment Hugo felt like an actor under a spotlight.

As he sat, sipping the sweet, creamy mixture from the long carton, he was able to see people coming and going. The electronic sign above the grand portico of the hotel opposite alternately displayed the time and temperature. Fifty-one degrees. He shivered and drew his jacket around him, regretting not having brought an overcoat.

He couldn't get the thought out of his mind. *Why do I sit in meetings with people like that, firing questions one after another, just to show off to their colleagues? I have enough money now, why don't I just retire?*

He knew why: there was nothing to retire for.

What would he do with his time? More importantly, who would he spend it with?

He sighed. Over the road, the sponsored display switched back to the time. In five minutes, they'd be restarting. Yet, as he swallowed the last of his hot drink, a feeling of excitement began to course through his veins. He knew that in a little over an hour the meeting would be over. After lunch, there'd be a meeting with the members of the finance committee, to run through the annual accounts. Professional people, who'd understand them.

Then one more dinner tonight and he'd be free.

As he pushed himself up, one thought filled his head: *let's get this over with*. The wine country was waiting for him. A solitary adventure, it was true, but he'd long since got used to that.

A surge of joy welled up inside him now and he almost skipped across the road, but settled for a brisk walk. So brisk that, as he reached the entrance doors to the foyer, he collided with a woman coming the other way.

He made a clumsy attempt to help the woman as she juggled to hold on to the papers she was carrying and shuffle them back into a neat shape. As she straightened up, she smiled, touching his elbow. 'My fault. I shouldn't be rushing around all the time.'

Hugo caught another faint hint of a familiar perfume and recognized her as the woman he'd brushed past when he was leaving the dinner the previous evening. This time, though, their eyes met, and as Hugo stood motionless, words queueing in his mouth but failing to come out, her smile left her face. Muttering an apology, she manoeuvred round him and began to hurry away.

Hugo thought he could hear his heart pounding in the fragrant silence she'd left behind.

He started after her retreating figure, managing to touch her coat sleeve.

'Marietta. It is you, isn't it? Please stop, don't run away.
She twisted to thrust his hand off her sleeve and broke into a trot, but after a few steps came to a halt. As she turned

round, she closed her eyes and Hugo saw her lips move, though trapped inside his cocoon spun from disbelief and shock, he failed to hear what she said. His ribs ached as though he'd been violently squeezed.

He managed to find some words. 'I'm sorry, I didn't mean to startle you...'

The woman clutched her papers tight against her chest, as though they would provide some sort of protection. Narrowing her eyes, she moved closer. 'Hugo. I can't...' She glanced to one side then looked back at him, her eyes searching his face. 'God, how many years has it been? I can't believe it.'

He shook his head, bewildered. 'You're the last person I'd have expected to see here.' He felt himself swallow. 'I mean, the commercial world was never your thing...'

Her smile was almost apologetic. 'Have you forgotten? This is a conference for charities.'

Hugo's mouth was bone dry. 'Yes of course, sorry, I'm just a bit in shock.'

She took a short breath and exhaled it. 'Me too.'

Hugo waited for her to speak again, then realized it fell to him to break the silence. 'Would you... I mean, have you got time for a coffee? Not now, I'm stuck in a meeting in there.' He wafted a hand in the direction of the hotel foyer behind him, as if that would help him explain. 'Later on maybe?'

Marietta's features tightened, and Hugo stood motionless. Willing her, praying for the first time in so long he couldn't remember. *Please Lord, let her say yes.*

Across the hotel driveway, the trees seemed to huddle in

a circle, shutting out the light from the sky, and the birds settled in the branches. Watching, waiting to hear what she'd say.

Marietta nibbled on her lip and looked away, and the inevitability of what was to follow rushed towards Hugo like a giant wave.

'Oh God, I'm so sorry,' she pointed in the direction in which she'd been heading, 'I was just on my way to get packed up. I've got two meetings this afternoon I daren't miss, and my flight leaves tonight.'

Hugo nodded and lowered his head, silently pleading to her to rescue him.

And then, just as she'd done so many times when they were young, she did. She reached out her hands and he clutched them with both of his, the only thing he had to hold on to.

She lowered her voice. 'Look, I tell you what. I'll need to beg a couple of favours, but maybe I can meet you around seven, that's if you're free? But I absolutely have to be away by eight.' She grimaced.

Hugo knew he was *not* free at that time; the closing dinner started at half past seven. But while no one would forgive him if he failed to show up to a business meeting, the dinner was something informal. Much more important was that the woman standing opposite him now was his first love. She was leaving tonight and he knew he might never see her again.

He heard himself speaking. 'What about the bar on the mezzanine floor?' He had a feeling she had just said the same words at the same time and, standing outside the hotel, with people coming and going all around them, they laughed together, as though they were teenagers again.

Marietta looked down at their hands, knotted together, and her voice was a whisper. 'But Hugo, if you want me to be on time, you'll need to let go of me...'

They had been little more than kids at the time.

It was at a barbecue, a family day arranged by his father's company, on the sports fields alongside its head office. The scent of freshly mown grass, bedecked with grand marquees and red and yellow bouncy castles, all with pointed roofs.

Mid July. It had started out as a beautiful sunny day. Adults chattering, clutching those fancy coupe glasses, full of what they would later tell their friends was champagne but which more likely was *Asti Spumante*. Long trestle tables, white tablecloths. Giant plates and paper doilies, cold sausage rolls and crumbly cheese sandwiches cut into triangles. Black Forest gateau, pink blancmange, jellies in the shape of rabbits for the children.

That peculiar hum, concocted from dozens of voices floating into warm summer stillness, broken only by the occasional squeal of laughter.

Then the first rumble. Before long the heavens had opened and people were dashing for shelter. Deciding not to follow the adults and their children inside, Hugo took cover under the open awning in front of the marquee. He'd stood there alone, listening to the comforting sound of the rain, pattering on the canvas above his head. A well of water broke free at the corner and sploshed down on the grass.

Then this funny-looking girl arrived and stood a few yards away from him. Her dark, wiry hair straggled down her face, which was the colour of milky coffee, and she squinted her eyes to look at the end of her nose and blew drops of rain from it. He'd tried not to laugh, turning and covering his mouth with his hand, but she'd noticed him watching and giggled even more.

He'd loved her sense of fun, right from that moment.

He'd loved her too, from about a minute later.

Hugo wasn't normally lost for words, but 'Aren't you going inside?' was the best he could come up with at the time. It also happened to be the very last thing he wanted this girl to do. She said no, and he'd felt a surge of relief.

'It'll be all older people in there,' she remarked, and stuck her nose in the air, mimicking imaginary characters inside the marquee behind them. *Which school are your children at? Oh really? Mine go to the private school, further up. Where do you live? Oh yes, I vaguely know it, aren't those the terraced houses with those quaint little gardens at the front?*

He'd laughed at the put-on accent.

'No thanks,' she'd added, her voice more like a growl now. 'I'd far rather stay out here. Besides, I love the sound of rain. So long as I'm not out in it, getting soaked.'

Did she work for the company? No, it was her dad who worked here. As she'd said this, she'd made a circular movement with her index figure pointing upwards, indicating the enormity of the place. At the time, she had no idea who Hugo was. Hugo had thought, but didn't say, that their two fathers had probably never met. He'd always doubted his father met many of his employees. He was not there that day either, the so-called family day.

Her parents had come here from Sweden when she was a baby, she told him, though her mother was Brazilian. What about him? What was his name?

As they'd talked, the dark clouds began to move away, and the rain was easing off. People were beginning to emerge from the marquee, glancing up at the sky. Hugo knew he had to seize the opportunity. 'Do you fancy going to the pictures next week?'

To his astonishment, she said yes. They went to see *The Graduate*. Hugo's school friends had told him about the sex scenes. Hugo remembered both of them being disappointed with the film, in his case probably because there wasn't that much female flesh exposed. They'd left early.

From that moment onwards, Hugo couldn't imagine life without Marietta.

Two years later came the Outward Bound course.

Hugo had been set to go to university and was looking forward to spending the summer holiday with Marietta. His father had other ideas, adamant that the young Hugo would benefit from some experience of real life before the next part of his formal education. His father knew the chairman of a company that owned a remote lakeside manor which had been converted into a corporate training establishment. It would do him good, his father had told him, prepare him for the career that lay ahead.

And which career is that? The one you want for me, or the one I want? Hugo had thought, remembering his father's

33

reaction when he'd first mooted the idea of studying economic development. He hadn't voiced that question. His father wasn't a man people willingly took on.

So Hugo boarded the train to Cumbria. A month of fell walking, orienteering, amateur dramatics. Gymnastic exercises in vest and shorts, at half-past-six in the morning, by the side of the lake. The smell of wet grass and pine trees, a heady mixture he would never forget. Bromide in the tea, it was rumoured, to quell the sexual appetites of the lithe young bodies interned together for so long.

He would remember too, the rowing instructor prodding him out of his daydreams as he wondered what Marietta was doing. *Sorry to butt in, only would Mr Whiting mind awfully at least trying to keep in time with the others?*

And the letters. He wrote to her almost every day, telling her how he longed to be home. Each letter answered by return. SWALK, said the flaps of the envelopes. Or she'd written *First Class Male*. Inside, she told him she missed him horribly and couldn't wait to meet him at the station when he came back.

Then three letters and no reply. Sick with worry, Hugo feigned a more credible illness and they let him leave a couple of days early. She wasn't waiting for him at the station, of course. She wouldn't have known he was back so soon.

The last letter was waiting for him when he arrived at his parents' house. The envelope was propped up on the telephone table in the hall and didn't say SWALK on it.

Only weeks later, when he was calmer, did something begin to trouble him about that letter, but he'd dismissed those vague thoughts from his mind. It was already enough for him to have to bear, the thought that the Angel of Desolation had visited him that day and laid out its plans for his future, better than his father could ever have done.

Now, forty years later and half a world away from where it began, he stood in the shower and turned the water as hot as he could stand it, letting it pound against his chest and splash all over his body. He wrapped himself in the huge, soft white towel and sat down on the end of the bed, staring into the void of his life.

God knows, it was so long ago. Was he doing the right thing?

If he didn't, though, could he go through the rest of his life never knowing? Long years ago, he'd resigned himself to doing just that. But now here she was, showing up in his life again, against all the odds. If he walked away he would never know the answer. This was his last opportunity to find out the truth.

Was he just being selfish though, disturbing whatever life she'd made for herself, just for his own personal satisfaction? He hadn't looked to see if she was wearing a wedding ring. She probably had a husband, children, grandchildren even.

And what about him? He'd be putting himself through the agony all over again. He'd buried the ghost of Marietta years ago, at least he thought he had. Was he now, suddenly, hoping deep down inside that there might be a second chance?

He covered his face with the palms of his hands and

dragged them backwards, stretching the flesh tight. He had to go. For one thing, if he just left a note, he'd be doing exactly what she'd done to him, as though he was trying to exact some kind of revenge. A dish best served cold, wasn't that what they said? Decades cold, in this case, like those mountaineers found years after they'd disappeared, ghostly images frozen in ice.

He just couldn't, wouldn't, let her think that.

He stood up. He'd go to the bar early. Take a newspaper, keep his head buried in it. If Marietta arrived early too, better still. Even so, he knew that whatever time they got there, they wouldn't have long. An hour, maybe, to catch up on more than half a lifetime?

Thank you oh ye gods of fate. Thanks a lot.

Intermezzo, like bars in airports and hotels all round the world, had no front wall. It was more like an open fronted cave, secured by a drop-down grill when it was closed, which wasn't very often.

Hugo felt a surge of relief when he saw the bar was empty. He chose a table at the far end, from where he could keep a distant eye on people walking by outside but not be easily seen himself. The last thing he needed was anyone recognizing him and stopping by for a chat.

As he nursed a red wine, he watched men in black ties and dinner jackets and women in long dresses passing by. A couple of guys sporting kilts; wasn't tonight's event a formal dinner, not a display of national pride? He knew he was on edge and getting irritable.

But now here she was, standing at the entrance, adjusting her eyes to the low lighting in the bar after the brightness of the lobby. She was pulling a small case on wheels, carrying her coat over her arm. He jumped up and strode over to meet her.

'Hugo, sorry I'm late.' She reached up to grip his shoulders and pecked him on both cheeks, as though they were meeting up for lunch after not seeing each other for a couple of weeks. She gestured at her thick cotton sweater and jeans. 'I'm hopeless at flying. I need to be ultra-comfortable. Fashion goes out of the window.'

'No, you look great, really good.' Hugo glanced towards the bar, but the waiter was already on his way over. Marietta asked for a sparkling water and began arranging her coat and handbag on a chair.

Hugo took the opportunity to study her close-up. She still wore a bob cut, as she had when they were teenagers, but her hair was flecked with grey now. Her skin was darker than he remembered but still as clear and fresh.

His smile was nervous. 'I didn't have time to tell you earlier on, but I saw you last night, at the dinner.'

Marietta's eyes flew in his direction. 'You did? Why didn't you come over then?'

'I'm sorry to say I didn't recognize you. I was sneaking out early, just after the film star finished speaking. I only saw you for a split second.'

'Ah, right. I suppose you were at the front of the room, mixing with the great and good? Lowly charity workers like me don't get to sit near the top table.'

'You seemed a bit fed up with the fellow you were sitting next to.'

'Oh dear, was it obvious?' She broke into a smile, but this time it didn't reach her eyes. She met his gaze. 'You know, Hugo, never in my wildest imagination did I ever think this would ever happen.'

The waiter had returned and before Hugo could say anything, began setting down small bowls of nuts and olives, scalloped mats and serviettes. He picked up the bottle of mineral water and started to pour it into the glass of ice and lemon in front of Marietta.

Hugo's eyes darted to the clock on the wall, then at the waiter. 'That's fine thanks.' The waiter took the hint and set the bottle down.

Marietta watched him walk away. 'I think you've upset him.'

Hugo nodded. 'I'll give him a good tip.'

'Anyway, yes, that man at the dinner last night... what a pain! He was some junior executive with an international bank. He was telling me about one of their branches in,' she shook her head, 'I can't remember where it was, Chile I think. Said they'd planned a sponsorship with one of the big charities, but then the bank's finance director discovered the government there didn't give tax relief on donations from big corporates. "How ridiculous is that?" he was going on. "How do they expect companies to help them when they make it so difficult?" So I asked him why they'd pulled out, if they made all that money there, couldn't they just help the poor people out anyway, without having to get a tax break? I swear he was about to say "we're not a charity you know" but then he remembered where he was and managed to stop himself.

He told me the banks are having to cut back like everyone else. I said right, okay, so how's your bonus going this year?'

'What did he say to that?'

'He told me to mind my own business.'

Hugo forced a smile. He had picked up one of the little wooden sticks the waiter had brought with the olives, and as he listened to Marietta's story of her encounter with the banker he unthinkingly began snapping it into small pieces. More than once he glanced at the clock on the wall whenever Marietta broke eye contact. A sickening feeling fluttered around his stomach. All he'd done was invite her to meet him for a coffee. Maybe she was hoping he'd be happy just to talk about their lives now. Was she hoping deep down that they might avoid a painful reopening of the past? The way she was chattering away now suggested she may well have.

The rise in the tone of Marietta's voice dragged him out of his ruminations.

'... I asked him if the banks *cared* about the opinion of the man in the street, so he comes out with some smart-alec remark about opinions being like bottoms: we've all got one, he says, but sometimes it's not a good idea to expose them in public. I nearly emptied my glass into his lap. I would have done but I knew I'd never get invited back here again.'

Hugo leaned forward and, clasping his hands together, shoved them down between his thighs. 'Listen, Mari, I could stay here forever, talking to you again. But I know you haven't got a lot of time...'

Marietta's smile left her face. 'And you want to ask me

something…' She took a deep breath and began nodding slowly.

'I need to, Mari. I think I have a right to know. If you'd decided we weren't right for each other, couldn't you have waited for me to come home so you could tell me to my face? Had I done something so bad that all you could do was leave a letter and then vanish out of my life?'

She bit her lip, looking down into her lap. When her answer came, it was the faintest of whispers. 'You're right, Hugo. I'm so very sorry.'

Hugo reached across the table and rested his hand on her arm. 'Mari, you know I couldn't have let you run off this afternoon. There was no way I could stand there and watch you just disappear out of my life for a second time without trying to find out what happened.'

When she lifted her head he saw the tears in her eyes, but she forced a smile through them. She rested her hand on top of his, as if she feared he might take it away again. 'You know, maybe someone up there *is* looking after us after all.'

Hugo snorted. 'Well, whoever it is hasn't been looking after us all that well for the last forty years.' He took a deep breath and let it out slowly. 'Sorry.'

Marietta reached for her handbag and Hugo caught his breath, but released it when she merely pulled out a tissue. She dabbed at her eyes and looked across at him.

'Mari, we could sit here and I could ask you about what you've been doing all this time, tell you a bit about my life, then off you'd go and catch your flight. Or I can ask the question and risk you getting mad with me and leaving anyway. So what do I have to lose? Either way, I wouldn't find out.'

When she spoke, it was as if her voice had passed beyond sadness into despair.

'It was because other people were involved.'

Hugo felt his whole body stiffen.

Marietta shook her head. 'No, not like that. There was no one else. But there were other people who would have got...' she turned away to stare at some unseen object in the distance, 'really, badly, hurt.'

Hugo's face contorted. 'Mari, don't you think *I* was really, badly, hurt?'

She flashed her eyes back towards him. 'Of course. I knew you would be. I *knew* you'd be hurt. But I also knew in time you'd get over me. I meant another kind of hurt.' She looked down at the tissue in her hands and tugged at it. 'I didn't want to destroy your relationship with your mum and dad.'

Hugo stared at her, furrowing his brow. 'My mum and dad? What have *they* got to do with it?'

She took another deep breath, then crossed her arms, as though the temperature in the bar had suddenly dropped. 'First, you need to make me a promise.'

'What promise?'

'I know your dad passed away, but I need you to promise me, however you feel when I've told you this, you won't ever, *ever* breathe a word of this to your mum.'

'I don't understand...' He shook his head.

'Hugo!' Her words snapped at him and she looked around, then lowered her voice. 'Unless you promise me that, I *will* get up and leave...'

His face projected his shock. Then he nodded. 'Okay, I'll make you that promise. I won't say a word. But you have to tell me exactly what happened.'

She searched his face, then nodded back. 'What happened was very simple. It was your mum and dad who forced me to go away. They told me to leave. To get out of your life.'

Hugo shook his head, as though by doing so he would be able to put all his thoughts back into a nice, orderly formation. 'How could my mum and dad have told you to do that? We were supposed to be getting engaged.'

'And *that* was the whole point. They told me, well, to be precise, your mum told me, they didn't *want* us getting engaged. She said I wasn't right for you. I never had been, but they'd gone along with it, thinking it would come to a natural end anyway. But she said when we announced the engagement they knew they had to put a stop to it. She told me if I didn't go, it wouldn't just be me who suffered, it'd be my mum and dad too. Don't forget, this was the nineteen-seventies. Remember what it was like then? A white man with, what was the word they used in those days, a "coloured" wife? Your father was a powerful man from a rich family. It wouldn't have taken much to destroy mine. For one thing, my dad worked for your dad.'

Hugo sat back, cupping his hands over his face. Only the faint tinkle of glasses being stacked on the bar across the room disturbed the silence.

'Hugo, I know I made a complete mess of everything. Even this, now, I should never have agreed to come here, not when I had so little time to explain. Maybe I should have brazened it out earlier on, pretended I didn't know you, you were mistaken. But you caught me off-guard, and all I've done now is make things worse, reopened all the old wounds.' She stood up. 'I'm sorry, I have to go. I just can't do this. It's all too late.'

Hugo jumped up and put his hands on her shoulders, pulling her close. He felt the stiffness in her body. 'Please, Mari, don't. I know you've got a flight to catch but listen, get another one tomorrow, I'll pay for it. Let's get away from here, find somewhere to have dinner and talk. You can't just tell me half the story then walk away and leave me like this.' His voice faltered. 'I can't handle it.'

Long-buried images drifted through his mind. The first time he'd stood with her like this, when they'd shared a clumsy kiss. He'd made out he was experienced, a man of the world already, yet their first attempt at sex had ended in failure. When his embarrassment had disappeared he'd admitted it was his first time as well and they'd dissolved into laughter. They'd hugged like this too, just before he boarded his train to Cumbria, and she'd run along the platform as he leaned out of the window. Just like in the movies. A month apart that seemed as though it would be a lifetime.

And in the end, it was.

As she began to walk away, Hugo held out his hand towards her, but she quickened her pace. This time she didn't turn round. He stood watching, tasting the saltiness.

Which particular type of suffering was this exactly, this one right now? Was it just what he'd had to put up with for more than half his life? So no big deal then. Or was this a new kind of suffering, where the gift seemingly handed to him earlier in the day was now being wrested back from his grasp? Maybe it wasn't a gift, just a temporary loan, and now there'd be interest to pay. The thought rattled round his head like a bat trapped in a barn: *I must have done something really bad in my life for this to keep happening.*

And at that moment the image of the last time she'd gone, the letter she'd left, came back to him. Suddenly, he realized what it was that had troubled him about it for so many years.

4

It wasn't just the fraudsters who needed be thankful for the surge in financial crime, Hugo thought. It had spawned its own multi-million-pound industry, pen pushers on six-figure salaries who'd never looked after a client in their lives but just loved calling meetings.

He'd been stuck in another of those meetings for the last two hours and all he could think about was the weekend. What had happened to the days when he'd spent his time meeting clients, decisions were sealed over lunch and a person's word was their bond? He sighed. All that was gone forever, but it didn't stop him feeling nostalgic.

He realized he'd felt nostalgic a lot lately.

His bathroom scales had persuaded him to use the stairs these days, though today he decided to treat himself to a ride in the lift. When the doors opened for him to get out, Laura was waiting to get in.

'Got to dash, sorry, PAs' meeting.' She held the lift door open with her foot. 'I've left a few messages. See you later.'

The door slid shut and Hugo shook his head and set off back to his office. He could hardly miss the little pile of pink post-it stickers and, half-sitting on the edge of his desk, he picked them up. More than once Laura had asked him if, now the world had entered the twenty-first century, he might give some fleeting consideration to using email for his messages, but he preferred it this way. So long as the brightly-coloured slips were staring at him on his desk, he couldn't forget about them, and when they were dealt with he could toss them in the bin. More recently he'd developed a habit of doing that before he'd dealt with them, and on one occasion an exasperated Laura had asked him if he'd prefer her to put his messages straight in the bin to save him the trouble.

The third one made his insides lurch.

Hugo, a Marietta Forsberg called – rang about the US conference & asked if you could call. Said she was going out in about an hour, so if not today can you call tomorrow?

L

10.05 a.m. x

He glanced at his watch. Twenty past eleven. He cursed and decided to try the number Laura had written underneath anyway. It rang several times without response.

He realized he'd never had the chance to ask Marietta where she lived now and slid his laptop towards him. He tapped out the first part of the number and squinted at the screen. Brazil, Rio de Janeiro.

If anyone bothered to look up from their computer

screens when he thumped his desk, he didn't notice.

During the night, he tossed and turned, tugging his pillow over, resting his head back into a few moments of coolness.

New thoughts merged into old ones. He hadn't thought to check the time difference between London and Rio de Janeiro. He knew that the east coast of North America was five hours behind, so if South America was the same and she'd called him at ten UK time, it must have been five in the morning there. Hadn't she been able to sleep? That must be a good sign, mustn't it?

But what could she possibly be calling him for, so long after they'd parted in the way they had? Marietta was strong-willed. Even as a teenager, she hadn't backtracked on the decision she'd made, no matter how much it must have hurt and angered her to have been forced out of his life. And when they'd met again, she was adamant she'd made the wrong decision in agreeing to talk.

So why would she change her view now?

He reached for the switch on the bedside lamp and, screwing his eyes up, rotated the alarm clock towards him. Almost half past two. He sighed and climbed out of bed, pulling on his dressing gown. In the kitchen, he made himself tea and brought it to the table, then opened up his laptop. When he searched for the time in Rio de Janeiro, a neat little clock image appeared on the screen. Twenty to twelve. He glanced up at the kitchen clock. Twenty to three; so Rio was only three hours behind? He sipped at the tea, trying to clear his head. He vaguely remembered he had a client appointment later in the morning, but if he got into the office early enough he could call her before he left.

He nibbled his bottom lip and raised his eyes to the ceiling, letting his thoughts drift round his mind. Did he really want to do this? Why would he choose to put himself through any more misery? He'd found out what he wanted to know, so what else did he need to do? Since he'd come back from San Francisco, he'd done what he had the first time Marietta had left him; he'd thrown himself into his work again. In the last few days, he'd even managed to convince himself she was right. It would have been wrong to scratch those sores now. He hadn't even told Laura about what had happened.

Fact: Marietta had left him because she'd been driven out by his parents. And he couldn't remonstrate with them. His mother was stricken with dementia and even if he thought she would understand him, he would not break the promise he'd made to Marietta. Nor would it serve much of a purpose to sit by his father's gravestone and shout at him, however loudly.

The bin wagon woke him at just after half past seven.

He'd gone back to bed at around four but had lain awake, still tossing everything round in his head. And then the mezzanine bars and rain-pounded awnings and papers fluttering around outside hotel entrances merged into one giant green and turquoise peacock, which winked at him before flying off into the night.

Now, standing on the platform, he sighed with relief when his train pulled in on time. Except it wasn't his usual one, which had left an hour and a quarter earlier. He rang Laura and again thanked Saint Mary and the Daughters of Providence and anyone else who was at the disposal of the needy that she was a part of his life. She would send the files round to the client's office, so he could go straight there.

Once he'd settled in his seat he opened his newspaper, but when he scratched the side of his face he froze. He'd forgotten to shave. He rocked his head back and silently cursed. Well, he couldn't ask Laura to send a razor and soap with the files. The client would have to accept him as he was. Not shaving wouldn't diminish his financial advisory skills. Lack of sleep just might.

Hugo dropped into the comfort of the quilted green leather chair.

Harry Parker's oak-panelled office had greeted him with the rich tang of furniture polish and cigars, and his client pushed the open box towards him. Hugo shook his head. 'I've given them up. Doctor's orders.'

Parker shrugged and returned to clipping the end off his cigar in a miniature brass guillotine which stood on his desk. Without looking up, he launched into a tirade.

'You won't believe this. A few days ago, this guy from my HR Department comes in here. He says they had the Fire Brigade round for an inspection, I was out at the time. They told him they could smell stale smoke in here. So this fellow from the fire station goes ferreting around, in my private office, and sees the cigar box. He tells my man he has to have a word with me, I'm not allowed to smoke in here.'

He struck a long match and circled it round the end of the cigar. Hugo watched silently as the flame leapt up and down. Parker turned the cigar round to check it was lit properly, then drew on it and released a billow of smoke into the air.

'So I said to my guy, you go and tell the fire chief or whoever he is to fuck off. I said, tell him *I* own this building and *I* own the company that occupies it. No one's going to tell me I can't smoke in my own fucking property.'

Hugo chuckled. 'What did he say?'

'Who, my guy or the fire brigade man?'

'Your HR man.'

'Oh, he didn't say anything. Well, not to me anyway. Whether he said anything to the fire people I've no idea, but they haven't been back since. Bastards. Who the hell do they think they are?'

With Parker still muttering obscenities about his perceived victimization, Hugo spread some papers out and Parker drew a couple of them towards him and began to read, nodding his approval.

Hugo's gaze turned towards the window. Outside, it was pouring down and the buildings across the road reminded him of a Turner Venetian scene he'd seen somewhere in a gallery, somehow managing to look as though they were being viewed through a curtain of yellow water. He realized he hadn't brought an umbrella with him.

'... Earth to Hugo, hello, Earth to Hugo?'

Hugo was startled out of his trance.

'For fuck's sake, are you joining this meeting or not?' Parker blew another cloud of smoke and rolled his eyes.

Hugo knew his client well enough to smile. 'Sorry, Harry, it's been a tough few weeks. A few old ghosts coming back to haunt me.'

'Your wife…?'

'That and other things.'

'You still find it tough I guess?'

Hugo rocked his head from side to side, considering the question he'd been asked about his wife, but knowing his answer related partly to Marietta too. 'Sometimes. I mean, work takes my mind off things, but every now and then the past has a habit of catching up with me.'

Parker barked a laugh. 'With me, it's more a case of the future catching up. Hasn't there been anyone else since…?'

Hugo sensed Parker had forgotten his late wife's name and came to his rescue. 'Sarah?' he smoothly interrupted. 'There could have been. Might still be, if I can let go of the past.' Hugo was surprised to hear himself talking to his client like this. He'd known Harry Parker for years, but they'd never been close outside the office.

'See,' Parker said, 'I've managed to avoid getting divorced despite being a shit husband. And I've got great kids. But the truth is, I wouldn't know what to do with myself if I ever stopped working.' He waved his hand around him. 'This is all that keeps me going. You know I've got the yacht in the Bahamas, but I've not set foot on it in two years. My wife and the kids spend most of the summer there. But, nah, it'd drive me crazy. Everyone's different, except all of us only get one life. It's all about doing what really means something to us. Making money does that for me.'

He shrugged. 'Sometimes, I wish it had been different, but it's no good complaining if you don't grab your opportunities when they come around. This isn't an audition for another life, this one's the full-scale production. Once it's gone it's goodnight Vienna.'

He glanced at his watch and fiddled with the strap. 'Anyway, enough of this philosophy crap, we've got work to do.' He glanced at Hugo. 'And if you don't mind me saying, old son, you could do with standing a bit closer to your shaver in the mornings.'

The cab windows were misting up, wrapping Hugo in his own closeted world.

What was it Parker had said? *This isn't an audition for another life.* So much of Hugo's life had been looking back on what might have been. Was he now going to let something that had happened all those years ago blight the future too? It didn't matter how much thinking, how much remonstrating he did, nothing in the world could change what had happened.

Back at his desk he draped his jacket, glossy with rain, over an empty chair. When he turned round he saw Laura heading towards him.

She handed him a sandwich packet. 'That was good timing. I hope you haven't eaten already, otherwise I've got cheese and tomato on brown for dinner tonight. Fancy a cuppa?'

'I thought you'd never ask.'

She returned carrying a china cup and saucer in one hand and an enormous mug with a picture of a beagle on it in the other. She set them down on Hugo's desk and pulled out the chair opposite him. 'Tell me to mind my own business, but do you want to talk about it?'

He returned her gaze. 'Talk about what?'

She raised her eyebrows. 'Hugo, we go back a long way. I can read you like a book.'

He grunted. 'Yes, you could probably go on *Mastermind*. Specialist subject, Hugo Whiting. You probably know more about me than I know about myself. But talk about what, specifically?'

She shook her head. 'Well, first of all, San Francisco? You came back earlier than you planned. And you haven't been the same since. You don't do over-sleeping, but you managed it this morning.' She pointed. 'And on top of that, you forgot to shave, when you had a client appointment.'

Hugo took a sip from his cup and set it back on the saucer. He leaned back and grunted. 'Where to begin…'

'Perhaps with a phone call from a certain Ms Forsberg?' Laura tilted her head to one side. 'I'm willing to bet that's got something to do with it. Like I said, you don't have to tell me, but if you want to…'

Hugo glanced around. Over in the far corner, a lone young woman was staring into her computer screen as though she was playing a game of who blinks first. Otherwise the office was deserted. He heard Laura's voice. 'It's Alex's birthday. They've gone out to the wine bar.'

So, on a soaking wet afternoon, Hugo told his most trusted ally what had happened at the conference. 'The thing is, when I crashed into her outside the hotel, she tried to run away. She made out she hadn't recognized me.'

Laura opened her mouth to interject, but evidently thought the better of it. She nodded her head neutrally as Hugo carried on speaking.

'To be fair, she promised she'd meet me and she showed up. Then she told me what I needed to know. After that, she didn't have to get in touch again, did she?' He shrugged. 'Now I've got no idea what to do. What do you think about what she did? Do you think she was wrong?'

'Do you mean when you were kids?'

He nodded.

'It's not for me to judge, Hugo. Nor anyone else for that matter. If you're asking me what I'd have done in that position, I'd probably have brazened it out till you got back, then told you about the whole thing. Or even called that place and got you to come back early. Then both of you could have had it out with that vindictive cow.' She clapped her hand to her mouth. 'Oh, I'm sorry…'

'No, you're right. My mother was a vindictive cow to do that.'

Laura took a deep breath. '… but remember, I'm only going on what you've told me. If Marietta's right, that her dad would have been kicked out of work, or the family deported, maybe I'd have done the same as she did. I think I'd have tried to find out what you thought first though. If your dad was so determined to take out his rage on her family, it'd have been up to you to make him see how stupid he was being.' She leaned back in her chair. 'You have to remember how young she was. It was a big risk either way. If you'd stormed back to your parents and they'd gone through with what they were threatening, who knows where it could have ended up?' She shook her head. 'It doesn't bear thinking about, the poor girl must have been frightened to death.'

Hugo sighed and nodded his head. 'I had meant to call her this morning, but then I overslept. Maybe that was an omen, because now I'm thinking, do I really want to call her back? For heaven's sake, I'm trying to get over all this, not start it up again.'

Laura studied his face. 'Don't jump down my throat, Hugo. But if it was possible for you and her to get back together, would you want that?'

Hugo shuffled in his chair, smoothing out his damp shirt. 'I don't know, Laura. I'm not sure she'd be interested...'

Laura smiled. 'Well, that's not what I asked you, but one thing's for certain: you'll never know unless you try. It's up to you of course, but if you're asking my advice...'

'Which I am...'

'... then I'd ask you a question. If Marietta wasn't interested, why did she call yesterday? I doubt she'd be ringing to ask if you noticed if she'd left her umbrella on the table in the bar.' She leaned forward. 'Hugo, do you really think she didn't know how you'd feel once she'd told you about what happened? Or that she ever believed it would be easy? *Oh, Hugo will be fine when I tell him. He'll say, poor you, I know how you must have felt, darling, now let's go off to dinner and after that we can jump into bed together and everything will be hunky-dory again.*' She tilted her head as if challenging him.

Hugo rubbed his finger on his lips, and Laura raised the beagle mug to hers, sipping slowly. Neither spoke, and into the void Harry Parker's words drifted back: *it's no good complaining if you don't grab your opportunities when they come around.*

Hugo stood up.

'Right, wish me luck.'

She answered on the second ring.

'Hugo, hi. I'd started to think you weren't going to call back.'

'I tried to call yesterday, but the message said…'

'Yes, sorry, I had to go out to work.' Her voice, from thousands of miles away, sounded as though she'd just landed on the moon. 'I keep going over in my head what happened in San Francisco. All I was thinking at the time was I had a plane to catch. If I'd have had time to think about it properly, I'd have realized I wasn't being fair to you, just going off and leaving you like that.'

In the deserted client meeting room, Hugo sat on the edge of the soft leather chair. 'I understand, Mari. It's okay…'

'No, Hugo. It's not okay. Yes, those things did happen a long time ago, but I just walked away from your life when we were planning to get married and I didn't even have the decency to tell you why. You had a right to know the truth. At the very least, I should have told you I'd call you when you got back. I didn't even ask you for your phone number.'

'But you found it anyway?'

'Oh, that bit was easy. The woman on the conference reception desk was Brazilian. When I got back home I rang her and she gave me your office number. Speaking Portuguese has its advantages.'

Hugo laughed. 'She wasn't called Nancy by any chance, was she?'

'Yes, and she knew you.'

'Nancy's Brazilian?'

'Originally. She said to tell you they've taken lion meat off the menu. What's that all about?'

'Oh, don't ask.'

'Hugo, listen. I want to ask you something. I don't know if you'd still be interested, but I've got a chance to go to Italy next week. To Rome. I'm working on a project with Save the Children...'

'You are an international jet setter.'

'I wish. I've only ever been invited to two conferences, and both of them have come within a few weeks of each other. This one's only three days, but then I'm going to take a break. I've been working almost non-stop for most of the last year. I asked them if they could leave the date of the return flight open so I can go home later.'

Hugo held his breath.

'... I'll probably stay a week, maybe a little longer. I know it's short notice, but I was wondering...'

A pause extended out from the word. He waited, but she had left the sentence dangling in the air. 'Mari, are you asking me if I'll join you there?'

'Well, I thought, if you could find some time, even if it was just for a day or two. We could, you know, have a proper talk. Maybe I could make a better job of explaining things this time.'

'So tell me where I need to go to and when.'

'Okay. But Hugo, you need to…'

The silences were beginning to say more than the words. 'I need to what, Mari?'

After a long pause, she continued. 'This isn't a story with a happy ending. I don't want you to do this thinking that way, you need to understand that. That's why I thought it might have been better for both of us if we'd left things as they were. But I saw how heartbroken you were when I walked away from you in that bar. Please don't…'

'Mari, I'm a grown man now. I've had time to come to terms with what you told me and I know you did what you thought was best at the time. I'll be okay. Just tell me the dates and I'll be there.'

There was a moment's silence. 'Don't you need to check your diary? Your schedule, or whatever you businessmen call it these days?'

'I just did. Diary, schedule, calendar, PA. Conscience. All clear. Now just please give me the details.'

5

Eighteen miles south of Rome, nestled into the rolling hills above the shores of Lake Albano, a mediaeval villa watches over the valley below.

The hillside on which the villa stands meanders down to the lake and rises again on the opposite side to snuggle up under Castel Gandolfo, summer residence of popes for centuries past. On clear days a keen observer would also be able to spot Saint Peter's Basilica in the far distance. The permanent and the temporary homes of the most favoured of the Roman Catholic hierarchy, two for the price of one.

Today Hugo had to settle for one. A mist had tucked itself comfortably between the hills like a damp blanket and he shivered as he pulled up the collar of his overcoat.

After Sarah died, some friends had told him about this place. They'd thought the quietness and peace, the sense of reflection that seemed to seep from its walls, would help him as he struggled to deal with what had happened. But, though he'd booked in for a week, in the end he'd checked out after two days. It was company he sought, not walls and isolation.

Now, Hugo had come back. Perhaps this time round, if

these walls that surrounded him contained anything that could truly soothe the soul, he would grasp the gift more willingly.

He'd arrived shortly after lunchtime and been shown directly to his room, which, befitting the villa's history, was simple and plain. He'd eased the windows open into the cool autumn air, and from somewhere in the distance came the muted, high-pitched whine of an electric saw, mingled in with the chirping of birds. The white lace curtains had fluttered back across the small polished table in the bay window, and his stomach had fluttered in time.

Leaning against the cold garden wall now, he shook his head at the irony. Fate had led him by the hand, back to Italy, of all places. He and Sarah had fallen in love with the house they'd bought in Tuscany from the moment they'd seen it. They'd spent whatever time they could there. But in the end they had both come to realize that the house needed more attention, more frequent human presence. They'd sold it to an American couple. Hugo remembered the day they left for the final time, the two of them fighting back tears as they said their goodbyes, making ill-thought-out promises to return soon.

Two years later, Sarah was dead.

He realized with a start that his mobile phone had pinged and, pulling it from his pocket, he saw Marietta's name on the screen, a text message. His heart jumped. Had she changed her mind? No, the opposite. Her conference had finished early, she was skipping the closing function and getting a taxi over. She'd be there by six so they'd be able to have dinner together.

Hugo tipped his head back and stared up at the bleak sky. More than forty years had passed, but finally the answers to the questions of a lost lifetime might be in sight.

He spotted her from the corner of his eye as she turned the corner onto the corridor. She was wearing a beige sweater and olive trousers, tucked into brown ankle boots, a light-weight coat dangling from her arm.

Standing outside the dining room, Hugo excused himself from his conversation with a couple of priests who had told him they were on a sabbatical. The word had faintly amused him, given he'd understood priests worked on the Sabbath, but he wasn't in the mood to debate the point. He greeted Marietta with a kiss on the cheek and caught the faintest scent of her perfume. The priests decided to introduce themselves too and Marietta told them she was in Rome for a charities conference. She glanced at Hugo with a broad smile and told them he was an old and very dear friend who acted as an adviser to a number of charities. Of course, she added, being a man from the financial world he probably had one of the better rooms here, with a view of the lake. Not like mine, she told them, overlooking the car park.

Hugo had to marvel at her cleverness. She'd managed to let the priests know the two of them were just friends, and that they were staying in separate rooms. Maybe she was even trying to get him a bit of business. Nothing she had said was untrue. Just, well, not quite the full story.

When they wandered into the dining room, Hugo's face dropped. One long table had been set for all the guests. He counted ten of them, and most were already in the process of pulling out chairs. He pondered the thought that at some point in the development of social etiquette, someone had decreed that it was a good idea to separate couples. Perhaps they feared they might talk to each other. Hugo looked downwards to hide an ironic smile; he and Marietta were not a couple anyway.

Whatever the case, he was forced to take a seat diagonally across from her and, during dinner, he noticed how she twice failed to respond when she was being spoken to. Several times she glanced up at the clock above the door.

He sighed with relief when, at just before nine, the other guests began excusing themselves and making for the bar. Hugo and Marietta declined an invitation to after-dinner drinks and headed outside into the chilly evening air.

The front of the villa was lit only by a Victorian-style wall light over the door and the amber glow filtering through the upstairs windows.

Hugo didn't know if it was cold or shock. Either way he couldn't control the trembling.

Marietta stared down at the paper handkerchief she was stretching between her fingers on her lap. It might as well have been Hugo's soul she was tearing apart.

Somewhere in the distance an owl screeched.

When he was able to speak, Hugo's voice was little more than a whisper.

'How did I not guess? There had to be some clue I missed.'

Marietta lifted her eyes. 'You couldn't have guessed,

Hugo. Even I didn't know for certain until I was three months gone.'

He covered his eyes with his hand, massaging his temples with his finger and thumb. 'But when you did find out, you decided not to share the news with me?'

'I didn't get a chance. Your mum found out first.' There was no trace of rancour in her voice, only the weariness of a lifetime.

'My mum? How could my mum find out, if you didn't tell her?' He stared at her. He wanted to scream, but the energy had deserted him.

'She was a doctor.'

'Yes, but not *your* doctor.'

She sighed. 'Do you remember what doctors' surgeries were like when we were kids? Front rooms in terraced houses? People sitting in stuffy little waiting rooms in front of coal fires, passing germs to each other?'

Hugo nodded, unsure.

'You probably don't remember. You hardly ever went to see a doctor, but there were two surgeries and they both moved into the same building. A new medical centre. Your mum's surgery moved in with the one I went to. I'd been having morning sickness for a few days, so I made an appointment to see the doctor. It was the first week you were away in the Lake District. I waited till you'd gone, I didn't want you asking questions till I knew for sure. Worse still getting in a state while you were away. As far as I knew, your mum hadn't even moved over to the new building by then. Anyway, I had the test, then I had to wait two days for the results to come back. I know my own doctor wouldn't have said anything, so all I can think is your mum was in there and spotted me and went poking around in the files. I don't know, Hugo, maybe they didn't lock the filing cabinets at night. All I know is she found out about the test. And the result.'

'So what did she say to you?'

'She phoned me one day, out of the blue. All nice and pleasant, asked me if I could go over to the house later on. She didn't say what it was about and I didn't ask, I never thought. When I arrived, your dad was there. That's when I started thinking something was wrong. I'd checked before I went, to make sure I wasn't showing, and I definitely wasn't. I'd hardly sat down when she started on me, she said she wasn't going to tell me how she knew, so don't bother asking. She must have known what she'd done was unethical, probably illegal too. She could have ended up in enormous trouble. Anyway, she asked me if the baby was yours.'

Hugo whipped his head sideways to look out over the wall, into the blackness. 'I don't believe it. What a fucking nerve...'

'Anyhow, I remember staring at her with my mouth wide open, like an idiot. I said, of course the baby's Hugo's. Who else's would it be? She asked me if I'd told you and I said no, I hadn't, I was waiting till you came back. She didn't seem all that angry at first, but she was as cold as ice. I was shaking like a leaf. Your dad hadn't said a word. I'd hoped he might be a bit more sympathetic, but that turned out to be a big mistake. Your mum asked me if I could understand what this would mean for your family's reputation.'

'Not a word about *your* family then?'

Marietta shrugged. 'You have to remember, Hugo, I was nineteen. And not a very experienced nineteen at that. Your dad was standing for MP, and he was a director of a big company. A company that just happened to employ my dad. Your mum said that having a son who "had to get married" would be a disaster for him. She told me it would be the end of your career too. They wouldn't accept you into the civil service if they found out. She said it was bad enough that their son was thinking of getting married to a "half caste" in the first place.'

Hugo thumped his fist down on the table. 'Damn them,' he hissed through gritted teeth. 'Oh, Mari, I'm so sorry.' He filled his lungs with cold night air and released it slowly as Marietta sat in silence. 'So did my dad have *anything* to say?'

Marietta raised her eyebrows. 'Like I said, my first thought was he was going to be a bit more on my side. That was naïve. Your mum was so... kind of, detached, but manic at the same time. It was like she was saying I was some sort of little tramp who'd come from a working-class family and seduced her son to get herself pregnant. She'd never really been very warm towards me, you know that, but I thought that was just how rich people were. Your dad had always been okay with me when he was around. That's why it was such a shock...'

He waited for the rest of the words to fall from her lips but was forced to press. 'What came as a shock, Mari?'

'It was your dad who came out with it. He said they were going to give me some money.'

Hugo's eyes narrowed. 'They tried to buy you off?'

'If that's the way you want to put it, yes. I doubt they'd have seen it that way. Your mum knew an abortion clinic, they both said it would be the best thing. I'd be able to have a new start and the money would make certain I'd have the best life possible. I told them straight out, the best life possible was for me to have my baby and for that baby to be brought up by its mother and father. Your mum just laughed.'

She began rubbing the tops of her arms, but couldn't prevent a shiver. 'I'll never forget that laugh. Like her voice had suddenly become deep, as if she was deranged. Her eyes were fixed and staring. She said that was never going to happen, I should take what they were offering, it was a lot of money. All I had to do was end the relationship, tell you I wouldn't see you again, have the termination and then go. She made it all sound so easy. She wanted me to write a letter to you in Cumbria. Just like that.'

'And you refused?'

'Of course I refused.' She glanced around, even though the garden was deserted. 'But after a while, I mean, when they realized I wasn't going to just go along with their plan, that's when the threats started.'

Hugo gazed into her eyes. 'Threats?'

She gritted her teeth. 'Hugo, this was the nineteen-seventies. My dad was an immigrant. My mum was even worse as far as your parents were concerned. Wrong colour of skin.'

'So they blackmailed you into having the abortion?'

Marietta stared at Hugo, and had he slapped her face it

couldn't have displayed more astonishment.

'Hugo, that's what I'm trying to tell you. I didn't *have* an abortion.'

6

It was as though a glass curtain had descended around him, blurring the world beyond. He cupped his hands over his face.

He heard Marietta's voice again as if from a distance. 'I'm sorry, Hugo, I know this is heartbreaking for you.'

Sobs punctuated the words that finally emerged. 'We had… *I* had… a son? And now he's *gone missing*?'

He gazed up into the night sky. Through his tears the stars seemed to bleed circles of watery light into the inky darkness around them. He tried to speak again but all he could manage was a course whisper. 'How?'

She inhaled a deep breath and held it as long as she could before releasing it. In the process she seemed to have resolved something: now she had come this far there was no option to go back.

'Erik and his wife were working with the Red Cross in Mexico.'

'Erik? Your dad's name.'

'Erik Hugh, to be precise. My dad's name and yours. At least, your Sunday best name.'

'But if he had a wife, how old was he, when he…?'

Marietta covered her face with both hands and at last stopped trying to hold back tears. The grief shuddered up through her body and she sobbed uncontrollably, so much so that Hugo ignored his own despair and moved round the table to crouch at the side of her, one knee resting on the chilly stone paving. He wrapped both arms round her, locking her upper body against his to try to stop her shaking.

The evening had brought clearer skies and far away the twinkling lights of Rome provided an odd reassurance. That the normal world was out there somewhere, going about its normal business. In this cold garden though, the light was weak, and it set the little table and the two lonely figures in stark relief among the shadows all around them, as though they were in a soft spotlight.

When she was finally able to speak, Marietta's words were as soft as the breeze. 'You'd have been so proud of him, Hugo. I'll never forgive myself for keeping him away from you.'

The two bottles of Irish single malt Hugo had bought at the airport had been planned for Christmas at home. Or to celebrate, with Marietta. Maybe both.

They'd returned to their separate rooms, the only easy decision they'd made all evening. Marietta had tried to answer Hugo's probing about what had happened in Mexico but her teeth had been chattering and her breathing became so rapid she'd begun choking and was sick. Hugo knew enough to realize she was in shock and had wanted to get the night manager to call a doctor but Marietta had refused. They'd moved inside and the manager had opened up a small private bar where there were comfortable chairs and Marietta had taken deep breaths and sipped at a brandy.

Hugo had noticed the manager glance at him several times as he'd stood next to them, holding the brandy glass, and had felt guilty at his own frustration at a time like this, realizing he'd have to wait even longer to find out what had happened to his son. The son he'd never even met, and who had now apparently vanished.

Now, the first bottle stood half empty in front of him. He took another slug and set his glass down, then rested his head on the table, running his finger through the little wet circles that intersected each other on the surface. Patterns created by the bottom of the glass that seemed to move further away, then come closer and grow thicker, in time with his soft breathing.

The old saying kept flying round his head. *Money can't buy happiness*, so the wise men said. He glanced at the golden liquid in the bottle. *Maybe not, but it can buy a fucking better class of misery.*

And on the subject of misery, what must it have been like for Marietta, that night at his parents' house? Like a frightened lamb, facing up by herself to the formidable force that was his mother and her ferociously ambitious husband.

She'd fought it all for what she believed in. For the unborn child that would become Erik.

How old would he be, would he have been, now? Hugo's

brain fought with the alcohol and the arithmetic. He was nineteen when Marietta left. He was sixty-one now. So if he'd been twenty when Erik was born, his son would have been forty, maybe forty-one.

Marietta had said Hugo would have been proud of Erik. Well, chance would have been a fine thing. He reached out for the bottle and, without lifting his head from the surface of the table, tilted it over the glass.

And what about Marietta herself? He still knew practically nothing about her life, apart from that she worked for a charity. Had there been someone else? He hadn't even asked. He opened his eyes wide. Was there someone now?

Brilliant, she walks out of my life without so much as a by-your-leave, and some other bloke steps into my place. Erik was *his* baby, but someone else gets to bring him up. And Erik never gets to meet his father. *What kind of bloody justice is that?*

He surveyed the haze in front of his eyes and pushed the glass to one side. Folding his arms, he rested his head on them, more comfortable than the bare wood surface. At some point later, he heard something shatter below him. He opened one eye and shifted his head so he could see the floor. Shards of glass were scattered around an expanding pool, tiny glinting islands in a yellow-brown sea.

He rested his head back down.

The boy's face was in the shadows, so he couldn't see it.

Hugo knew the boy was in danger and wanted to help him. Now, though, the boy turned towards him and his face was suddenly caught in the light. But it was not the face of a child; it was an adult's face.

You can't help me. You don't know me.

But you're in danger...

No, only my mother can help me.

Where is your mother?

There was a knocking on the door, and they both looked towards it, he and the boy. The knocking was loud and Hugo had to cover his ears, but the boy seemed untroubled.

When Hugo opened his eyes he spotted his watch on his wrist. He looked down. He was still wearing his clothes, too.

He tilted the watch but the figures swam in front of his eyes. There was the knock again.

Holding on to the edge of the table, he forced himself up. He felt something crunch under his foot and lifted it enough to drag it along the floor and dislodge the broken glass.

He opened the door but whoever was standing there was made of light.

As his eyes adjusted, Marietta emerged. She was fully dressed, and had he not seen the redness in her eyes it might have occurred to him that they'd organized to go out for the day and he'd forgotten.

He glanced along the corridor and wafted his hand towards the table. 'Be careful, there's glass all over the floor. Sorry.'

Marietta wrinkled her nose as she inhaled the stale alcohol, but didn't comment. She edged round the bits of glass and pulled out a chair. 'Have you had any sleep?'

Hugo nodded at the table. 'Not much.' He ran his hand through his hair. 'Sorry about the mess…' He went into the bathroom and ran the cold water for a few moments before filling his toothbrush mug. He downed the water in one and filled the mug again. He squeezed his forehead. 'God, I'm going to have the mother of all headaches in the morning.'

She looked him up and down. 'I'm sorry to be the bearer of bad news yet again, but it already *is* morning.'

Hugo gestured at her jacket. 'Are you leaving?'

She raised her eyebrows. 'I had thought we could go down to breakfast, then go for a walk, talk about all the things we couldn't face up to talking about last night. It doesn't look like that's going to happen any time soon.'

'Sorry, Mari.' He rubbed his eyes.

She reached out and gripped his wrist. 'Hugo, I understand how hard this is on you, that's why I tried to run away when we were at the conference.' She sighed. 'I seem to spend my life running away. I knew how you'd be when I told you. At least in my case I've had time to come to terms with everything that's happened. You haven't.'

Hugo's lips were pressed tightly together but he forced the edges upwards into something resembling a tiny smile. 'You know, I tried to trick your mum and dad into dropping some kind of clue. I spoke to your friends, but they were as shocked as I was that you'd gone off so suddenly. I even went to the travel agents in the town, like some kind of private detective.'

For a moment, her eyes sparkled, a glimmer of

everything that was good about her. 'I knew you would. That's why I used a travel agent in London.'

He nodded. 'Eventually I realized you weren't going to come back and I was going to have to start a new life. I threw myself into my career. It wasn't the one my mum and dad wanted for me, it was my decision. I was past caring by that time. I started being rebellious, standing up to my dad. I wasn't going to let anyone push me into something I didn't want to do.' He glanced at her. 'I even had a few dates.'

She smiled wearily. 'It's all right, Hugo. I didn't expect you to become a monk.'

'I always thought I'd find you again one day.' He glugged down the rest of the water. 'Now, though, I just keep thinking, I'm not a young man any more, I haven't got a new career to bury myself in. But the shocks keep coming back. When we were in America, I suppose I started thinking, you know… maybe there could still be a chance for us. It's not as though we're that old. I haven't even asked you, is there someone else in your life now?'

She shook her head.

Hugo shrugged. 'Maybe I was getting ahead of myself, thinking we could start again after all this time. Then, what you told me, about Erik… it's just so hard to take.'

Marietta breathed in deeply and flicked the corner of her eye with the end of a finger.

'Mari, did Erik and Maria have any…?'

'Children?' She shook her head. 'No. They couldn't.'

'Oh God, what a mess.'

He woke again in the middle of the morning, realising he had his arms wrapped around Marietta from behind. Daylight had crept into the room round the edges of the thick curtains and bathed it in a half light. He let his eyes wander about, trying to sense if she was awake. Her silence was so absolute he was certain she could not be sleeping.

He whispered her name and her reply was instant. 'Yes?'

'I'm so sorry.'

'For what?'

'For all this mess. For all the years we've lost.'

He waited for a reply that didn't come.

He whispered into her back. 'Did you know I got married?'

'Yes, I know about that, and your wife died. I'm sorry.' She loosened his grip and wriggled round to face him, brushing his face with her fingers.

He tried to force a smile. 'When Sarah died the way she did, unexpectedly, I went into a kind of shock, so I know what it's like. I wish you'd let me get you a doctor.'

She shook her head, searching his face with her eyes. 'You know, Hugo, when you think of the worst things that can happen to people in their lives, the biggest nightmare is losing a child, because we feel responsible for them, no matter how old they are. If anything goes wrong, we blame ourselves as parents. I had to be realistic and accept that Erik wasn't going to come back, that most likely he was dead. I lost a daughter-in-law I loved very much too, someone who was like a friend to me. Those things stay with you forever. Oh, one day you learn how to smile again, eventually you even remember what it's like to laugh. But there's always something that stops you being totally free.'

She stroked his forehead. 'And here I am, talking to you about something you already know, losing someone you loved dearly.'

Hugo took a deep breath and blew it out steadily. 'It sounds like nothing in the world would have stopped Erik going up there.'

'Maybe, but what I blamed myself for was denying him the chance of being with his own father. Now look what's happened. What were the chances I'd ever meet up with you again? Both of us in different lines of work, living in different continents. Yet what happens? The nightmare begins all over again. Now you have to go through everything I went through. Only at least I had the joy of knowing Erik, you didn't even have that.'

She dropped back into the softness of the pillow, which muffled the words she spoke. 'So, what do we do now?'

7

The pungent aroma of smoke drifted through the woods, where the chirping of birds blended with the almost perpetual chain-saw in the distance.

They walked side-by-side and Hugo attempted to break the tension. 'Mari, what's done is done. We can't turn back time.' His voice was little more than a whisper.

'Except that you still keep thinking, what if?'

'I don't think anyone could criticize me for that. I just wonder if you couldn't have told me after you got to South America. You'd have been out of the firing line by then.'

She laughed, but without any trace of humour. 'And then what? You'd have had one almighty row with your parents, stormed out of the house and flown over to join me? Hugo Whiting, the son of a rich businessman, the big-shot politician, shearing sheep and mending broken gates.' She blew out her cheeks.

'If I'd had to, yes. But better still, I'd have brought my family back home, where they belonged.'

'Oh, right,' she shot back. 'Hugo with his wife and child, riding triumphantly back into town like someone out of the wild west. You, drummed out of the family. My dad with no job, my sister having to ditch school in the middle of her exams.'

Hugo's heart quickened. 'That's not fair, Mari.'

'But it's true, isn't it? You might not like to hear it but that's how it would have been.'

He took a deep breath. 'All I'm trying to do is understand, put myself in the same situation. I'm not trying to dole out blame.' He looked away. 'Well I am, in a way. I'm blaming my parents. They were beyond forgiveness.'

Marietta closed her eyes for a moment. 'Look, Hugo, you're right. Everything you've said is right. I'm sorry.'

Hugo sighed. 'Mari, the last thing I want is you and me to end up tearing each other apart.' He stopped and turned to face her. 'You know, I was thinking, what if we got away from here, stay somewhere else for a few days? It just feels a bit claustrophobic here. Why don't we give ourselves a bit of time to get to know each other again before we start making decisions?'

When she looked up at him, she tried to force a smile, though it didn't succeed in reaching her eyes, which were glossy with tears. Hugo reached out and wrapped his arm round her, pulling her close to him. She rested her head against his chest, stroking the soft warmth of the sleeve of his overcoat. 'I guess I've been on edge ever since I called you in England. I was really worried you wouldn't call me back.'

Hugo stared down at the ground and brushed a stick to one side with the toe of his boot. 'Mari, if Erik asked about who his dad was, I guess you had to tell him I was dead?'

She looked at her feet. 'Yes. I'm sorry, that was probably

the worst thing of all. But as long as Erik thought you were alive, he was always going to try and find you one day. It wasn't such a strange thing for a kid in that part of the world not to have a father. There were plenty of those. We talked about it once, when he was very young, then he forgot about it for a long time. It was only when he was in his teens that he asked again. Yet nothing had changed by then. Erik had his own life, his family and friends, he was settled. If I'd tried to get in touch with you at that point, all the old problems would still have been there and the fallout would have been even worse. I had to stick to the story. After that, it didn't get mentioned again. Now and then, I might start thinking, maybe there was some way I could tell him the truth. But both your parents were still alive and you were married. How many other lives would have been disrupted, as well as Erik's, if I'd just shown up with him one day?'

Below them the Roman autumn carpeted the ground and, as they walked on, his arm round her waist, twigs snapped and piles of dry leaves crackled under their feet. Ahead of them, weak sunlight broke through branches, forming a halo of light.

'Can you ever forgive me for what I've done, Hugo?'

'You don't need me to forgive you, Mari. But if it makes you feel better in any way, then yes, I do.' He squeezed her closer again and stopped walking. 'Mari?'

She looked up.

'Will you tell me about Erik? I mean, what he was like?'

She allowed herself a tiny laugh. 'Like you, to look at. But he wasn't good at the things you were good at. He was hopeless at sport, for instance. And not much good at maths or science, anything like that.' Her eyes glistened at the memory. 'What he was really good at was things like art and drama, and geography, history, politics. And languages, of course. After he graduated, he got a job with UNESCO. It looked good on his CV, but it wasn't what he wanted to do in the long-term. A couple of years later he got a job with a smaller charity and that's when he started getting involved with looking after street kids. So did I, after a while.'

Hugo nodded. 'I read about the street kids after the conference. I thought the movie star lady sounded really sincere.'

'Yes, she's done a terrific job raising the profile. But it's astonishing how it goes on and people hardly know about it outside Brazil. Can you imagine that happening in Britain, kids as young as two or three on the streets without any parents? Being looked after by other kids not much older themselves? How can that still be going on in the twenty-first century?' She tugged on his sleeve. 'You know, Hugo, I'm hoping one day all this sadness will bring you something positive. Erik's life needs to be celebrated. He was a truly amazing person, and so was his wife.'

'What was she like?'

They began walking again and Marietta's eyes smiled as she fixed her gaze on the track ahead. 'Maria just made up for the fact that they couldn't have children by looking after other people's. They'd have made wonderful parents, the two of them. We all lived together on a small farm, I suppose in Britain they'd call it a smallholding. It's really not that big. We were surrounded by animals. "Child sub-stitutes", Erik used to call them. And the two of them would bring kids home from the streets if they were ill. The children didn't usually stay long, though. Most of them get sent out on the streets to beg and thieve, anything to bring in some income for the family, and they can't do that if they're hidden away in someone else's house. Almost all of them went back on the streets eventually. There was only one who stayed, because his whole family had disappeared. And at least some of the others have got themselves off the streets now. They come back to visit now and again.'

'You still have this farm then?'

'Oh yes, that's where I live.' Marietta stopped and pointed ahead of them. 'Oh look! A little seat for people with tired legs.'

The trunk of a long-fallen tree lay suspended a few feet from the ground, anchored at one end by the stump of another tree and at the opposite side in a clump of low branches. Fungi clung along the underside.

When they sat down, Hugo took Marietta's hands into his own. 'What happened to Erik and Maria in Mexico, Mari?'

She latched her fingers between his and fixed her eyes on their interlocked hands. 'Somebody Erik knew rang him one day, a guy who worked for the Red Cross. You've prob-ably read about the drug gangs up there. The problem's out of control as far as the police are concerned. I think half of them are on the gangsters' payroll anyway, so the honest ones never know who to trust. As always, it's the kids who suffer the most. A lot of them were made homeless in the drug wars. Erik said it was heartbreaking, there were children as young as three or four nursing baby brothers and sisters, all of them orphaned. There were so many kids displaced, the workers couldn't cope.'

'So Erik and Maria went there to help?'

'Yes. They used to call me when they could, it all sounded a bit scary and I worried for them. Then Erik rang this one time and told me they were coming back, they'd managed to sort out some arrangements, the kids were going to be moved away from the area. The Red Cross had a temporary camp over to the west and he said they'd set off back as soon as they got them all in the trucks. Then it all kicked off.'

She squeezed her eyes shut and Hugo tightened his grip on her hands.

'Anyway, there was this one boy, a bit older than the others, apparently the police knew he had some information on the drug families. Someone tipped the families off, and they raided the camp in the early hours of the morning. I didn't get much information after that. The police said some of the workers heard a commotion going on and tried to stop them taking the boy.'

She glanced away and sniffed, as though summoning the courage to face up to the memory. 'Maria and three other workers were shot for their trouble, two of the kids as well. But Erik was never found.'

Hugo lowered his voice. 'So can I ask, what did the police do about trying to find him?'

She raised her eyebrows and sighed.

Hugo stroked the back of her hands. 'It's okay, honestly,

you don't have to talk about it if…'

'No, I need to talk about it, Hugo. And you deserve to know. It's just that the police in Mexico are riddled with corruption, so you're never certain whether you're getting the right answers. The Brazilian police weren't much better. They can't even get involved looking for someone unless the police in the other country agree. They did make some calls, or at least they said they did, but they never came back with anything.'

'Was there no ransom demand?'

'No, that's the odd thing. The police in Rio were puzzled about that too. But like I said, one way or another we got nowhere. Apparently there are experts, hostage negotiators you can employ privately. But for one thing there wasn't anyone to negotiate with, and apart from that it's dangerous work so they cost a fortune. They're really for the wealthy families, no one's going to employ a skilled negotiator for a five hundred dollar ransom, it's cheaper to just pay up.'

Hugo hoisted one leg to straddle the tree trunk and wrapped his arms round her. They sat without speaking for several minutes, Hugo rocking her gently, feeling, rather than seeing, the sadness. He nuzzled his face into the side of hers. 'I'm sorry about how I was with you when you told me.'

She touched his hands. 'You feel cold. Let's get back, I've brought you nothing but bad news. I bet you wish now I'd gone back to Brazil, and stayed there.'

Hugo smiled. 'Is that really what you'd have wanted?'

She shook her head. 'No, not for one moment.'

8

The restaurant was within walking distance of Vatican City.

Marietta reached across the table and rested her fingertips on the back of Hugo's hand. 'Thank you.'

'For what?'

'For being… well, just for being you. The same old, reliable Hugo I always remember.'

'Less of the old.' Hugo smiled. He realized both of them had started to do that during the evening. 'I still can't believe all this is happening, I thought I'd go to my grave not knowing. I very nearly didn't go to that conference, you know. I really didn't want to. But we look after a lot of money for that charity and there are plenty of our competitors who'd love to get their grubby hands on it.'

'Your mum and dad must have been disappointed you didn't go into the Foreign Office?'

'Yes, they were.'

'Tell me about what you do now. What's it like, apart from making loads of money?'

Hugo shook his head. 'Honestly, there's very little to tell. I liked it to start with, for a long time I suppose. But I hate it now.'

Marietta's eyes searched Hugo's. 'So why do you keep doing it?'

There was no humour in his one-syllable chuckle. 'What else would I do? I like the clients, some of them anyway. And Laura, of course. She's more a pal than an employee. As for the job itself, well let's say, I wish I'd have been a doctor or a scientist, something like that. Something useful.'

She screwed her face up. 'Oh, Hugo…'

'No, listen. A friend of mine's daughter was diagnosed with leukaemia when she was young. The consultant at the hospital was a specialist, devotes his life to curing cancer in children. Goodness knows how many lives he must have saved. That's a proper job, he can go home every night and feel satisfied with his life. I kept asking myself at the time, what will I have added to this wonderful universe by the time I check out?'

'Aren't you being a little hard on yourself?'

Hugo grinned.

'What's so funny?'

'Just that Laura said the same thing to me not long ago.'

Marietta nodded. 'Well, you've helped people keep their money and not lose it, haven't you?'

'Okay, but if that's the best anyone can say about me when I'm gone, it kind of proves my point. I can see my gravestone now. *Here lies Hugo. He helped a few people not to lose their money.*' He wrinkled his forehead. 'By the way, I keep meaning to ask you: that letter you left me, there was something about it that bothered me, but I couldn't put my finger on what it was at the time. I know it sounds stupid, but it was the way it was propped up against the vase on the table in my parents' hallway.'

'I wouldn't have thought there were many studies carried out into how a letter can be propped up, Hugo…'

'No, but you didn't have a key to my mum and dad's house, did you?'

'Course not, but what's that…?'

'So *you* didn't put the letter there?'

'No, I handed it to your mum.' She rolled her eyes. 'She didn't exactly invite me in as I recall.'

'Right, so she must have been the one who stood it there. The thing was, it was propped up neatly. It kind of looked proud to be there, like when it's your birthday or you've passed your exams. It was as though the person who'd put it there couldn't wait for it to be opened. The irony was, I almost missed it. The envelope was the same colour as the flowers in the vase.'

Marietta pressed her lips together, then shrugged. 'I guess your mum was glad to see the back of me. She had a different future in mind for her precious only son.'

Hugo took a sip of wine and set the glass back on the table. 'And what about the future now?'

'What future is that, Hugo? Do you mean mine, or yours?'

He raised his eyebrows. 'Well I kind of hoped there might be a chance they could be similar.'

Marietta took a deep breath and blew it out again, puffing up her cheeks. 'I don't know, Hugo. This was all so unexpected. I know we agreed not to worry this thing to death but I'm still trying to get rid of the feeling I've let you down so very badly.' She held her hand up to stop him protesting. 'Anyway, I wanted to ask about your wife, but if you prefer not to talk about her it's fine.'

Hugo shrugged. 'No, it's okay.'

'How did you meet?'

'It was when I was in my late twenties, her name was Sarah. We were introduced by some friends. A bit of a whirlwind thing really, we got married the year after. She was six years younger than me. Her mum and dad knew mine, I think they met each other a few times at social dos.'

Marietta allowed herself an ironic smile. 'Ah, so Sarah got your mum's approval then?'

Hugo grimaced. 'Ouch. Anyway, we had a few problems, but all in all we were good together. And we once bought a house here,' he waved his hand vaguely, 'in Italy. After a few years, though, there were some problems.'

'Do you mean the normal problems all married couples have?'

'One of them was she started drinking too much. I'll never know for sure, but I think one of the things was she knew about you, and what happened. Even if I hadn't talked about it, the friends who introduced us all knew about you and me. They'd probably have talked about it between themselves, before she and I got together. Sarah only ever asked me about it the one time. She wasn't bitter about it at all, but I always wondered afterwards if somehow she felt second-best. Maybe that's where I went wrong, I should have talked about it more with her. I think what happened was she created her own version of you and me in her own mind. Maybe she thought there'd only ever be one woman for me and no one else could take her place.'

'Another *Rebecca*? If that's true, it must have been traumatic for her.'

'Maybe. The other thing was not being able to have children and for some stupid reason she blamed herself for that.'

'Can I ask, how did she die?'

'A few months before, she'd had a miscarriage. Then one day, I'd just gone back to work after the Christmas and New Year holidays, and when I got home I found her unconscious. She was rushed to hospital but it turned out she'd taken too many anti-depressants and she'd been drinking heavily too. The coroner wasn't convinced it was suicide, she recorded a verdict of accident or misadventure.'

The waitress had reappeared, carrying a dish of pasta, which she set down in the middle of the table. Hugo stared absently as she topped up their wine glasses, and the thought occurred to him, not for the first time: people tended to think about women who had children and women who didn't; very little was ever said about the other group, the small, silent movement of women who nearly had children.

Now, here was a member of yet another group, women who *had* borne a child, but didn't have them any longer.

'Hugo, are you okay?' Marietta's voice broke into his thoughts as he watched the waitress walk away.

He sniffed air into his lungs and forced a smile. 'Yeah,

I'm fine thanks. Maybe we can try and enjoy dinner now and talk about something a bit lighter? What about you, were your mum's relatives in Rio or did you move there later?'

'No, I went to Venezuela first.'

'*Venezuela?*'

'Yes, I went to live with my mum's sister, Aunt Assunta. Now there's a good Catholic name if ever there was one.'

'But what about your mum and dad? Didn't they know you were pregnant?'

'Not at that stage. I was hardly showing at all. Remember, I was a skinny little thing. I just made up a story that I wasn't doing well at college, wasn't enjoying it. I told them I wanted to go and stay with my aunt, have a year out if she'd agree to have me. I made out a good case. I could learn Spanish, see the world a bit. Other kids were taking gap years, so it wasn't unusual. I said I'd come back in a year and start a languages course. It wasn't a total lie, I didn't know how long I'd stay at that point, I wasn't thinking that far ahead. Of course, the first thing they asked about was you, or more precisely, us, what was going to happen there? I had to make out I'd changed my mind, I didn't think it was working. They were dumbfounded, as you can imagine. I told them I'd explain everything to you in a letter. I said it would be best that way, avoid a confrontation. They were really upset by that. They said I should go up to the Lake District and tell you face-to-face. Or at least wait till you came back.'

Hugo smiled. 'At least someone was on my side then?'

Marietta barked out a laugh, but it was without any

trace of humour. 'You don't know the half of it, Hugo. It was my side no one was on.'

'Sorry, that wasn't a very good joke, I know.'

'I begged my mum and dad not to tell you where I'd gone, just to say it was South America. I know it wasn't a nice thing to do, leaving a letter like that, but I was scared if I did tell you to your face you'd start firing questions and I'd blurt it all out.'

Hugo rolled his eyes. 'I didn't even know you had any relatives in Venezuela.'

'No, it was my mum's little secret. Assunta had two children before she got married, by another man. Ramón wasn't the father of the girls. Mum was too ashamed to talk about her and she didn't want me to tell other people about her either. What with that and the fact my mum suspected Ramón was carrying on with other women as well. She used to cross herself every time his name was mentioned! But deep down, she knew they were good-hearted people. She just told me to keep a knife under my pillow in case Uncle Ramón came calling in the night.'

'And did he?'

Marietta almost choked laughing. 'No, I don't think I was his type at all, too thin. I think he liked his women meaty. Anyway, I was relieved I'd never mentioned Assunta to you. When I got out there, I didn't even tell her about the baby for a couple of weeks. I'd been trying to pluck up the courage. Then one morning I was out in the yard feeding the chickens and I started feeling sick. There was an old loo out there and I ran in and started throwing up. The next minute the door swings open and Assunta's standing there with a face like a bolt of thunder. She just glared at me, never said a word, all she did was jab her finger towards the house and walk off. When I'd finished being sick I followed her into the house and she forced me to tell her everything. The first thing she did was cross herself! I thought she was going to faint on the spot.' Marietta chuckled. 'Aunt Assunta of all people, with two of her own children born out of "holy wedlock".'

Hugo realized that, for the first time since they were kids, he and Marietta were laughing together again.

'Anyway, when she was over the shock she asked me exactly when I'd been planning to tell my mum. She made me call her that evening and stood over me like a vulture. Of course, my mum put two and two together right away. She was even more upset than before I left. She wanted to know if I was planning "by any chance" to let you know. Her and dad came out to Venezuela just before Erik was born and that's when I finally told them the whole story, about what your mum and dad had said to me. They told me you'd been to see them.' She squeezed Hugo's hand. 'I knew you would, of course.'

'So what about you? Did you find someone else?'

'The short answer to that is no. Most people in Venezuela live in cities, there's so much poverty in the rural areas, eventually people move out. Ramón's place was miles from anywhere, so there was very little chance I was going to meet anyone my own age. I just devoted myself to bringing Erik up. Then, when we moved to Brazil, we lived out near the University.' She smiled. 'Ironic, isn't it? When I was in Venezuela there was no one young enough. When

I got to Brazil, there was no one old enough! I met a couple of guys over the years who were just about in my age range. We went out on a few dates, but nothing more. After a while, I just accepted that's the way things would be. Besides, I was a "fallen woman", single with a child. Not exactly the best candidate for all those good Catholic boys and their mums. Once I got involved in helping Erik with the street kids, most of my time was taken up with that anyway.'

Hugo smiled. 'What was it like, the place where your aunt and uncle lived? I get the impression it was a bit crazy.'

'Yes, it was. It was a few miles from the capital, Caracas. They called it a farm, but it was more like a shack in the middle of a dusty old yard.' Marietta smiled at the memory. 'It was a lot of fun living there, once I got used to it. They were a big, happy family, in a strange sort of way. They kept a lot of animals, and Uncle Ramón was the local odd job man.' She covered her mouth with her hand to hide her laugh. 'There was no limit to Ramón's talents in that respect. He used to drive around in this great big yellow truck. It looked like it was falling apart. He'd go off and do these "jobs"' – Marietta scratched the air with her fingers – 'but he wouldn't come back for days. And he used to brew his own liquor. Rough as they come, he was, used to get drunk and shout a lot. But for all that, he never laid a hand on any of us.'

'Is that where Erik was born then?'

'No, that was in the hospital in Caracas. He grew up on the farm and they treated him just the same as their own kids. But when Erik was about fifteen or sixteen, Ramón died. He'd probably poisoned himself with booze over the years, but the official cause was oesophageal cancer. Assunta couldn't manage the farm on her own. Her own kids had grown up and left for the city by then. She decided to sell up and move to an apartment nearer to them. I just felt it wasn't the right thing for Erik and me so we weighed up the options and decided to move to Brazil. It was a more modern country and he settled down well and managed to get a university place. Even at that age he was talking about helping the kids in Rio.'

As pale fingers of morning light crept across the walls, Hugo knew he would not let Marietta go again. He eased up behind her, wrapping one arm around her body, feeling her warmth.

'Mmm, what time is it?' Her voice was thick with sleep.

'Dunno, but the alarm's not gone off yet, we've got plenty of time.' He slid his hand over her exposed breast.

'Not *that* much time, Hugo. You've obviously forgotten how long it takes us women to get ready to go anywhere.'

He groaned.

Marietta rolled over to face him. As she spoke, she toyed with the hair on his chest. 'You know, we've lost all those years we should have been together. But I don't want to pretend they didn't happen. And I definitely don't want to pretend Sarah didn't exist. I want you to tell me everything about your life, and I'll tell you everything about mine. That's the way we get back those lost years. One day, if you'd like to, I hope you'll be able to come out to Brazil.'

'I'd love to do that.'

'There is one thing though. I don't ever want to take you for granted. Just because we're here now, it doesn't mean I expect anything from you. You have your own life.'

For the first time, Hugo noticed the way Marietta's accent had changed over the years. It wasn't so much the way she pronounced words, but how she strung them together, emphasised certain things. It reminded him of the young Ingrid Bergman, though he knew the Swedish connection had to be coincidence. Marietta had grown up in Britain.

He pulled her closer. 'Mari?'

'Yes, Hugo?'

'I love you.'

She levered herself up on her elbow and her reply was matter-of-fact. 'I love you too, Hugo. I've always loved you, from the moment I first saw you, when we were standing under that awning and I must have looked like a drowned rat. I never stopped loving you.'

He nodded slowly. 'Then if I love you and you love me, it's about time we *did* start planning that future we were talking about.'

9

Hugo had a sense of déjà vu. He was certain this had happened to him before.

Two customers hadn't returned their cars on time and another had wrapped his round a tree. The rental company could offer a small Fiat if they could wait fifteen minutes for it to be cleaned?

An hour later the car appeared, uncleaned, and not long afterwards they were entering the autostrada north of the city.

Hugo glanced at Marietta. 'You've never said how you got involved with the street children.'

'Through Erik and Maria. It was impossible not to know about the work they were doing. Also, now and then they'd bring one of the children back to the house if they were ill or they'd been attacked.' Marietta spotted the look on Hugo's face. 'Yes, that happened a lot. Quite often by the very people who were supposed to be protecting them.'

Hugo shook his head. 'Isn't the government supposed to be doing something about it? Don't those children go to school?'

Marietta snorted. 'Well, they're supposed to. But who's

going to check? There's no one employed to go out on the streets and find kids who should be in school. Let alone drag them in.' Her voice rose an octave. 'You know, the most frustrating thing is that so many people have no sympathy at all for those children and their families. They just see them as a nuisance.'

Hugo stared at the road ahead. 'I'll never forget the young girl in that film at the conference. The one standing under the lamp post.'

'Yes, I'm sorry to have to say but street children get raped. Sometimes by the security people, or even the police. After a while, they decide if that's going to happen to them anyway, they might as well get paid for it.'

Marietta frowned and tapped Hugo's thigh. 'Hey, I thought we'd done our soul searching for a while.'

Hugo smiled. 'You're right, but what you've done in your life just seems so rewarding and I'm trying to put my own career into some sort of perspective.' He squeezed her hand. 'And please don't do a Laura on me, *what about all those poor souls with all that money you've helped?* I just feel now, I'd have loved to have been there with you, helping those kids.'

Marietta couldn't stop herself laughing. 'Have you forgotten something, Hugo? If you and I had stayed together, I'd never have been there in the first place!'

Italy was closed for lunch.

The streets of Siena were emptying as quickly as the restaurants were filling and only foreign tourists remained on the pavements, bending to study menu boards before looking at each other and walking away.

The waiter brought water and bread before taking their order. He returned with a bottle of white wine nestled in a bucket of ice and as he uncorked it, Marietta looked over at Hugo.

'Don't you ever feel like going back to the house you and Sarah had over here?'

Hugo shook his head. 'I just know it'll have changed too much. I prefer to keep it as a good memory.'

'Like us?'

Hugo raised his eyebrows. 'I don't want *us* to be just a memory, I'd like to think we had a future too. Except the other day you didn't seem so sure.'

Underneath the table, she wrapped her ankles round his. 'I'm sorry. I was just trying to protect myself. I didn't know what you wanted to do after...' she waved her hand vaguely, 'when we leave here.' She leaned forward and took his hands in hers. 'Of course we can try and have a future together, if that's what you truly want.'

'It *is* what I truly want, Mari. You told me you'd always loved me. It's been the same with me too.'

He sipped some wine and set the glass down. 'I keep meaning to ask, do you live on your own now, in Rio?'

'Yes,' Marietta replied. 'The house is a bit dilapidated these days, but it's home. It's too big just for me, of course, but I need some spare space. A friend I work with on the streets has a very wealthy husband, he's an industrialist. He's very sympathetic to the cause and he's happy for us to take kids back to their home now and again when they're not well. But I can't expect them to do everything, so kids come to my place sometimes. It's a lot harder looking after them now, without Erik and Maria.'

'Is it mainly women that work with the kids?'

'The regular ones are women, but there are men who get involved now and then.' She chuckled. 'Once, we were trying to help some kids who were living under a bridge. There was water running along cracks in the brickwork every time it rained and the ground was soaking wet. The whole place had this horrible smell, like dank soil. Just the stench of it made you feel cold. Anyway, six or seven of us went over there, all women. We took plastic sheets and buckets, but none of us knew what to do about the cracks. Somebody must have put the word out though, because after a couple of hours this bus pulls up. It was a bit unnerving because the buses don't normally go down there. The next thing, the driver jumps out and opens the side locker, then he starts dragging out these bags of cement. It was hilarious, the passengers were still on the bus, staring out of the windows, wondering what on earth was going on.'

'Did anyone know how to mix it?

'No, that was the thing, the driver says, don't worry, I'll come back when I've finished my shift. So later on he comes back again, but this time there were no passengers on the bus, just a couple of guys in overalls. They stayed till it got dark, fixing the cracks. The funniest thing was, the ladder didn't reach the middle bit of the arch under the bridge, so one of the guys jumps back in and drives the bus right up to it, then they all scramble on top of it and carry on filling in the holes. The council could hardly complain.

The guys might have been misusing public property, but they were repairing public property too, at their own expense.'

The waiter had returned and set plates of pasta in front of them, pausing to top up their glasses. Hugo dug his fork into the soft tagliatelle. 'I guess you need times like that, it must feel like an uphill battle sometimes?'

Marietta nodded. 'Sometimes, yes. Like when shop owners and passers-by shout abuse or throw stuff at us. Rotten food, soiled clothes, or worse. Once, this car pulled up and someone chucked a box of rat poison out of the window, told us to give the kids a treat for dinner. But the good people make up for it.' A smile folded out from her lips to her eyes. 'Sometimes I feel on a real high, especially when I get into bed at night and think about the kids on the streets sleeping a bit better. Dry and warm, properly fed. There are more good days than bad ones.'

'Is it a full-time job for you?'

'It could be if I wanted it to be. Sometimes things settle down, though. If we can get plenty of water and food to the kids, and none of them are sick, we don't always need to be there. But sometimes we have to work at night, if there's a specific threat to any of the kids.'

'Isn't that dangerous for you?'

'Yes, it can be, but we take it in turns to stay with them in groups. It's a bit eerie at first, but you soon get used to it. After a while it becomes therapeutic, people working together through the night, without actually needing to speak to each other. There's so much love out there.'

As they ate, Hugo stared out of the window towards

Siena's famous square and Marietta's voice cut into his thoughts.

'You look miles away.'

He looked back at her and smiled. 'I was, in a way. I was thinking about having to go back to London, how different it all is from what you've been telling me.'

Marietta's smile was tinged with sadness. 'You know, it's just like old times, you and me, sitting here together, nattering away. The only difference is now we're telling each other about our past lives, instead of planning our future like we used to. But it still almost feels like we've never been apart.'

Hugo took a deep breath then blew it out. 'But we *have* been apart, for a long, long time. And when I listen to you, everything you've done for other people during your life, it just makes me think. You know, I read something in the newspaper a while back. They were saying the top handful of billionaires are richer now than the poorest half of the whole world. Those people have more money than they could possibly spend in several lifetimes. How have we managed to get ourselves into that situation?'

She chuckled. 'Well, it's going to take a lot more people than you and me to change that. And as for you, dear Hugo, you can't just abandon the people who need you. You said yourself, at least some of your clients are worth your time.

Hugo nodded his head slowly, and picked up his wine glass. 'Mari, I'm not sure whether this is the right time, but there's something else I wanted to talk to you about.'

She searched his face. 'Am I not going to like this?'

'I don't know, I'm not sure *how* you're going to react, to be honest.' Hugo's features tightened and Marietta's smile dissolved into a look of apprehension. He set his glass down and gripped her wrist. 'I wanted to ask if you thought we could try and find out what happened to Erik.'

Marietta's pain was instantly evident in her eyes, which she turned to stare out of the window. Hugo kept hold of her hand.

When she looked back at him, she shook her head. 'I don't know, Hugo, I'm not sure I could…'

He nodded briefly. 'I understand, Mari, but it's just that you said about these negotiator people charging a lot of money, and I *have* a lot of money. I'd never want to get your hopes up and then you get let down again, but if you felt you could handle it, I'd like to give it a try.'

She swallowed hard. 'It's such a long time ago, Hugo, the chances of finding him alive after all these years are so slim…'

He began stroking her wrist. 'I know, Mari. But even if we only found out what happened… it might just give us both some kind of closure.'

They picked at their food in silence but after a minute Marietta spoke in a low voice. 'Would you let me think about it, Hugo? More than anything, I want us to enjoy being together again for a while. I just don't know if I could take any more pain, if we started to get somewhere but then it led to nothing.'

10

The heavy curtains kept out all trace of the sunlight, which was settling over the ancient buildings of Siena like a warm blanket. In the darkness Marietta felt around for her travel alarm clock and pressed the button for the backlight.

She pushed herself up to lean on one elbow. 'Hugo, it's nearly half past eight.'

Hugo tugged back the sheets Marietta had dragged up with her. He groaned. 'They don't stop serving breakfast till ten.'

Marietta rested back down. 'Actually, I don't want breakfast, I ate far too much yesterday. I'll end up as fat as a pig if we stay here much longer.'

'Okay, but if it's all right with you I'm going to go down for a coffee and have a walk around, clear my head. I don't know about eating too much yesterday but I certainly drank too much.'

Out in the frosty *Piazza del Campo*, the scene of the annual *Palio* horse race, Siena was heading to work, wrapped in quilted coats and jackets. Hugo made his way into the labyrinth of interconnecting streets that fed the main square like the spokes of a wheel. Bright windows displayed a delicate balance of the old and new, traditional Italian craftwork merging uneasily with the Asian souvenir shops. The glorious perfume of baking bread tempted him into a *panificio* with a huge black and silver sign above the window. He ordered a brioche and a thick, sweet *caffè corretto* with a grappa, to keep out the early morning chill. Then, suitably recharged, he set off on his quest.

It was almost lunchtime before he arrived back at the hotel.

Their footsteps echoed in the late-night deserted streets as they walked arm in arm through the old city, passing through individual pools of lamplight.

'You're in a good mood tonight,' Marietta said.

'Why wouldn't I be?' he replied. 'I haven't felt so happy for a long time.' He pulled her closer to him. 'And getting a table in that restaurant was a stroke of luck. It's normally booked up weeks in advance. I had to go in and speak to them personally. By the way, I keep forgetting to tell you something.'

'That you love me?'

He laughed. 'I hope I'll never forget to do that. But after Sarah died, a friend of mine who's into fishing suggested I went with him. So I went a couple of times and I got hooked.'

'You, Hugo, going fishing?' She stopped as she felt Hugo laughing at the side of her. 'What are you...? Oh, very funny.' She slapped his arm. 'Hooked. I was a bit slow there. But I just can't picture you, of all people, sitting under an umbrella all day long. You never had enough patience.'

'Well, for a start, I don't sit under an umbrella. But if you'd stop interrupting me I'll tell you what happened.'

'I'm all ears.'

'Anyway, four of us organised this fishing trip in Spain, near Granada. Then, just as we were getting ready to fly home, I spotted this house with a *For Sale* sign. It was a few miles south of the city, right next to the river...'

'Hugo?' She stopped and turned towards him. 'Are you about to tell me you bought a house there?'

'I surely am.'

She smiled, shaking her head. 'You really are full of surprises.'

'Yes, and for once, a nice one. It's been a real bolt-hole for me. A few of my pals have been out there. I haven't been for a couple of years though.'

'Who looks after it, then?'

'There's a lovely old man, lives in the village. He keeps an eye on it and does the garden for me. The local people are really friendly, they took me under their wing. And there's a restaurant close by, so I can get drunk and stagger home. I feel bad about not going out there for so long, but I've been so busy. I was thinking, though, maybe we could go and stay there if you'd like, you could help me turn it into a proper home. It could do with a female touch. We could go into Granada and choose some furnishings.'

As they turned the corner they found themselves in a half-darkened street, another victim of the Siena council's cutbacks. Halfway along, a single café remained open, the paving stones in front of it glossy in the bright amber light spilling from inside.

Hugo pointed. 'This place looks nice. Let's go in and have a nightcap.'

After the cold bite of the streets, the warmth inside embraced them.

'*Buona sera, Signore, Signora*. Please, come, sit down.' The voice came from a small man with a beaming smile who gestured towards a table in the corner, where an ornamental flame flickered inside a pyramid-shaped cage, splashing dancing orange patterns across the white linen tablecloth.

Apart from a young couple at the far end of the room, who were obviously finding their mobile phones more interesting than each other, all the other tables were unoccupied.

The man took their coats and as they sat down he exchanged a few words with Hugo before nodding and hurrying back to the bar.

Marietta raised her eyebrows. 'I didn't know you could speak Italian, Hugo.'

He shrugged. 'I'm not sure it's all that good, he might come back with something totally different from what I asked for.'

'And what *did* you ask for?'

'Wait and see.'

When the owner arrived back he offloaded tiny trays of olives and pickled gherkins from his tray, before setting down two flute glasses on round paper mats. He returned to the bar and came back with a heavy silver ice bucket.

Marietta watched as the man expertly removed the cork with the minimum of noise and filled their glasses. She pointed to the bottle. 'I don't know very much about wine, but I do know what that is. Some American guys on my conference in Rome were talking about *Cartizze*.'

Hugo smiled and rolled his eyes. 'You know, I've never tasted the stuff. I bought a bottle for a friend once, took it to his dinner party, chilled it first so it was ready to drink. He took it off me, said thanks and shoved it in the fridge. The worst thing was the stuff they served up at dinner was rubbish, I had a headache the next morning.'

Marietta chuckled. 'The people on the conference were saying how expensive it is. What's the occasion? It's not your birthday, I remember that much.'

Hugo made a show of patting his pockets. 'What's the occasion? Dunno, I've forgotten. Anyway, do we need an excuse to drink good wine? Ah, wait, here we go.' He pulled a small, shiny, red and gold bag from his inside pocket, holding it out.

Marietta's brow furrowed as she opened the bag and drew out the small box. 'Hugo, dinner at that expensive restaurant tonight and now this, you're spoil…' Her words hung in the air as she darted a look at Hugo and then back at the open box. Then she closed her eyes and whispered something Hugo couldn't hear. When she opened them again, the tiny stone, sitting in its delicate basket of gold filigree, shimmered as it reflected the orange flames of the space heater.

Hugo's voice entered into the silence. 'I know we've only been back in each other's lives for a short while but I think all the other years count too. Maybe it's time we were married now, before people start talking about us. That's if you're still prepared to have me.'

When Marietta looked at him, the same flickering flames danced in her eyes. 'It's beautiful, Hugo. And of course I want us to be married. I think we both deserve that now, don't you?'

Hugo steadied her shaking hand and, forty years after he'd planned to do something just like this, slipped the ring onto her finger.

Outside the cafe, Marietta turned to take a last look at the place where Hugo had, for the second time in their lives, proposed to her. It was only then that she noticed something odd.

None of the tables had tablecloths, except the little one where they'd sat in the corner and which was now being cleared by the owner.

The man saw her watching. He smiled and waved, and she waved back.

11

Marietta was turning the ring round on her finger. 'How come you managed to get exactly the right size?'

Hugo adjusted the pillow behind his back as they sat next to each other on the enormous bed. 'Well, you were never a jewellery sort of person. I could see you hadn't changed when I sneaked a look into that little fold-over case you keep your bits and pieces in. There was only one ring in there. Anyway, I borrowed it, I was praying you wouldn't notice it was missing.'

Marietta giggled.

'What?'

'That ring was my mum's. I just keep it there.'

Hugo snorted. 'Well, I got lucky in more ways than one then.'

She turned her head towards him. 'And by the way, Hugo Whiting...'

'This sounds serious.'

'Yes. Last night? How come that café was the only one in the whole street open at that time, and...'

Hugo opened his mouth to interrupt.

'... *and*, there was only one table in the whole place with a tablecloth on it? Just, conveniently, like it was there, waiting for us. You set that up with the owner before we got there, didn't you?'

Hugo's face was a picture of innocence. 'Who, me? I'm flattered you think I can control how long a man keeps his café open.'

Marietta laughed. 'Do you remember the first time you bought me a ring?'

'No.' He frowned. 'I mean, I never bought you a ring. We were going to go and choose one but then...'

'... I know about that. But there *was* one you got for me. It cost you two shillings from Woolworths.'

Hugo narrowed his eyes. Then he broke into a grin. 'Oh God, I know... when we went for that dirty weekend in Bournemouth! Yes, and didn't I make a big fool of myself somehow?'

'You sure did. You were going through all sorts of surnames we could use...'

'And you kept saying, why don't you just use your own name? It's much easier and you won't slip up.'

She sighed. 'Things were so different in those days. You were so worried about your parents finding out. And then what did you do? The woman's standing there frowning at us with the guest register and she looks down her nose and sniffs. She says, *What name is it?* And you get all tongue-tied and blurt out, *Er, it's Mr and Mrs Smith.* So she scowls at you and writes it down. She hardly spoke to us all weekend. When you said good morning to her on the Sunday she looked you up and down and said, *Well it is for those of us who observe the good Lord's word...'*

Hugo's face lit up. 'You know, I was thinking, maybe you'd come back with me to England if you don't have to rush back home. Just so I can sort things out there. Then we could get married in Venice, since you seem to love Italy so much.'

Marietta rested her hand on his. 'Venice? Gosh, I've never been there. Will I get a real wedding ring this time?'

'Probably. I thought we could come back on the Orient Express, from Venice to Paris? Like a kind of mini honeymoon. Then if you like we could fly to Spain and stay in the house.' He shrugged. 'After that, it'll just get boring. Getting on with the rest of our lives, while we've still got a bit of time left.'

'Oh Hugo, that sounds wonderful, you're so romantic.' She turned to fix her eyes on his, taking both his hands in hers. 'Can I ask you though, what exactly does getting on with the rest of our lives mean?'

'What do you mean, what does it mean?'

'Well, presumably you can take time off work for the honeymoon and come out to Rio, like you wanted to do. But what about after that? I won't be able to drop everything I'm doing over there, not right away anyway. I guess what I'm asking is, are we going to have a long-distance marriage, at least for a while?'

Hugo gave a brief nod. 'Just hear me out on this, Mari. I've been thinking about it for a while. I *am* going to go back to London, but not to work. I'm going to hand over my clients to one of my colleagues and quit.' He saw Marietta open her mouth to interrupt but gripped her hands.

'I've told you how I feel. I don't have anyone to leave my money to and if my parents hadn't acted the way they did, Erik would have inherited some of their money anyway. So let me ask you a question: what would *he* have done with it?'

Marietta bit on her bottom lip.

'I think we both know the answer to that, Mari. It's not too late.'

Marietta took a deep breath and her cheeks puffed out as she blew the air out in a long stream. She shuffled closer and wrapped Hugo's arm round her. 'Hugo, I want to tell you something. I've come to a decision too, and I *would* like to see if we can find out what happened to Erik. That's if you're still sure about it.'

He nodded. 'I'm absolutely sure, we owe it to him. Let's do this for Erik.'

In the afternoon, after they'd booked flights from Rome to London for the next day, they went for a walk through the ancient streets of the town.

'How do people get started, working with street children?' Hugo asked. 'I mean, Erik was obviously destined for that kind of work, but I'm guessing not just anyone can head down to the street and start getting involved?'

'No, you can't just walk into one of those little communes. The kids wouldn't trust you, after all they've been through. Erik had a pal called Adriano, the guy who introduced him to Maria. Adi was already doing work with street children, but he wasn't actually on the streets with them, not most of the time anyway. He was more involved in fundraising. Erik was the opposite, he wasn't the type to be desk-bound. He did start off doing that, working on the financial side, but he was always restless, he wanted to get involved at the sharp end. It was Adi who took him down to the streets, and it just carried on from there. Of course, we had the advantage that our house was fairly big, even though it was run down. It had some land attached to it, that's if you call some patchy grass and a load of dust land. But we worked hard on it, all three of us, and we got it looking pretty good. There were a lot of rooms, so if we needed to we could bring kids back there.'

Hugo sighed. 'It must have been incredibly hard for you after…'

Marietta heard the faltering of his voice as he looked away. She squeezed his arm.

'I'd got used to picking myself up when things went wrong. When I was younger, Aunt Assunta did her best for me, but she was struggling herself with bringing up her own kids and having a husband who went missing for days on end. Obviously I kept in touch with my mum and dad and my sister, but it's not quite the same as having them around when you need them. So it forces you to be strong.'

The corners of her lips make an attempt at a smile but it was no more than a twitch and her eyes told the real truth.

Hugo shook his head. 'You know, you and me, we paid the full price for someone else's ambitions, didn't we?'

Marietta raised her eyebrows and nodded. 'I just knew, somehow, after what happened with your mum that night. It could never be the same again. As much as I wanted to, I was never going to be able to hold on to you.'

In that moment, one thought flashed through Hugo's mind: Erik might have inherited his love of the arts and music from the father he never knew, but there was no doubting where his bravery had come from.

12

They elected to travel to the airport by the scenic route so they set off early the next day.

West of Siena the first flutters of snow announced that autumn would soon be turning to winter and there was already a thin blanket of snow by the time they came to a halt behind a line of stationary traffic.

After ten minutes they hadn't moved an inch and Hugo left Marietta in the car to go and see what was happening. When he returned, cold droplets were melting in his hair and running down his cheeks. Marietta fished tissues from her handbag and began dabbing him dry.

Hugo pulled a face. 'I don't think we're going to get through for a while. There's a boat fallen off its trailer. They're all standing there waving their arms about and shouting, but nobody's doing anything about getting the boat back on. I think we're going to have to turn round and try another route.' He put the car into gear and began reversing.

Marietta pulled her phone from her handbag and searched the route on the navigation app. 'According to this, we've still got over four hours to go if we go this way.

I reckon we're going to be pushing it. If we head back towards Siena we can join the autostrada. It's only three hours that way.'

Hugo nodded. 'Okay, well we're going to need to fill the car up anyway, so we can stop at a services on the motorway. We'll have to miss the nice views this time round.'

The service area loomed up ahead only a few miles after they entered the motorway and after he'd fuelled the car, Hugo went into the shop to pay. Seeing there was only one person serving and several people queueing, he stopped to flip through the rack of compact discs. It was the usual fare of Eros Ramazzotti and Andrea Bocelli, but his face broke into a grin when he saw an English CD on the stand.

Returning to the car, he hunched over as the snowflakes swirled around his head and stopped to sweep the wet drops from his hair. When he got back into his seat, his smile was still lighting up his face.

'What are you so amused about?' Marietta rooted in her handbag for more tissues.

Hugo tossed the small plastic bag into her lap.

A puzzled look crossed her face but when she looked inside the bag she let out a whoop. 'You're joking, they're selling this here, in Italy? *British Hits of the 60s?*'

'Crazy, isn't it? I haven't even seen that one in England.' He pointed to the CD. 'That's the soundtrack to our youth, Miss Forsberg.'

Marietta studied the back of the case. 'Wow, look at all these.' She held up a finger. 'Actually, no, don't look. You drive and I'll read them out.'

'*Flowers in the Rain*. I think that was the first record they ever played on Radio One. And Sonny and Cher. The Beatles, *I Feel Fine*. That's the one with that twangy noise at the beginning.'

Hugo waved his hand towards the dashboard. 'Well, come on, put it on then.'

Marietta slid the disc in the player and the husky voice of Chris Farlowe was the first to emerge from the speakers. She laughed. '*Out of Time*. That'll be us if we don't get a move on.'

Hugo glanced at the clock.

... *You're out of touch my baby, my poor discarded baby...*

Marietta rocked her head in rhythm with the music. She glanced at Hugo. 'Not very nice words, are they? I never really thought about that at the time. You couldn't hear the lyrics as well in those days, in glorious mono...'

... *You can't come back, and be the first in line...*

'Arrogant so-and-so, I wouldn't *want* to come back to someone like you, mate.'

'Mari, it's only a song...'

'Yeah, I know, but it's typical of the sixties and all that misogyny...'

Hugo tutted. 'God, look at this idiot behind. Fast lane of the motorway with snow falling and he's about two yards off my back bumper. I swear every Italian male thinks he's a Formula One driver.' He indicated to get into the inside lane, but one after another, cars were hugging the backs of the ones in front.

Out of the corner of her eye, Marietta caught a glimpse of the car behind in the side mirror. She turned her head. The BMW's headlights were flashing rhythmically and she flicked her hand at the driver.

Chris Farlowe was still doing his throaty best. *A girl who wants to run away, discovers that she's had her day.*

Hugo shoved his foot down on the accelerator, but the tiny Fiat struggled to oblige.

You're all left out, out of there without a doubt.

The driver of a flat-backed truck in the inside lane had had just about enough of being part of a procession of funeral-paced traffic. His indicator was a threat rather than a warning and began flashing at precisely the moment he swung the truck into the outside lane. Hugo swore and dabbed on the brake as hard as he dared, but yelled out when the front end of the Fiat nudged the back of the truck, which pulled away again before swerving into the central barrier. It bounced back and, as if in slow motion, performed a pirouette. Two heavy shunts rattled the back of the Fiat and Hugo heard Marietta scream as the front end began shoving the truck along.

And then he didn't hear anything else.

The spinning front wheel slowed, so that it would have been possible, if anyone had been standing nearby, to make out the spokes. Then, gradually and noiselessly, it came to a halt.

Even the white frosted feathers from the heavens were beginning to melt.

… you're out of time…

The song, oddly, kept playing.

BOOK TWO

13

The boy stood under the cover of the porch.

His dark hair almost reached his shoulders. It was wet and straggly. Though he was tall, his deep brown eyes seemed to flicker as he spoke, betraying his nervousness.

'I'm sorry. Are you Mr Whiting?'

Hugo craned his neck to see round the boy into the garden behind him. 'What do you want?'

'I'd have called if I could but there was no telephone number. My name is Paulo. Paulo Mendes.'

'Are you Spanish?'

'No, Brazilian.' He looked down at his shoes before raising his eyes to meet Hugo's. 'Would it be okay for me to speak with you?' His eyes darted past Hugo, into the house behind.

'I'm not in the habit of letting complete strangers into my home. Tell me why you're here, or I'll close the door.'

'I was a friend... I mean, I knew your friend.'

A soft evening rain was falling, pitter-pattering on the

121

big, leathery leaves of the fig trees around the porch. Hugo stared at the boy. He'd seen faces like this before, looking back at him from the pages of the local newspaper. Perpetually in distress, always harmless to look at. The moment you tried to be kind to them… your wallet was snatched, your car hijacked. Or worse.

'It's a long story…'

'I'll bet it is,' Hugo interrupted. He shook his head. 'You should leave now. You have no business here.'

'I'm sorry I couldn't call ahead, Mr Whiting…'

'How do you know my name?'

'I told you…'

'Yes, you told me. Now I'm telling you. Please go away, I've nothing to discuss with you.'

The boy lowered his eyes. 'I came a long way… I hoped maybe…'

'Please, go now. Before you get yourself into trouble. And don't come back.'

Only the closing door broke the eye contact.

The big man wiped the surface of the bar with a towel and with his free hand set down a generous glass of brandy.

Hugo picked the glass up and took a sip. He spoke to the man's back as he watched him tidying bottles on the shelf. 'Somebody came to my house last night, in the pouring rain. Did you hear a car go past?'

'*Está aquí.*'

'What's here, Toni?'

'*He* here. Your visitor.'

'What do you mean, he's here?'

122

Toni pointed at the ceiling. 'He staying here. He outside door when I open up this morning.'

Hugo knitted his brow. 'This morning? Where's he been all night then?'

Toni turned round. He raised his eyebrows and gestured vaguely around the room. '*Señor* Hugo. This my place. Is not much, but I run it good. This morning, two people come, man with pastries, and boy, sitting on step. He want room.' He shrugged his shoulders. 'If someone want room, they pay me. I don't have no cameras following them around.'

'Did he say how long he wants to stay?'

'No,' Toni replied. 'He come in, drink coffee, eat. He pay me for room then he go up there. He still up there. I don't ask no questions.'

'But it's a long way to walk to the town. And anyway, there's nowhere open late there. It was raining last night. Where's he slept?'

Toni guffawed. 'Hey, maybe he stay out in the fields, with the cows. All I know is he here now.'

Hugo drained his glass and pushed it back towards Toni. Without a word, the barman brought the bottle and refilled it.

'So you've no idea how long he plans to stay?'

'No, he pay me for one night, but he ask if he can stay longer if he want.'

'And what did you say?'

'I say okay. I need money like everyone else. Anyway, his passport here. He not go nowhere without that.'

'Have you looked at it, Toni?'

'*Sí*. I have to look at it, is the law. He from Brazil. Long way to come to see you. Why he not stay at your house?'

Hugo rubbed his bottom lip between his finger and thumb, ignoring the question. 'Can I have a look at it? His passport?'

The big man reached back to the shelf behind him. He tossed the document down in front of Hugo.

Hugo flipped through the pages and found the photograph. That was him all right, and that was the name he'd given. Paulo Eduardo Sousa Mendes da Silva. Born 3rd November, 2002, Rio de Janeiro. He noticed the passport had been issued just a couple of months ago.

'Know anything about Brazilian names, Toni?'

The barman stretched his face and held his hands up in the air. '*Señor*, I very happy. You think I am great man. *Muchas gracias*. First, you think I watch people all night even though they not even come here yet. Now, you think I some kind of expert on Brazil. I Spanish, *Señor*.'

Hugo smiled and scanned the pages of the passport, having no idea what he was looking for. He knew that Brazilian and Portuguese people had long names. When he was a kid, his parents had bought him a football annual at Christmas, and it was only then that he realized why two of his favourite players didn't have a first name like everyone else. Their names were so long they had nicknames.

He closed the passport and dropped it on the bar, sliding down from the stool.

The barman looked over. 'You want me to phone when he come down?'

'No,' Hugo called back over his shoulder. 'He's nothing

124

to do with me.'

Hugo was standing with the gardener when the boy came again.

The arrangement suited both men. Hugo loved gardens but disliked gardening. He knew too that there'd been little else but gardens in Salvador's life since the old man's wife had died. Over the years he'd turned Hugo's ragged, over-grown plot into a fragrant mass of colour, like a painter's palette. Hugo would gaze at it in the mornings and inhale it in the evenings.

It was impossible to guess the old man's age. Sometimes, Hugo could see in his face only the deep wrinkles of sadness, but on occasion, when he spoke about his two sons, both of whom had long since moved away to the city, his brown eyes would gleam like autumn olives in the rain.

Now, they watched together as the solitary figure picked his way up the narrow path which meandered by Hugo's house and eventually led to the road. Salvador threw a questioning look towards Hugo, who turned away to face the boy.

'So, here you are back again.'

The boy nibbled his lip but didn't answer.

Hugo directed his gaze down to the bottom of the path. 'You don't seem to have come in a car. But then again, you don't look old enough to drive anyway.'

The boy flashed a truculent glance back. 'I have a car, back home.'

Hugo tilted his head. 'Where did you stay last night?'

He felt a tap on his elbow and turned round. Salvador

was shuffling past. 'I go now *Señor*, come back tomorrow.' Hugo patted him on the shoulder and the boy stepped aside to allow Salvador to pass, then looked back at Hugo. 'I waited till the bar opened. Then I went there.'

'But it was after nine o'clock when you came here. What did you do after that?'

'I went to the parking lot for the visitors, at the Centre. There are benches there.'

'You slept all night on a bench, outside? It was pouring down.'

For the first time, Hugo saw the boy smile, which made him look even younger. 'Well I didn't sleep much. But I stayed dry. One of the benches is set back, in the wall.'

Hugo regarded the boy. 'I saw your passport. You have a lot of names, but none of them means anything to me.'

'One of them is the name of the woman who took me into her home. Her name was Maria. Maria Constança Yasmin da Silva. Before that I didn't have a proper name registered.'

'There must be millions of Marias in Brazil. Just like in Spain. Is that name supposed to mean something to me?'

The boy studied his trainers. 'This Maria was married to a man called Erik Forsberg.'

Hugo's heart felt like it was trying to claw its way through his ribcage. He glanced over his shoulder at the low garden wall and took a couple of steps back to lower himself down.

He drew in a deep breath. 'This woman you talked about. This Maria Cons…'

126

'Constança.'

'Why isn't her surname the same as Erik's?'

'It's Brazilian. Well, Portuguese. Our surnames don't work like that.'

Out of the corner of his eye, Hugo caught sight of Salvador, picking his way through the fields towards his house. He tried to stop his mind racing. He looked up at this unexpected visitor, this kid who was threatening to disrupt the life he'd carved out for himself, after Marietta had left it for the final time. After he'd tried to shut the memories out of his mind in much the same way as he'd shut himself away from everyone else.

He tried to analyse the sequence of events. What did he have to gain by the boy's arrival? What if he was who he said he was? So what? It didn't make any difference. He wasn't Erik. Wasn't even related to him. Or to Marietta. He was just someone who, what had this kid said, they'd taken into their home, maybe helped him out? There were lots of kids they'd helped out. Didn't Marietta say there was one who stayed on? If this was the one, well he was fine now, wasn't he, if he could afford to travel all this way on his own? What the hell did this boy want from him?

Worst of all, his very arrival threatened to bring back the ghost of Marietta herself.

Hugo pushed himself up. 'You say you've come a long way and I'm sorry about that. But I'm afraid you've wasted your time, there's nothing here for you.' He turned away, keeping his eyes fixed on the boy until he was forced to look away so he could begin walking towards the house.

At the door, he glanced round and their eyes met again

for a split second.

Then the boy shook his head and began walking back down the pathway.

14

H ugo found comfort in the white bookshelves and vases and pots brimming with green leaves that surrounded him in his study.

A large, brightly-lit window faced out to the gently rolling hills, and in the distance he could see the clusters of small urbanizations which lay south of the city of Granada. Only a few months ago, those same hills had been covered with a thick coat of snow.

Years earlier, Hugo had read a novel about the troubles in Ireland a century before. He could no longer recall the title, but the bit he remembered most was about a man trying to deal with the aftermath of his wife having died while giving birth to their son. He had left the boy in the care of a relative before retreating in despair to a remote island, where he settled himself in an abandoned stone cottage. He'd stayed there for several weeks, during which time the only person he'd seen had been a priest who'd passed by one day, and who continued to return every day afterwards with food and water. The priest had asked the man if he'd wanted to talk, but the man had raged. Raged at God, raged at the world. Raged at the very fact he was still on this earth, while the reason for his existence lay cold in the peaty soil across the short stretch of sea within their view.

In his damp hovel, the man had tried to come to terms with his grief. In time, he would talk for long hours with the priest, and after a while he had begun the task of writing something he called *The Rules of Life*. One day he would present *The Rules of Life* to his son to read. What gift, more precious, could a father give? The boy would have a head start, understand the mistakes adults make, try to avoid them. Learn, while he was young, the things his father wished he himself had known at that age.

The idea had intrigued Hugo ever since he'd read that book. He'd have loved to have done the same for his son. Or daughter. Or grandkids.

Except that he didn't have any of those. Not now, anyway. He could still write the book, but who would it benefit?

His shoulder was playing up and he knew he needed to avoid the feeling of depression that would come over him if he allowed anything, or anyone, to carry him back to the past.

Somewhere out in the garden, a movement caught his eye and he saw Salvador spraying a Mexican orange bush he'd planted there a couple of summers back. The old man's lips were pursed together and Hugo knew he'd be whistling one of his tuneless melodies.

When Salvador straightened up, Hugo saw him holding the small of his back and thought how he seemed to have aged recently. Another winter had passed and here, high up in the hills, it had been far more bitter than down near the coast. Hugo knew at least one of the old man's sons lived somewhere near the sea and had been trying to persuade his father to go to live with him and his family. But Salvador was fiercely independent and Granada ran in his blood.

Hugo sighed as his eyes travelled to the bottom of his computer screen and he realized he'd not even written a thousand words today. His book would be a long time coming at this rate.

His thoughts returned to the boy who had twice come to his house. He leaned back in his chair, eyes closed. Wasn't this what he was supposed to be good at, analysing things? What facts did he have? The boy knew his name. He also knew about Erik. The age was about right, too. And somehow this boy had managed to travel thousands of miles, apparently to find him. Yet Hugo hadn't given him any opportunity to explain why.

He shook his head. When would he realize he didn't work in the big city anymore? This was not a business deal, where he would work out the pros and the cons, play the hard guy. Due diligence, as they called it. Why hadn't he just given the kid a little time, let him explain? This boy might well be the last link to a family he had so nearly gained, but just as quickly lost. A wave of panic rippled through him. Where was the boy now, anyway?

He pulled his jacket from the hook near the door and went outside. Careful not to approach the old gardener from behind and startle him, he ambled round in a wide circle until he came into his peripheral vision. Hugo spoke to him in Spanish: *let's both have a break, let's go down to Toni's*. He knew Salvador no longer drank alcohol, but they could stroll down to the bar together and Hugo would enjoy a glass of red wine while the old man would talk or play chess with the regulars.

Maybe Toni might know something.

Sitting on a stool, leaning on the bar, Hugo was conscious of Toni glancing over at him as he filled customers' glasses or pushed cups under the hissing spout of the coffee machine.

The big barman wasn't able to restrain himself for very long. 'So, you no going to ask?'

'Ask what, Toni?'

'About your friend. He not here now. He stay two nights, then he say he have no money left. I tell him, you stay as long as you want, pay me when you can. He say no, he should go, get his things together. He only bring one small bag.' Toni mimed pulling straps over his shoulders, a backpack.

Hugo put his glass down, twisting it round with his fingers as he stared into it. 'So, did he say where he was going?'

'No, *Señor*, all I know is he go towards the town. But how he stay there if he not able to pay to stay here?'

Hugo waved to Salvador, who was sitting with a couple of the regulars around the chess board, and started off back to the house.

He stopped at the foot of the little lane and leaned

against the stone wall. His shoulder was hurting badly today and he longed for the return of the warm weather. But the sick feeling inside him troubled him more.

Toni had told him the boy had gone towards the town. He was also out of money. Beyond that, he had no information. That was the last link.

But it was also the first.

It was past midday. This was Spain though, lunch and siesta wouldn't begin for another couple of hours or more. He'd go into the town and ask around.

In the general store he couldn't get a word in edgeways as he scanned the shelves and *Señora* Ana chattered away. She was keen to reassure him. The days were getting warmer, the artichokes were very nice, that's a good year for *rioja* and did he see the young foreign boy who'd come here?'

Hugo swung round so quickly he felt another twang of pain.

'Which boy, Ana?'

The woman was nodding towards the tiny square beyond the window. 'He sleep over there, all night I think. My daughter see him in morning.'

'Which morning, Ana? This morning?'

She shook her head. 'No, it was two times I think. Dolores see him. He gone now.'

'Where? Do you know where he went, Ana?'

'I don't see him now for two days maybe. One time he come in here, buy bread, cheese. I ask him, why you stay outside? He say he come to see someone. But people no sleep in street here, *Señor*. This not big city. My daughter say she see him go towards *Parque Nacional* one day. He no sleep here last night, or night before I think.'

Hugo rubbed his chin. The boy must have left at least twenty-four hours earlier. But evidently he'd stayed around for several days before that.

The desolation that gathered in the pit of his stomach felt like a brick.

The heavy-set man at the tourist centre was sweating profusely and clearly had better things to do with his time than answer questions from this Englishman about who might have been sleeping in his car park.

Hugo had been down the day before, but everything was boarded up. Today the Centre was opening for the first time after the winter closure. The man was struggling to prop up the canopy over the opening in the front of the hut and Hugo took hold of one end to help out, which seemed to pacify him.

'Someone say a young man stay here on one of the benches. But he no here when I arrive this morning. I tell you, *Señor*, if someone stay here, he vanish with no trace. He no leave any mess. If he come back, I tell him you ask for him.' He waved his arm in the direction of the gritted open area in front of them. 'Poor *bastardo*, he have to be very desperate if he need to sleep here. He freeze his *cojones* off.'

Hugo flopped down into one of the bucket chairs.

He didn't need to ask, Toni came over seconds later with a large glass in one hand and a bottle of Spanish brandy in

134

the other. He poured out a slug and slid the glass towards Hugo before resting his back against the counter.

'I went to the town the other day.' Hugo volunteered.

Toni shrugged. '*Sí?* You often go to the town.'

'No sign of the kid. Ana said he slept out in the square for a couple of nights, then went towards the *Parque*. No sign of him over there either. He must have got the message and gone back home.'

Toni waited a moment. 'Salvador was here before.'

'*Sí?* He often comes here.'

The big man screwed his face up at the *touché* moment. 'At *ten?*'

Hugo looked over the rim of his glass. 'Yeah? That's early for him.'

'Then he go up to your house.'

'Ah, I went out for a walk. Anyway, he doesn't need me there, he knows where everything is.' He went to take another sip, but out of the corner of his eye he spotted Toni watching him.

'Why are you telling me this anyway, Toni?'

'No reason.' The big bar owner rocked his head nonchalantly. 'I just think he look, I don't know your English word, *preocupado*.'

'Worried? I don't know what he has to be worried about. He's fitter than any of us, and probably a whole lot richer.'

Toni grunted, nodding. He went back behind the bar and began washing glasses.

Hugo frowned. 'Are you suggesting Salvador's getting…?' His words trailed away.

The big man held up a glass to the light, inspecting it for

marks, then polished it with his towel. 'Getting what, *Señor*?'

'No, nothing. I was just thinking…' He put his drink down and stood up.

Hugo avoided the lane and headed back to the house through the open fields, playing out the scene with Toni in his mind. What had the big fellow been wanting to say? Salvador was looking older, frail? Shouldn't be working at his age? What?

He knew the old man wanted to carry on looking after the garden. It was his project, his pride and joy. What else was he going to do if Hugo called a halt, 'for Salvador's sake'? Who was he, Hugo, to make judgments like that?

Perhaps he could find him some help with the heavier jobs. He'd ask Toni if he knew someone. The trouble was going to be the old man's ego. How would he react, not only being taken off part of the job, but also having someone else working with him?

Hugo shook his head and sighed. He could do without this new problem. He had enough on his mind with this Paulo business.

He found Salvador round the back of the house, atop a ladder, pinning back an unruly climbing rose. He finished tying the wire, then nodded in satisfaction before climbing back down.

Hugo held the bottom of the ladder. '*Quetal*, old friend? How are things?'

'*Bien, Señor…*' Salvador brushed his hands together and Hugo noticed he didn't make eye contact. He took the old man's arm, and together they walked round the side of the house to the small table underneath the jasmine arch. Hugo pulled a chair out for him to sit down and went inside, returning a minute later with a jug of fresh orange juice and glasses.

He watched as the old man sipped at the cold drink. 'Salvador, are you not feeling well?'

Salvador nodded his head. '*Sí, Señor. Pero...*' He set the glass down on the table, but kept it between his hands and stared into it.

'But what, Salvador?'

The old man sighed, holding out his hands in a gesture of hopelessness. He seemed as though he was about to say something else, but returned his hands to the table. Hugo thought he looked like a dog that had just been caught eating the chocolates from the Christmas tree. He rested his hand on Salvador's and shook his wrist.

'What is it, old friend? You can tell me.'

'I think you will be very angry with old Salvador...'

Hugo knitted his eyebrows. 'Why on earth would I be angry with you?'

'*El niño*. The one who come the other day.' He looked up. '*El Portugués.*'

'*El Brasileño,*' Hugo corrected him. 'He's Brazilian, Salvador. But what about him? He's gone.'

'He *no* gone, *Señor.*'

'*What?*' Hugo jerked back.

The old man winced. 'He stay at my house.'

Hugo lowered his head in a futile attempt to make eye contact, cupping the old man's hands between his own.

'Salvador. Listen to me. *El niño,* the boy? You're saying he's been staying at your house?'

Salvador lifted his eyes and nodded. 'He still staying. He there now.'

Hugo jumped up so quickly he almost toppled the chair behind him and the old man wrapped his arms around himself as though bracing for an attack. Hugo came round behind him and squeezed his shoulders, planting a kiss on the top of his head and Salvador looked up, his mouth wide-open.

'Would you mind if I went to your house, Salvador? Now? You've no need to come with me.'

'*Sí, Señor.* Door not locked.'

The old man's words drifted into the breeze as Hugo vanished through the side gate.

15

As he stood in the porch outside the old cottage, Hugo couldn't help but reflect on the irony.

Not long ago, it had been the other way round. Now, here was Paulo filling the door frame while he, Hugo, stood back, as though on foreign territory.

It wasn't exactly the same though. Apart from the fact it was daytime and it wasn't pouring down with rain, Hugo did have somewhere comfortable to go if Paulo was as hostile as he himself had been.

Hugo nodded towards the inside of the house. 'Could I come in?'

A tiny fire smouldered in the grate under a mantelpiece crowded with lace mats and photographs: the old man's sons and their wives, their children too. Salvador and his wife on their wedding day. In the corner, an ancient television was showing an American western with Spanish subtitles. Paulo switched it off.

Hugo pulled out one of the chairs at the table. 'Can I sit down?' He realized he was treating the house as though Paulo owned it.

Paulo sat down opposite him, but said nothing.

'I'm sorry for how I've been with you, Paulo. Truly sorry.'

The boy nodded.

'I've had a lot of hurt in my life in recent years but I thought I was settled again. When you told me who you were, where you'd come from, I just couldn't take it all in. It was too much, almost as if everything I've found here, all this peace and tranquillity, was going to disappear again.'

Paulo listened, looking down at his hands, clasped together on the table in front of him.

'But I was wrong to treat you like that. I hope you can forgive me.'

Paulo shrugged his shoulders. 'I wanted to give you time. I thought, maybe after a few days you'd change your mind, let me explain. But I ran out of money. I had my plane ticket, but everything else was pretty much gone. After a few days, I knew I'd have to go back home.'

'But you didn't, though, did you? You came here.'

The boy's face muscles tightened. 'Please don't blame Salvador, it wasn't his fault. I went into the town, slept there a couple of nights. I wasn't sure whether to try one more time, go back up to your house. But then I thought you'd be even more angry if I showed up again. I was waiting for the bus to get to the railway station in Granada, so I could go to Madrid, to the airport. Then Salvador saw me.'

'Salvador was in town?'

'Yes, with a lady. She took him there to do his shopping. He was just getting back in the car when he saw me across the road, at the bus stop. I'd been to get something to eat for the train journey. He came over, asked me where I'd been, where I'd been sleeping. I only had twenty euros left. Salvador said I must come back with him, to his house. He said if I still wanted to go he'd ask the lady to drive me to the station, but first I must eat, get my clothes washed. He said I could stay here as long as I wanted. He wanted to speak to Toni, see if they could get you to meet me, give me a chance to explain. Salvador said Toni would know how to sort things out, but I was to stay with him till they figured out what to do.'

Hugo folded his arms and rubbed them vigorously, as though a sudden cold front had come down. 'It seems a few people have been far cleverer than I have.' He glanced at the fire, dying in the grate, and felt a shiver. 'You know what, it's warmer outside than it is in here.' He stood up. 'Come on, let's go up to my house. The first thing we need to do is put Salvador out of his misery. He was convinced I was about to sack him for letting you stay here and not telling me about it. If you want, you can come and stay with me. It'll give us a chance to have a proper talk.'

He pointed to the grate. 'Would you do me a favour though? Put another log on the fire? We don't want Salvador freezing to death when he gets home. Right now he's miserable enough as it is.'

Salvador was nowhere to be seen when they got back.

Hugo left Paulo downstairs, drinking coffee and eating apple cake in front of the fire. The window of the spare bedroom hadn't been opened for several months but with a couple of thumps from the heel of his hand he managed to force it open. Sweet air from the jasmine bush underneath drifted in, overpowering the smell of dampness that had assailed him when he first opened the door.

He brought clean sheets from the airing cupboard and began making up the bed, but now he noticed a movement out of the corner of his eye and saw the boy leaning against the door frame. His tattered rucksack dangled from his hand.

Hugo gestured for him to come into the room. 'Sorry, it was a bit musty in here. Nobody's stayed for a year or two.'

'It looks a lot more comfortable than the bench in the park.' Paulo flashed a quick smile and Hugo felt a stab of pain somewhere inside. He hurriedly changed the subject. 'How come you speak such good English?'

'I had to. For the tourists, in Rio. I lived on the streets for years. There are lots of Americans there, and Europeans who speak English. If you can't speak English, they just walk away and you don't get any money from them. Also *Vovó* helped me with it.'

'*Vovó*?'

'Sorry. I don't know the word in English. Like the mother of your mother.'

'Ah, grandma, grandmother.'

'Yes, that's what I always called her, she was like that to me. Except, when she died, it was like I'd never been in her life. I didn't find out till weeks after. She hadn't said when she was coming back, so I didn't think anything was wrong, but when I went downtown one day I saw this woman who knew *Vovó*. I think they used to work together. She said they were all really upset about what happened. Then she could see, I didn't know what she was talking about.'

Hugo nodded. 'I'm sorry, that must have been a terrible shock.' Not knowing what else to say, he glanced out of the window. 'We're a bit isolated up here. Not many people come this way, especially at night. Apart from you, that is.' He smiled and pointed. 'When a car comes along that lane at the bottom, it lights up the whole house. It did come as a bit of a surprise when someone suddenly knocked on my door late on and I hadn't seen a car approach.'

Paulo shrugged. 'I didn't know how to contact you, I didn't have your phone number or address. I suppose I was worried too, maybe you'd have told me not to bother coming. I was two days in this hostel in Madrid. The people there tried to get me some information, but they couldn't find anything. They said maybe if I got to Granada and asked at the *Correos* they might know. In the end, I decided I'd just come here and try to find you when I arrived. If you wouldn't see me, I'd go away. But I had to try.'

'But how did you manage to find me if you didn't have an address?'

Paulo unzipped his rucksack and rummaged through it. He held out an envelope. 'I found this at *Vovó* Marietta's.'

Hugo took the envelope from him and glanced at it. He recognised Marietta's handwriting and noticed the Italian stamp. It was addressed to a *Sra R Serafim* at an address in Rio de Janeiro. He ran the tips of his fingers over the writing. The boy was looking at him, waiting.

Hugo lifted his gaze. 'If it's okay, I won't open this right now...'

Paulo nodded. 'Sure.'

'But are you saying Marietta has written my address in this letter? I didn't think she ever knew the address here?'

'There's no address in there,' Paulo nodded at the envelope, 'but she wrote about you in it. She says something about the town, where it was, that you fished in the river and stuff. Also it was near the *Parque Nacional*. I went on Google Earth, there was only one town like that, and it wasn't very big. I got to Granada and there was a bus to the town. Then I asked at the *Correos*, about an English person, and they knew you. But I only got there late in the afternoon, just as they were closing. The last bus had already gone so I walked here. It was dark and I got lost. That's why I came so late.'

Hugo held out the envelope. 'Who's this R. Serafim?'

'Rosa. A *freira*, a friend of *Vovô*'s.'

Hugo sat down on the end of the bed and laid the envelope at the side of him. He sighed. 'It's a long way for you to come, though, Paulo. I mean, without having the full address, and without knowing how I'd react. How come you took such a chance?'

Paulo tilted his head to one side. 'Lots of reasons. Your son was very good to me. I used to call him *Pai*, like, papa, because that's how he was to me. He started coming down to the streets, *Mãe* too, sorry, like, mom. Maria, the one I told you about. There were about ten of us there, in a commune. Sometimes they'd give us money, but mainly they brought us food and bottles of water. This one day when they came, I was sick. *Mãe* had been over the week before and I was okay then, but this time it was really bad.

144

I hadn't eaten for four or five days and we had no bottles of water left. I was throwing up all the time. I had to keep going to the public toilets. They're disgusting.' He screwed his face up as though remembering every detail. 'The other kids were keeping away from me in case they caught anything. Anyway, *Pai* phoned the doctor, but he wouldn't come down to the street, so *Pai* brought the truck and they took me up to their house. The doctor came there and then I had to go to the hospital. I don't really remember much about the next few days. I was having these, I don't know the word in English, *alucinações…*'

Hugo nodded. 'You were seeing things that weren't there?'

'Yeah, that's it. Anyway, I ended up being in there for weeks and they told me I nearly died. When I was well enough to come out again, *Pai* and *Mãe* took me back to the house.'

Hugo stood up. 'I'm sorry. It can't be very pleasant for you having to relive those times. Look, we'll have plenty of opportunity to talk, but let's get you settled in first.' He gestured around the room. 'This should be nice and comfortable for you now. When you're ready I'll show you where everything is downstairs.'

Paulo nodded. 'Would it be okay if I had a shower, then got some sleep? It wasn't too comfortable on Salvador's sofa.'

Hugo made tea and sat alone at the table, mulling over the conversation.

Somehow Paulo had managed to avoid the real question,

which was why he'd come halfway across the world to find him. It surely couldn't be because Erik and his wife had been good to him; that didn't make sense. Hugo understood that they'd taken him in when his life was in danger, and he felt he owed a lot to them. Yet that didn't explain why, now they were gone, he would choose to undertake such a risky gamble. Or where he'd got the money from.

Paulo had said there were lots of reasons he'd come. But he'd only talked about one.

Well, all that could wait for now.

It was early evening before Paulo reappeared.

Hugo was in the kitchen and pots and pans were rattling on the hob. The rich savour of wild boar, onions, tomatoes and garlic was drifting through the downstairs rooms.

Paulo sat down and Hugo poured out a glass of orange juice and set it in front of him.

'Did you sleep well?'

'Yeah.' Paulo rubbed his eyes and blinked. 'I needed that.'

Hugo joined him at the table, a glass of white *rioja* in his hand. He pointed to the glass. 'Sorry, would you like…'

Paulo shook his head.

'What are you doing in Brazil now?'

'University. I'm studying economics, I'm in my second year. I always liked things like economics and math.'

Not for the first time, Hugo noticed Paulo's use of American words. His English was virtually fluent. He must have learned it from television; he guessed Marietta would have had one. Or maybe he'd picked it up from American tourists.

'I did the state exam for uni when I was sixteen. They call it the *vestibular*, but it's got some other name now. That's the toughest bit, ten kids chasing every place. You have to study like crazy. I did thirteen tests and every one of them was over four hours. It's easier if you can get on a private course first but it can cost you five or six hundred dollars a month.'

'What about you? Did you manage to get some private tuition?'

'No, but I did okay at school, so it was just brushing up really. I was lucky.'

'It doesn't sound like luck to me. Sounds more like it was your own hard work that got you there.'

Paulo shrugged and Hugo noticed he lowered his eyes before replying. 'Well, maybe, but I was lucky *Pai* and *Mãe* took me in, else I'd never have got that far. They made me go to school. It was different, after all that time on the street. I guess I kicked up a fuss at the start. But they helped me, made sure I did my homework and handed it in on time.' He chuckled. '*Mãe* used to check with the teacher. One thing I was definitely lucky with was being ill when I was, otherwise they probably wouldn't have taken me in. Crazy, isn't it? When I was doing the *vestibular* there were rich kids complaining about their parents getting on their backs all the time about studying. What chance do they think the others have, the ones on the streets?'

Hugo stood and stepped across to the old cast-iron stove. The stew was bubbling away noisily on the hob and he stirred it, before carrying the pot to the table between thick oven gloves.

Paulo ate as though he hadn't seen food for a week and as Hugo watched, the soft drumming of rain began again on the roof of the adjoining conservatory.

Somewhere between mouthfuls, Paulo glanced up. '*Vovó* spoke about you a lot.'

'I think she might have mentioned you too, but not by name. That's why I didn't put two and two together when you first arrived. Did you lose your parents?'

'I don't have any family left now. My parents, two brothers, a sister, *Pai* and *Mãe*, *Vovó*. Everyone's gone.'

Hugo felt himself shiver. His features tightened. 'Snap.'

Paulo stared at him.

'Sorry, it means same for me too.'

'That's another reason I wanted to come here. I thought maybe you could give me some advice. I know you worked in the finance business.'

Hugo furrowed his brow. 'Why, is that what you're thinking of doing?'

'Maybe.' Paulo shovelled more stew into his mouth.

Hugo nodded. 'Well, I'll try to give you whatever help I can, so long as you remember I've been out of that world for a while. Out of interest, shouldn't you be at uni now, or is it end of term?'

Paulo gave a sheepish look.

Hugo smiled. 'Ah, I see.'

The boy put his spoon down. 'The summer break finished in February. But I didn't find the letter till afterwards and the next vacation isn't till July. So I went to see my tutor and told him I wanted to try and find you. He was really good about it. He said we'd have to keep it quiet, the

148

uni kicks people out if they have a bad attendance record. He said he'd cover for me until the end of the July break but after that, if I didn't show up again, I wouldn't get back in. He sorted out a schedule of work I can do online.'

Hugo shuffled in his chair. 'Were you very young when your parents died?'

'When my dad died, yeah, but my mom's a *desaparecida*.'

'She disappeared?'

Paulo nodded. 'After I was in the hospital and then at *Mãe* and *Pai*'s house. When I went home, she wasn't there. I asked all the neighbours, they said she hadn't been there for a week.'

'So you had a home at that time, I mean, not just on the streets?'

'Sure, some of the kids on the street still have families in houses.'

A distant memory flashed through Hugo's mind, Marietta saying much the same thing.

'We lived in one of the *favelas*. Me going on the streets was no big deal, the streets are not safe but the house wasn't safe either, so what's the difference? We needed money and I could go and earn some. The main thing was I wanted a bit of space, because we were like herrings in that house.'

'Sardines,' Hugo mumbled.

'Yes, sardines. In a can.'

'So did the rest of the family live there too?'

'Well, my real father died before we moved to the city. My brothers and sister, we all lived together at the start. My sister's older than me and after a while she met this guy and went somewhere else to live. I don't know where, she never

149

got in touch. Anyway, that day I got back to the house, only my youngest brother Lucas was there. One of the neighbours said the older one had gone out on the streets, trying to get some food.'

Hugo frowned. 'So when your mother disappeared, your two younger brothers were left on their own in the house?'

Paulo shrugged his shoulders. 'Yeah. It wasn't unusual. I stayed there a couple of days, but my mom didn't come back. I never found out what happened to her. I had a friend whose mother disappeared one time, but she turned up a week later. She'd moved to another part of town because the landlord was chasing her for rent. She never told her kids she was leaving. I guess I kind of hoped it would be the same with my mom.'

'How old would you have been then?'

Paulo tilted his head. 'Eight or nine, I guess. I can't remember.'

Hugo leaned towards him. 'Hang on, so how old were your brothers?'

'Lucas is five years younger than me, so, maybe three at the time. Roque would have been six, I guess.'

'And Roque was out looking for food for Lucas?'

'Yeah, well, for both of them.'

Hugo took a deep breath and blew out, sitting back. 'So what happened after that?'

'Well, I looked around for mom, asked people. No one knew anything. My mother was...' he grimaced, 'she'd been on the streets herself, I think. In a different way, at night. Maybe someone killed her, it's happened before. Some men kill women because they don't want to pay afterwards.'

He turned his head away. 'I know she wasn't the best mother in the world but it wasn't her fault. I don't blame her. What a shit rotten life. My papa dies, I never knew the full story but he probably drank himself to death. Then she moves to the city, thinks everything's gonna be great there, new life. And what? Trying to bring four kids up in a two-room dump. No work, no money for proper food. She did the best she could for us. I still miss her.' He shook his head as though it might erase the memory. 'Anyway, I took Lucas down to the streets and we stayed there for a few days. Roque wasn't down there, he'd disappeared. I've no idea where he is now.'

Hugo emptied his wine glass and refilled it. 'So, you were eight or nine and you were left looking after a three-year-old on your own?'

'At first, the other kids looked after Lucas while I went to try and earn some money. But I couldn't keep asking them to do that. They needed to go out and get money themselves. I was getting really desperate. Then, *Mãe* and *Pai* came down one day. They'd heard what had happened and asked me if I wanted to go back to their house again and bring Lucas. I didn't have any choice. Later, I went back to the streets, but I was spending less time there and more time at *Mãe* and *Pai*'s house. Lucas stayed too, but when he got older he started going off to the street again, not coming back at night. After that he got involved in a drug gang and then one day...'

For the first time, Paulo's voice began to break. He sipped at his drink and Hugo decided to change the subject.

'You say Marietta, *Vovó*, she talked to you about me?'

'Yeah, lots of times. One time she was clearing out some drawers and she had all these photos.' Paulo's eyes seemed to smile at the memory. 'I'd never seen photos before. I mean, paper ones, people have them on their phones now. Anyway, she was sorting through them. It took her all day, because she kept stopping and looking at them for a long time. Sometimes she was smiling, other times she was crying. There was this one photo, when she was young, she showed it to me. She was sitting next to this boy about the same age. They were in this, I don't know the word, like a round thing.' He opened his arms out and described an arc round the front of himself with his hands. 'They had this kind of bar across the front of them. *Vovó* said it was taken at a fun fair. I asked her who the boy was and she said it was *Pai*'s father.'

Hugo lowered his voice to a whisper. 'Paulo, when this happened, that day, was *Pai* Erik still around, I mean, was it before he went up to Mexico?'

Paulo frowned, and tilted his chin back for a second. 'No, because I remember *Vovó* was looking at photos of him too. That's when she was crying. It was after *Pai* went missing.'

16

When the morning came, Paulo seemed to be practising answering every question with one syllable. Hugo concluded he was tired after sleeping rough or on ancient threadbare settees over the last few nights and didn't push him. There was plenty of time.

After breakfast, they strolled along the bank of the narrow river which flowed down from the mountains and meandered through the *Parque Nacional*, passing the little houses scattered along the low hillside and on towards the town beyond.

The mid-morning sun winked from the silvery, shimmering water as birds flew busily overhead, going about the everyday business of life. A splash betrayed the presence of one of the small brown trout that made their home in the river and Paulo's eyes followed the ripples on the surface.

Hugo glanced sideways. 'Is everything okay, Paulo?'
Paulo looked across but just as quickly averted his eyes.
'Paulo…?'
The boy stopped walking and began scratching at the ground with the toe end of his trainer, hands in the pockets of his jeans. 'It's just I don't understand why you did what

you did.'

Hugo's attempt to make eye contact failed. 'What do you mean, Paulo? What did I do?'

'What you did with *Vovó*, when you were both young.'

Hugo shook his head briefly as if he thought that might clear it, and his brow furrowed. 'Am I missing something here? What exactly is it you think I did?'

Finally, Paulo met Hugo's gaze and Hugo saw the sadness in his young features. 'She loved you, very much.'

Hugo cleared his throat and spoke quietly. 'And I loved her very much too, Paulo. But you're still not making sense. What am I supposed to have done?'

Paulo set off walking again and Hugo stood with his arms spread, turning to appeal to a witness who hadn't shown up. He called after him. 'Paulo, would you just tell me, what is it that's upsetting you all of a sudden?'

The boy stopped and looked back. Hugo could see his face was flushed. 'She was having your baby, but you sent her away.'

Hugo's mouth hung open. He rubbed his forehead with his fingers. 'Is that what you think happened, Paulo?'

Paulo returned his eyes to his feet.

'Paulo, is that what you think I did? Are you saying that's what Marietta told you? Because I don't think she'd have said anything like that to you.'

Paulo stabbed his finger towards Hugo. 'No, she didn't say that.' He swung his arm as if swatting a fly. 'She never said anything against you, ever. Always, she said how much she loved you. But how could she love you so much, and you go and send her away?'

Hugo felt the blood race to his cheeks. He opened his mouth to speak, but checked himself, not wanting to utter words that would destroy any relationship the two of them might have built up before it even got started. He knew the boy was bound to be emotional. He had every reason to be.

He stared towards the river, his eyes following the different circles of ripples radiating out on the surface and disappearing just as quickly. When he felt his heartbeat slow to a calmer rate he turned his head to look back at the boy, who was biting his lip and gazing towards the hillside. He kept his voice low and steady. 'Paulo, I really do think we need to have a good talk if we're going to make this thing work.'

Paulo was sitting on the bank, scanning the surface of the silver water and hugging his knees into his chest

The moment of anger appeared to have passed and Hugo felt content to listen to the river's musical notes as it wound its way around the jagged rocks, feeling the warm breeze caress his face.

He stood up and stretched his back, turning away to ensure Paulo couldn't see his face. 'I think I can understand how you might have got that idea, but I hope you understand better now. That's how it happened, how Marietta and I lost forty years of our lives together. Because of the selfishness of other people, people who were close to me, my own family. And do you know what? After all that, Marietta still cared about my parents' feelings. She didn't want to upset their lives, so even though she knew my wife had died, even then she didn't bring Erik back to England.

Because she knew my mother and father were still alive. That's the woman she was, Paulo, and I can assure you I loved her every bit as much as she loved me.'

Paulo continued to stare towards the river. When he spoke, his voice was so quiet Hugo had to strain to hear. 'I'm sorry. I didn't know…'

Hugo managed only a nod, because at that moment the relief flooded up through him, shuddering to the surface. He realized he'd never told this story to anyone, not even Laura.

Keeping his back to Paulo, he surveyed the mountains around them, seeing nothing. Then he turned and held out his hand and Paulo gripped it, pulling himself up. Together, they began the walk up the narrow pathway to the house.

17

Weekend came around with no further mention of Paulo's future plans and more questions were burrowing into Hugo's mind.

On the Friday evening, Hugo suggested going down to Toni's for dinner.

The moment he saw them coming through the door, Toni bounded over to greet them.

'*Señor* Hugo, please, come in. And young *Señor*, how are you?' He shook Paulo's hand vigorously. 'Are you going to eat? I bring you some wine.'

'Don't go crazy, Toni,' Hugo called after his retreating footsteps. 'No need for *1999 Gran Reserva* tonight.'

'*99* not good now,' Toni called back over his shoulder as he disappeared through a side door.

Hugo smiled and shook his head. 'He doesn't often display his emotions. I think he and old Salvador were in league.'

'In league?'

'Planning things together. Making sure *you* stayed *here*.'

Moments later, Toni was back, the familiar towel over one arm and the neck of a bottle of wine gripped in his enormous hand. He uncorked the bottle and filled their glasses. '*Señores*, we have beautiful *cordero*, fresh lamb, tonight.' He kissed the tips of his fingers. 'Also fresh vegetables, potatoes. You not be disappointed.'

Paulo smiled, watching him rushing round. 'When I was staying here I only ate bread and cheese and a few pastries. And I've only ever had wine since I came to stay with you. When I was growing up it was just water, or a Pepsi if I got lucky and someone left some in a can. I never even had beer till I started uni.'

Hugo grimaced. 'It must have been incredibly tough, life on the streets.'

'It was exciting when it first started, after living in the *favela*. Like a new world. Nobody to tell us what to do, good friends. We were safe together. It was hard, but there were good times.' He stared towards the window and laughed. 'Sometimes, after we'd been begging on the streets, we'd use the money to buy bus passes. Speculate to accumulate! Beg for the money, pay to get on the bus, then beg from the passengers. It was crazy. If we could find a bus stop with lots of people waiting, we could hide between them and try and get on free. We'd go up and down the bus asking for money, some of us on one side and the rest on the other. It was really funny, if one of the passengers put his hand in his pocket all the kids on the other side of the bus would rush over!'

'How come the bus drivers didn't throw you all off?'

'Sometimes they did, but mostly they couldn't be bothered. Some of them would let us on anyway if we agreed to clean the bus after they'd finished their shift.'

Paulo rolled his eyes. 'Sometimes, if there were girls with us, they'd try and make another deal. Most of the time it was okay though, we all looked out for each other. It was tougher if you got sick like I did, it could be horrible. And some of the police were really bad with us.'

Hugo nodded. 'Yes, Marietta told me. You know, people here in Spain sometimes think the police are heavy-handed. I don't think they're anywhere near as bad as the ones you had to put up with.'

'One really bad thing happened, at the *Candelária*, that's the big church in Rio. I wasn't born at the time but they say there were all these kids sleeping rough at the side of the building. Lots of men came during the night, with masks on. They shot at the kids and some of them were killed. Most of them were asleep till they heard the shooting.'

Hugo closed his eyes. He remembered the movie star, all that time ago in San Francisco, launching the *Light a Candle* charity. The brochures they'd sent out mentioned *Candelária*.

Toni was back at the table, setting down an enormous plate of steaming vegetables and a wooden board stacked high with lamb. Hugo watched him walk away, then turned back to Paulo.

'I read about the *Candelária*. The men that killed the kids were police, weren't they?'

'Yeah, but only two of them went to jail.'

Hugo sighed. 'In Britain I used to read the newspaper every morning. I don't remember ever seeing anything about that. I suppose it was all a bit too far away to make the international news. It didn't affect the western economy.'

He studied Paulo sawing away at the lamb. 'Did your family move straight into a *favela* when they arrived in the city?'

Paulo snapped the heel from the loaf of bread in the centre of the table. His mouth was half full as he spoke. 'No, we had an apartment first. It was small, but it was okay, I liked it. But it looked out over a big square. Then one day the police came and told everyone they had to get out of the apartments. They said the government was going to pay everyone compensation, but we had to be gone in ten days. Everything, furniture, clothes. They wrote down people's names and addresses but the money never came.'

Toni appeared at the side of them. 'Everything good, no?' He topped up their wine glasses. 'One day I will grow my own vegetables.' He pointed towards the window. 'Look at all that wasted land. Anyway, *Señor* Hugo, when you going to take this boy to the river to fish? Or better, take him to a bigger river. Bring me back something my customers can eat.'

Hugo glanced at Paulo. 'Have you ever been fishing?'

Paulo shook his head.

'Would you like to?'

'I don't know,' Paulo managed, through a mouthful of lamb. 'I don't know anything about fishing. Only the boats that go out from Rio.'

Hugo smiled. 'Well, this won't be anything like that, but you might enjoy it. I haven't been out fishing this year and the weather's a lot better now.'

Hugo woke during the early hours of the morning. He turned his pillow over and gave it a punch, then for good measure turned himself over too. Neither helped him get off to sleep again.

As hard as he tried, he couldn't rationalize the way this boy, who'd plummeted into his life, seemed to deal with things. Hugo had spent a lifetime solving problems in a logical fashion and over time he'd developed a gut instinct which he trusted far more than any computer. Diverse particles of information had a habit of lodging, unused for long periods, somewhere in the recesses of his brain. Then, when situations arose, they would send a message to his consciousness, telling him that some of those particles were not sitting comfortably in each other's company.

This was a kid who'd spent much of his childhood 'on the streets', a phrase that tripped off the tongue easily enough but had a deeper meaning when you thought it through. Cold pavement slabs, dirt, begging, stealing, drugs, city-centre public toilets, no baths or showers, disease, sickness. Rejection, abuse, dreams knocked back time and again. Yet here was Paulo, almost fluent in a language that wasn't his own, knowledgeable, even a little eloquent. Not shy or uncomfortable in the company of people he didn't know so well.

Over dinner the evening before, he'd made a casual reference to the massacre of young, sleeping children by the so-called forces of law, while hardly stopping shovelling down lamb and topping up his glass with wine.

And what about his outburst a few days earlier? Why did Hugo walk out and abandon Marietta when she was carrying his child, he'd asked. No, not asked: virtually accused him. There was no way in this wide world Marietta would have told him that, or even allowed him to think along those lines. So where did he get that idea?

New, abstract thoughts were tumbling through Hugo's mind in the darkness, like the contents of a litter bin caught by a gust of wind.

How was it too that Paulo had apparently worked so hard to get into university and yet could come here in term time, assisted by a conveniently tolerant tutor who was prepared to cover up for a long absence?

Then the coincidental meeting with Salvador, just as the old man was getting into his friend's car after a rare excursion to the town. Exactly at the moment Paulo was waiting for the bus that would take him to Granada, and onwards to home. Just as his money was running out.

What was beyond dispute was that Paulo, or someone Paulo knew, had access to the house where Marietta had lived. She herself had said the place was run down, so that couldn't have been hard. And, once inside the house, presumably the letter and the photographs he'd talked about would be easy to find. What had Paulo told him that anyone who'd managed to get into that house would not have known, or been able to discover?

In short, how could he be sure Paulo *was* the boy Marietta had spoken about, the one kid who'd remained at her house when all the others had gone back to the streets?

Not for the first time he wished Marietta could find a way to speak to him.

Paulo appeared after ten, his long hair sticking out and up in various directions.

The sky was gunmetal grey and he rubbed the back of his neck as he craned to peer out of the kitchen window. He shook his head and crossed over to the table to pour himself a coffee. 'That's too bad.'

'What's too bad?' Hugo cracked an egg into a pan and a sizzle rose up.

'The weather. I guess the fishing trip will have to wait.'

'Why, what's wrong with today?' Hugo turned round to face him.

'It looks cold out there.'

Hugo rolled his eyes. 'I'll lend you a coat. Anyway, it'll be warm by midday. We don't want it to get too hot, otherwise the fish are going to start going deeper down. We need them up near the surface where we can see them.'

Paulo blinked and pulled a face. 'Why did Toni say we'd have to go to a bigger river to catch something we can eat?'

Hugo slid the eggs onto a plate and put them down in front of Paulo. 'He was joking, that's not the reason we go fishing. It's the sport. It's like a battle of wits between us and the fish.'

'It seems like a waste of energy, if you can't eat them.' Paulo sipped his coffee. 'I keep meaning to say, I'm sorry about what I said the other day, about you and *Vovó*.'

Hugo shrugged. 'Forget it, it was my fault, I should have told you the story earlier. It's just that it still hurts, even now. That's why I've not opened that letter you gave me. I guess we're both just a bit raw.' He tapped Paulo on the shoulder. 'Come on, eat up. We'll get going when you've finished.'

'What am I supposed to do with these?'

Hugo was fiddling with a rod and turned to see Paulo dangling the thigh-length waders from his hands, measuring them against his legs. He stifled the urge to laugh. 'You need them because you don't want to get soaked.'

Paulo nodded towards the rod in Hugo's hands. 'How will I get soaked dangling that thing into the river?'

'Because you *won't* be dangling this thing into the river., you'll be going in with it. You didn't think we were going to sit on those chairs all day, did you?'

'Well, yes, I did actually,' Paulo waved an arm at all the boxes and bags around him. 'Otherwise, what's all this stuff for?'

'You'll see, later. For now, you need to get those boots on and come with me. You'll enjoy it once you get the hang of it.'

Paulo sat on the wicker basket and, amidst a litany of grunting and swearing, managed to drag the boots on to his legs before attempting to stand up.

'They're too big!'

Hugo glanced over just in time to see Paulo wobbling, looking in grave danger of toppling over. He turned his attention back to the rod, speaking over his shoulder. 'Well, they'll have to do. They look fine to me,' he lied.

As they followed the bank, Hugo kept his eyes on the surface of the water.

Paulo's eyes switched between Hugo and the river. 'What are we looking for?'

'Fish, of course.'

'I know that, but aren't there fish everywhere in the river?'

'Sort of, but they go to their favourite places to feed. That's how we know where to cast the line. They don't always come up to the surface, so you have to learn to spot them. After a while, you start sensing where they are, but it takes time and patience.'

Paulo pointed back over his shoulder. 'What about all our stuff back there?'

Hugo didn't look up. 'Oh, that'll be okay. We just need to do some checking out first, pinpoint where the fish are.'

'Like a stakeout?'

Hugo furrowed his brow. 'Well, I wouldn't have called it that myself, but I suppose that's what it amounts to. Fish tend to hide behind rocks and face upstream, so they can see the flies coming towards them. So we need to stay downstream of them, otherwise they'll spot us. Just remember, if you can see a fish, there's a fair chance it can see you...' His voice trailed off. 'Aha, there we go, look.' He tapped Paulo's arm and pointed to the water.

Paulo followed the direction of Hugo's finger, then looked back, shaking his head. 'I can't see anything.'

Hugo crouched down. 'See, over there? Just below the surface. Look, on the far side of that rock.'

Paulo continued to gaze across the water. Then, his face lit up. 'Yes, there, I can see it.'

'Decent size too for a brown trout,' Hugo whispered. 'Let's...'

At that very moment, there was a noisy splash, and ripples pushed out in a circle across the surface of the water. Silently, they watched. Within seconds, the fish had returned to its position behind the rock.

Hugo kept his voice low. 'He's picking up flies. That'll keep him occupied. Come on, let's go and say hello.'

Half way down the steep bank, Hugo turned back to Paulo and whispered. 'This is why you've got those waders on. Can you manage to get into the water without splashing? I'll come down behind you.' He pressed himself back, to make space for Paulo to pass.

Paulo began edging down the bank, keeping his eyes on the shadow of the fish. He was inches away from the water when his heel caught the mud and he plunged straight in, coming to rest on his haunches, a spray of water flying up all around him. Sitting inspecting his hand, which was speckled with tiny stones, he let loose a barrage of Portuguese expletives which the fish was no longer around to hear.

'How long have you been a fisherman?' Paulo tugged a bottle of beer from the cooler box and levered off the top with his teeth.

Hugo stared. 'Where'd you learn to do that?'

'They don't have bottle openers on the street.'

Hugo thought they probably didn't have unopened bottles of beer either. He shook his head and decided not to go there. 'To answer your question, only since my wife died. I was a late starter. It helped me come to terms with things.' He glanced at Paulo. 'By the way, we call ourselves anglers, not fishermen. Fishermen are the ones who go out to sea in boats and sell the fish they catch, like the ones in Rio you were telling me about. Plus of course there are lots of fisherwomen, so it avoids the gender thing.'

Paulo nodded. 'So do you angle most days?'

Hugo opened his mouth, but closed it again. He stood up. 'It depends on the weather. We're much higher up here than in the coastal towns, so the weather isn't as predictable. I'm afraid to say I'm a bit of a fair-weather angler.'

'So what do you do when you're not doing angling?'

'Oh, I'm never stuck for things to do. For one thing, this book I'm writing. That takes up a lot of time. Not that I've been getting much done recently.'

Paulo frowned. 'Because of me?'

'No, I wasn't getting much done before you arrived either. I did manage some new stuff this week but it's the first time for a while.'

'What's the book about?'

'Well, it started out being a story about a lottery winner. I dealt with a lot of people who won the lottery, so it's what you might call home territory.'

'Did you look after their money for them?'

'Among other things. Most of them were like fish out of water.' He chuckled at his unintended joke.

'You mean like, thrashing around?' Paulo grinned, evidently pleased with his quick answer in a language that wasn't his own.

'Yes, that's a good way to put it. When you win a lot of money, and you've never had much before, it can be a shock to the system. Of course, no one has any sympathy, people don't see having money as a problem. But it can be, it can break up families.'

Paulo shrugged. 'I guess it's a bit like living on the streets. Only, the opposite way round. None of us had any money, and nobody had any sympathy for us either.'

Hugo forced a smile. Since he didn't know how to respond, he said nothing.

Paulo shook his head. 'If I ever got rich I'd know exactly how to spend the money.'

Hugo barked out a laugh. 'Spending the money was the least of their worries, Paulo. It was other people and their jealousy. It didn't help much having the newspapers on their backs either.'

'But you said the book "started out" being about a lottery winner, isn't it anymore?'

Hugo laughed. 'Well it is, but so far I haven't managed to get the story to work out the way I want it, so I've ditched the idea for a while. I'm working on something completely different now.'

'Can I read it when it's finished?'

'Sure, if I ever get it finished.' He glanced over towards Paulo, who was swigging beer from the bottle, and it occurred to him that this boy didn't miss a thing. He was as sharp as a knife.

18

Hugo set the tray down on the garden table and rested his hand on Salvador's shoulder. 'How are you, *amigo*?'

Salvador looked up and smiled, but the smile didn't quite reach his rheumy eyes. 'I am eighty-six soon, *Señor*. For old man, I do good.'

Not for the first time Hugo noticed how, as people get older, they volunteer their age without being asked, just as young children do. It was the people in the middle who were coy about it. He poured two glasses of water. 'How did you manage during all that wet weather?'

Salvador frowned. 'I no like it, *Señor*. My bones ache. But what can I expect? I grateful just to wake up every day.' He waved a crooked finger in the direction of the garden. 'I know you like flowers with perfume, *Señor* Hugo. But I think, is enough *jazmín* now. Maybe we need more *madre-selva* and *aliso*, over there.' He pointed towards the border that followed the length of the conservatory, twisting as he rummaged around in his waistcoat pocket. He pushed a scrap of paper in front of Hugo and tapped it with the tip of his finger. 'Names in English. But first I move all that long grass away.'

Hugo rubbed his chin. 'Yes, but if your bones are aching like you said, maybe you should leave the digging until later in the year, when it starts to cool again. You can still plant the...' he lifted the paper, 'honeysuckle and alyssum.'

The old man shook his head. 'No, *Señor*. Later, ground more hard.' He smiled. 'No need worry, *Señor*. I do small amount each day. Two, maybe three, weeks, all finished.'

Hugo leaned forward across the table, speaking with a conspiratorial whisper. 'You know, I don't know how long Paulo will stay. He has his university work, but maybe we need to get him out here in the garden sometimes.' He glanced towards the house. 'He needs some fresh air. Do you think maybe you could teach him something about gardens?'

Salvador tightened his lips together, his head cocked over to one side, considering. '*Sí*, I think so. Is good idea for someone young. You know, *Señor*, you very lucky. Paulo good boy. When he stay with me, he good guest. Always wash plates after we eat, fold blanket every morning. He talk to me about people he call father and mother, and his *abuela*, your friend. They take him into house because his family go, *desaparecidos*.'

Hugo nodded. 'Yes, they all disappeared. And you're right, Salvador. He is good. But he won't stay here, it's too quiet and there's no work for him. Anyway, he has to get back to university.'

The old man's eyes shone. 'Maybe if I teach him good he stay here, be gardener.'

Hugo smiled. 'It's a nice thought, Salvador, but I don't

170

think so. He seems to want to work in the city, in business.' He stood and pushed his chair back. 'But first he wants to learn as much as he can from me. He'll stay as long as I still have useful things to tell him. After that, he'll go back to Brazil, and who knows what after that?' He sighed. 'Anyway, for now we'll fish, talk, go places together. See what happens.' He picked up the tray. 'But let's find out if he's ready to start his gardening career. He makes a lot of noise around the house when he's not doing his university work and I need to get on with writing my book.'

As he headed towards the kitchen, another, unexpected, thought presented itself. If Paulo's motives in coming all this way were not quite as he was making out, there was no one more likely to discover that than the wise old man he'd just been talking to.

The heat had gone from the day and they were sitting on opposite sides of the wood fire. Paulo was drinking Coke from the bottle, Hugo a glass of *rioja*, which glowed like a ruby in the flickering flames.

As he held up his glass to admire the richness of the colour, Hugo glanced over at Paulo. 'Did you enjoy your day fishing?'

Paulo made what Hugo thought was an apologetic gesture. 'Sort of.'

'Ah, only sort of?'

'It was a lot of effort for one little fish. And when I fell in the water and the big one swam off it was really annoying. It was a bit boring after that.'

'What if we went and found ourselves a bigger river one

weekend? We could drive south and stay in a hotel, see if we can organize a real test. Gypsy barbel. Now that would give you something to get your teeth into. And I don't mean eating it.'

'Yeah, cool.'

'You still haven't told me much about your journey here. It must have cost an arm and… a lot of money, coming all this way?'

'It did, but *Māe* and *Pai* left me something in their will. I didn't find out about it until years after they died, when I was older. I don't think they had much. I guess charity workers don't earn a lot.'

Hugo twirled the stem of his glass between his fingers. He was not going to push the boy. He would only find the answers he was seeking if he let him talk at his own pace, even if it took several days.

Paulo's voice broke into his thoughts. '… I think *Māe* and *Pai* gave most of their money to the charity when they were alive, but they still left me ten thousand *reals*.' He held up a hand. 'I can tell you in US dollars, maybe four thousand. When *Vovó* died, she left me some money as well.'

'Well, you must have used a fair bit of that, travelling over here to find me'

Paulo raised his eyebrows. 'I used *all* of that travelling over here to find you. It was a good thing I had a return ticket. At least I could get back home again.'

19

Tourists in shorts and short-sleeved shirts, some sporting wide-brimmed hats, were now beginning to appear each day, making their way towards the *Sierra Nevada* mountains towering up ahead.

Hugo and Paulo mingled in the mini-procession until they reached the *Parque Nacional*. Paulo had been in Spain for several weeks now, and Hugo was conscious he still hadn't asked for any real advice about what he'd maintained was his proposed career. The thought crossed his mind, maybe the lad was just enjoying what was probably his first ever holiday.

They found a table with benches shaded by small trees, near to the coolness of the water. Paulo eased the strap on the cool box from his shoulder and dropped it down onto the table.

Nearby, a young couple ate sandwiches and cake and laughed as their young daughter played with a small dog, throwing sticks for it to fetch back. The girl was dressed in a loose, elasticated blouse and cut-off jeans and had a yellow baseball cap on her head, with the peak pointing backwards.

Hugo rested his chin in the palms of his hands and stared idly at the stick throwing game taking place. He smiled when the girl squealed in delight each time the dog completed a successful mission. For some reason he could not have explained he was concerned that the girl's forehead would get burnt by the sun. He turned to look over at Paulo.

'I know you wanted to talk to me about your business ideas. I'm glad if you're having some fun here too, but don't be afraid to ask.'

Paulo leaned his elbows on the table. 'It's just that this guy started coming into the bar where I worked. He runs this financial consultancy in Brasilia, but he comes over to Rio on business. We used to talk when the bar was quiet. He told me about his family, said his kids were over-privileged, living in a decent home, but he and his wife came from poor backgrounds. He told me he'd got lucky, he had the right breaks at the right time. I always used to think he sounded modest, but he isn't at all, he's a big-head. But I guess maybe he just thought I was a bit like him when he was a kid. He was never on the streets though. Anyway, this one day he came in and told me he had a proposition.' He glanced at Hugo. 'Is that the right word?'

Hugo nodded, not knowing whether it was the wrong or right word, given he wasn't sure what Paulo was going to talk about and didn't want to interrupt.

'He told me he wanted to sponsor me to go into the financial business if I was interested. He said I could go to a special business school, in Rio or Brasilia. His company would pay the fees. He wants to open up an office in Rio one day and he told me if I shaped up and passed all the exams I'd be able to work in it. He's thinking about opening an office in New York and he reckoned I might be able to go there one day.'

Hugo slid the cool bag towards him and unfastened the top. Opening two bottles of beer, he handed one to Paulo. 'That all sounds exciting.'

'There was no one I could ask about it though. I knew about you, and I thought if I was able to find you, you'd give me some advice. It's a really tough decision. It was so hard to get into uni and I'm not sure I want to give it up that easily.'

'This business school, Paulo? Couldn't you do that after you've finished your university course? Then you'd have a proper professional degree and the specialist knowledge as well.'

Paulo glanced away. 'That's what I don't understand. The guy seems to say one thing, then another. You never know where you are with him. He's always in a rush and he doesn't explain things properly. If I do it, I want to try and work it so I can finish uni first.'

Hugo wiped his brow with the back of his hand and looked up at the sun. He took a swig from the bottle and watched from the corner of his eye as the little girl's dog put the stick down in front of her and stood wagging its tail, eyes full of anticipation. He turned back to Paulo. 'You know, I've been meaning to ask. The other day when you first mentioned this financial thing, you said it was *another* reason for trying to find me?'

Paulo nodded. 'Yeah. Another reason is you're the

nearest thing I've got now to family.'

Hugo felt a lump suddenly rising in his throat and his voice came out as a whisper. 'Well, that's reason enough…'

Paulo frowned. 'You know, the hardest thing was finding out where you were. I searched all through the drawers and cupboards in *Vovó's* house…'

'You wouldn't have found me in there, Paulo.'

'What?' The boy knitted his eyebrows, then shook his head. 'Oh, very funny.'

Hugo smiled. 'Do you live in Marietta's… your *vovó's* house?'

'I can go there if I want to, but I don't live there anymore. *Vovó* left the house to the charity, they wanted to open it as a centre for the street kids. They had all these plans for it, but they haven't got the money. They'd have to get a warden, then they'd have to make lots of alterations because it wouldn't be a house anymore, so there are government regulations. I live in a house near the college with three other guys. I went over to *Vovó's* place because I was looking for anything that would give me an idea of where you were, a phone number or something. I found the letter I gave you, and *Vovó's* notebook.'

'Weren't you ever tempted to spend that money on something else, a car or whatever?'

'I told you, I already have a car. It's old, but it gets me around, I share it with my friend. Then I had the evening job in the bar. It didn't pay very well, but it was enough for me to put away some more money.'

'You've done well.' Hugo took a deep breath and exhaled slowly. 'You're obviously ambitious, I can see that. So, what kind of advice do you think I can give you?'

'I don't even know what it's like to work in a financial company. Were you the boss of yours?'

Hugo pulled another bottle of beer from the chiller box. 'One of them.' He rubbed the cold bottle on the back of his neck. 'Hell, it's hot today.'

Paulo swivelled round. 'I guess what I really want to know is, would you do it if you were me?'

'What, join this guy you've been telling me about? I'd need to know a lot more about him first. And about the whole idea. Even then I could only give you a personal view. From what you've been telling me though, it does look like you're in a pretty good position. You've got where you are by hard work. You're at university and you seem to be doing well there, your tutor obviously thinks highly of you. Have you talked to him, by the way?'

'Yes.'

'And?'

'He wanted to know what you thought.'

Hugo laughed. 'So, between us, we're not helping you much, are we? Just out of interest, what will happen if you do pack in uni? Say you give it a try with this guy and you don't like it. Is there any chance you could go back and carry on with the course?'

Paulo shook his head. 'I wouldn't dare ask my professor to cover for me again, even for a short while. The system in Brazil is crazy. You have to choose what degree you want to go for, then you have to stick to it. There's this girl I know, she started off on a physics course, but after six months she decided she wanted to go into medicine. She wasn't allowed to carry over any of her credits and they told her she'd have to do the whole entrance exam again. Can you imagine, fifteen hours a day studying, when you've already passed one set of exams a few months before? Then, thirteen four-hour tests all over again.' Paulo held out his hands. 'How's she supposed to live while she's doing all that?'

'Where is the college you go to?'

'North of the centre. They call it College City, students everywhere.'

'And the place where you live, what's that like?'

Paulo grinned. 'It's not exactly in the smart neighbourhood, but it's okay. At least I have a room of my own, and it's not far from the bars and cafes. It's pretty lively there. That's where the bar is I used to work at.'

'Will you be able to go back to work there?'

'Nah, I don't think I can rely on a job there after all this time.' Paulo swallowed a mouthful of cold beer. 'If you had your time again, would you go into the same business?'

'No.' Hugo's reply was instant and surprised even himself. 'If you'd asked me that a few years ago I might have given you a different answer. But I know for sure now, making money and being happy are not always the same thing. I mean, if you look at rich people, a lot of them don't seem to smile much. Nothing seems to make them happy. They go into expensive restaurants, they complain, the table's not in the right spot, the food's overcooked, the staff are too slow. Maybe it's just me, but I'd rather go to a cheaper place where you can have a laugh with the waiters and relax with people you feel good with.'

He shoved the empty beer bottles into the bag.

'Anyway, the best advice I can give you is to think very carefully why you'd quit university after all the hard work you've done to get a place there. Even if it all goes the way this guy's suggesting – and that's a big if – is that what you really want anyway? And if it is, does it have to be him you go with? I'm sure there'll be other opportunities for you in the future. But hey, if you can tick all the boxes, go for it.'

Paulo looked up at him. 'You know, I'm surprised. I thought you'd tell me to do it. After the career you had, I mean.'

Hugo stood up and slung the cooler bag over his shoulder.

'Like I said, things change.'

20

The hotel faced the rocky slopes that rose up above the little town huddled around the banks of the river.

As they'd driven along the winding road through those same southern Andalucían hills earlier, the roofs of the houses, basking in the sun, had appeared butter yellow. Now, it seemed the rain that had been soaking Granada earlier had followed them here and the warmth of the coffee lounge was beginning to steam up the windows.

Paulo finished his chocolate cake and wiped his mouth. 'I saw this film once, about the Holocaust. It was called *Schindler's List*.'

'You know about the Holocaust then?'

Paulo rolled his eyes. 'Sure, some of those war criminals came to Brazil afterwards?'

'Of course, I'd forgotten about that.'

'Anyway, I was just thinking about the guy who was in charge of the camp. The one who kept shooting people. And then Schindler tells him, the real power is the power *not* to kill them. So the next time the guy's ready to shoot someone, he tells them "I pardon you".'

'Why are you telling me this, Paulo?'

'Well, I was just thinking it's a bit like letting the fish go after you've caught it.'

Hugo raised his eyebrows. 'I hadn't thought of it that way. You have a very deep way of thinking about things, Paulo. Maybe you should have studied philosophy.'

Paulo glared out towards the gloom shrouding the hills and his reply came over his shoulder. 'No thanks. I'd have to do the *vestibular* again!' He turned back to face Hugo. 'You know, you still haven't read *Vovó*'s letter.'

Hugo's mouth tightened. 'I know, it just feels like I'm invading her privacy. It was different with you. You had to read it to find out what you needed to know, where I live and all that. I suppose I'm a bit afraid of what I might read in it. It's a long time since... what happened. Some nights I still wake up in tears.'

Paulo shrugged. 'There's nothing wrong with that. I've done the same thing and I wasn't even there. But I don't think *Vovó* would have minded you reading the letter.'

Hugo breathed in deeply, then released it. He slipped his hand in his inside pocket and withdrew the envelope.

Paulo could not disguise his surprise. 'You've got it here, with you?'

'I've had it with me ever since you gave it to me.' He hesitated, staring at the writing on the front, then glanced back at Paulo before nodding decisively and sliding out the letter. Marietta was dead and nothing would bring her back. It was the future that counted now, and it occurred to Hugo that maybe the boy sitting opposite him might be a big part of that, if only...

He left that thought to dangle alongside the letter in

front of him, adjusting the distance so he could read the scrawly writing.

My dearest Rosa,

I can't believe what's happening, the thing I've dreamt about for most of my life becoming a reality at last! In Italy too, a country I have come to love so much in so short a time!

From Italy we're going to travel to Paris. The plan at first had been to go on to Brazil after that, but Hugo owns a house in southern Spain which he bought a few years ago. It's in a little town not far south of the city of Granada. He says there's a lovely restaurant within walking distance and it's right on the edge of the national park so the scenery should be spectacular. He's suggested going there for a few days. It sounds idyllic! Hugo wants to do a bit of fishing in the river that flows past the house. I've never really been keen on the idea of fishing, but he says it's helped him through difficult times and he's promised me he's kind to the fish!

He needs to go to London before anything else, to sort things out there, so I'll be leaving beautiful Italy in a few days.

I haven't time to write a long letter, Rosa, Hugo will be back very soon, but I will keep you informed and *will let you know as soon as I have a date for returning to Rio. I'll write a longer letter to you when I get a chance.*

Till soon, with much love.

M xx

Hugo lowered the letter onto the table, keeping one corner between his fingers.

There was a soft rattle as Paulo set down his cup. When Hugo glanced up and saw another cup in front of him, the coffee untouched, he was surprised to realize it was his.

Images of those few days in Siena floated around in his mind, and Marietta's word, idyllic, seemed to create a fitting subtitle.

Paulo's quiet voice shook him from his memories. 'After I read that, I found a phone number in her notebook, next to a letter H. I guessed it would be yours and when I checked, it was a London number. They told me you'd retired and they put me through to a guy who said he'd been a colleague of yours.' He chuckled. 'I think he thought I was going to be a new client. If he knew I only had a couple of hundred dollars I think he would have put the phone down right away. Anyway, I told him I was sort of family and he said he heard you'd gone to live somewhere in Spain, but that was all he knew. I think he just wanted to get me off the phone.'

Hugo was hardly listening. Occupying his mind was one thought. *Here we go again, another letter that somehow doesn't seem quite right.* The little mystery of the placement of Marietta's letter forty-something years ago was just an exercise for his own curiosity. Whatever was troubling him about this one now struck him as something much more than that.

The waiter from Lisbon proved to be a welcome distraction for Paulo during the evening. Pleased to have an opportunity to speak Portuguese again, he perched on a stool at the bar, swapping jokes and stories.

Hugo settled in an armchair in the corner with a book on his lap. Not for the first time he patted the pocket of his jacket to check the letter was still in there and was comforted to feel and hear its soft rustle. He closed his eyes and thought about what he'd read. Marietta, happy once more after all she'd been through. Making plans, looking forward, excited at the prospect of introducing her new husband to her best friend. The end of the long and painful saga, but coming so late in his life and hers.

Why had his mother acted the way she did? Why didn't his father stop her? He pictured the scene in the kitchen, the night his mother made him his favourite food, poured out white wine and lies. Didn't she think he'd ask questions? That he wouldn't simply accept that Marietta had gone and that was the end of it? Whatever the case, they'd created years of misery for their own son and made sure they never saw their grandson. Then there was Marietta, her mum, her dad, her sister. You could even add Sarah, haunted by Marietta, to that list. Good people. What right did his parents have to ruin all those lives by their own selfishness and prejudices?

A cackle of laughter broke into his thoughts. He looked up to see Paulo swatting his waiter friend on the arm. He thought again about Paulo. He'd obviously told the truth about trying to phone Hugo before he arrived; his description of the phone call with his former colleague rang true enough. After that, Paulo had turned detective. There was just about enough information in the letter to help him find the town where he lived and it was a tiny place. Once he got there, finding a lone Englishman would be fairly straightforward.

When he'd first appeared, Paulo had been timid and nervous. Then he'd become resentful, never having learned the real reason Marietta had left Britain when she did. After Hugo had explained, he'd apologized and tried to make up for what he'd said, but Hugo felt that the little episode had driven some sort of wedge between them. Since then, as the days and weeks had flown by, Paulo's confidence had increased and a little sliver of warmth had started to creep into their relationship.

So why the brick in his stomach now?

He closed his eyes and allowed all the different thoughts to form an orderly queue. Their backgrounds could scarcely have been so diverse. His background had been privilege and wealth, Paulo's deprivation and abject poverty. His own education a smooth and facilitated ride, whereas Paulo's had been the result of sheer graft and determination. Yet if he set aside his nagging concerns, their histories were intertwined, because of the presence of Marietta in each one.

Hugo realized now, whatever those concerns might be, no matter how much they were still gnawing inside him, he was enjoying this time he was spending with Paulo. They'd eaten together, strolled along the riverside day after day, fished side-by-side in the little river, talked. Shared their separate histories with each other.

He knew too that Paulo seemed to be setting great store by his advice; advice that could steer him in the right, or the wrong, direction. So now it wasn't just their past; their futures had become bound together too.

Paulo would not be staying much longer though. He needed to be back at university and then he'd be out of Hugo's life again, just as quickly as he had come into it.

Hugo felt the butterflies in his stomach. For some reason he didn't fully understand, Paulo seemed to have given himself another challenge over the next couple of days. For Hugo, all this was nothing more than a fishing trip. But for Paulo it seemed to be something much bigger, an opportunity to prove himself to Hugo. And in Paulo's simple, youthful view of the world that ambition was encapsulating itself in one event: a memorable catch, before they went back to Granada.

Hugo was no psychologist, but he had little doubt the boy's tenacity was rooted in the frustrations and disappointments of his childhood. The problem was, the wild rivers of this region had other ideas and the even wilder temperament of the gypsy barbel that swam in it held no sympathies for life's unfortunates. Their business was the business of nature, survival.

All in all, this was a venture that might very easily end in disappointment. And if it did, would that hasten Paulo's departure?

Hugo had to get this right.

The problem was, he wasn't even certain what 'this' was.

A few weeks earlier Paulo had been happy to allow a cold day to end any prospect of a fishing trip. This cold and wet morning he couldn't wait to get going.

'Is this where we're going to angle?' Paulo asked as they got out of the car.

Hugo tried unsuccessfully to hide his smile.

'What's so funny?'

Hugo shook his head. 'No, nothing. It's just, well, we don't say we're going to angle, we say we're going fishing.'

'But you said…'

'I know,' Hugo interrupted. 'Don't ask me to explain. I can't.'

Paulo rolled his eyes. 'I don't think I'll ever understand English.'

Hugo pointed. 'Let's head up there, to that bridge. Bridges are always a good place to begin. That way we get a choice of both sides of the river. Come on, give me a hand with this stuff.'

'I suppose we're going to put these fish back as well?'

Hugo laughed. '*These* fish? We'll do well to catch *one*. And just to tell you, I ate a gypsy barbel once. It was horrible, tasted like a lump of cardboard.'

Two hours and several casts later, they hadn't hooked a thing, despite moving upriver twice. It was almost midday, and Paulo was restless. 'What have we got to eat?'

They hadn't brought the cooler box. 'We don't want to be lugging loads of stuff around for miles,' Hugo had said. He rooted in the tiny canvas bag and tossed a small tin foil packet to Paulo. 'Smoked salmon. Looks like it's the only fish we're going to see this morning.'

After lunch, rain clouds settled above them, threatening to bring their expedition to an early end. They moved even further upstream, but Paulo trudged along the bank with his hands stuffed into his pockets and Hugo was longing to get back to the hotel. Suddenly Paulo grabbed his sleeve. Hugo turned round to see Paulo pointing towards the water.

A moment later he spotted it. The first glimpse of a shadow, the tiniest of movements. As they moved closer they could see the fish clearly from behind.

Hugo whispered. 'It's a barbel all right, not big, but a lot heavier than the brown trout at home.' He passed the rod to Paulo who took it from him as though he'd been handed the keys to the kingdom.

Hugo stepped back. 'Try from here.'

Paulo edged closer to the bank. His breathing became slow and deep and Hugo saw the resolve in his face as he lifted the rod. Then he closed his eyes and Hugo's brow creased. Had Paulo lost his nerve? Hugo took a step forward, ready to offer help, but in an instant Paulo opened his eyes wide and whipped the line up ahead of the fish.

The response was instant. The line snapped tight.

'Let the line go out if you can't stop him pulling.' Hugo

was having to shout over the roar of the water. 'Keep the rod up, too, let it absorb some of the power of those runs. When he stops for a rest, start taking in line again.'

For five minutes Paulo, with Hugo by his shoulder, reeled in when he could but let out the line when the surging runs began. Hugo marvelled at how quickly Paulo was taking control.

Until the line went slack.

Paulo cried out and began winding frantically but no matter how much line wrapped onto the reel, the fish had gone.

Except, not quite gone. As if in a show of triumph, moments later it exploded from the river ten feet away inside a wide halo of silver pearls of water. The ripples coursed across the surface towards them, gradually melting in front of their eyes.

Paulo stared, first at the water, then at the rod, then back at the line. He stood, open-mouthed, surveying the water. Hugo reached out and ran his fingers down the line, taking hold of the hook. He held it out. 'Sorry, pal, there's your answer. He's straightened the hook.' He watched as Paulo plucked it from the palm of his hand. 'I did tell you this can be a battle. Looks like this is one we've lost.'

In the morning Hugo found himself eating breakfast alone. He watched the little rivers of rain dancing down the misted-up window and, in the warmth and comfort of the hotel's café, craned his neck to peer outside.

He grimaced. If they were going to make a catch, this would need to be the day. It was Sunday and tomorrow was

Toni's birthday. The regulars were planning a raucous evening back in Granada.

On the journey back the previous afternoon, Paulo had become morose. Neither of them had spoken a word, although a look of determination had set into Paulo's youthful features. Hugo knew he was desperate to make another attempt at a catch, but the rivers would be swollen now after the overnight downpour.

At just after eleven, two things happened. The rain stopped and Paulo came bouncing into the lounge where Hugo was sitting reading the morning paper and clutching a cup of coffee. Paulo dropped down next to him on the settee so heavily the coffee spilt into the saucer.

'Whoa,' Hugo cried out, holding the cup and saucer away from him. 'Slow down, you've already missed breakfast.'

'Yeah, I know, sorry,' Paulo replied. 'I'm starving though.'

Hugo thought about the new language he was learning from this teenager. 'Starving' was now not only what children in parts of the Third World were, but equated to something more like 'feeling peckish'. He'd already discovered that Paulo had only two body temperatures, boiling and freezing.

'We could go and get an early lunch soon,' Hugo suggested. 'Well *you* could. The Spanish don't start eating till about three, so we'll be able to get a table easily enough.'

Paulo wrinkled his nose. 'Nah, tell you what, I'll grab a packet of nuts or something. We need to get going if we want to catch something today.'

Hugo stared at him. Where had all the kid's desperate hunger gone in thirty seconds? 'Paulo, it's been chucking it down for hours. I know it's stopped now, but the river's going to be flooded.'

'It's okay, I don't mind,' Paulo replied levelly.

'Well, the fish might. I doubt we'll even see any today, let alone catch one.'

The excitement on Paulo's face dropped away instantly. 'We can still do it even if the river's high, can't we?'

'Technically, but it would be a massive challenge...'

'Well, I'm game.'

Hugo sighed and stood up, folding the newspaper and tossing it on the table. The irony was not lost on him: the boy who'd tried to get out of a fishing trip on a moderately cool day a few weeks back was the same one dragging him from the bliss of a calm Sunday morning now. And why? So they could take on the dangers of an overflowing river?

All, apparently, to prove this thing. But the thought rattled into Hugo's head: who was he proving it to?

21

Hugo was already chilled to the bone when the boy grabbed his arm and pointed. 'That flat rock, a couple of metres from the far side? Something's moving.'

Hugo screwed his eyes up. 'I can't see anything, but your eyes are better than mine. If you're right, we're going to have to be really clever. The bank on the other side is steep. And it's going to be drenched.'

'What about going across the bridge?' Paulo's excitement was palpable.

Hugo held his chin. 'Too far. If there is a fish there, by the time we get down to the bridge and back it'll be gone. The only way is to wade across behind him and then try casting into that deeper water ahead. We might get lucky if he sees the fly and doesn't see us.' He pointed. 'Look, see that bush across there? If we can clamber up the far bank we might have a chance.'

They waded through the shallower water but the scramble up the far bank was much harder. By now they were plastered with mud and Paulo hauled and slithered his way up and held out a hand for Hugo.

When they left the cover of the bush, Hugo's heart sank.

He turned back towards Paulo, who was right behind. 'I'm sorry, pal, I think it's just some weed floating under the surface. I don't think it's a fish.'

Paulo's face dropped in disbelief, but when he stretched forward he shook his head. 'No, look! There *is* a load of weed, but there's definitely something else, deeper down.'

The fly arced into the air and caught in the breeze, dropping into the water well away from where Paulo had aimed.

Hugo whispered, 'It's okay, just let it drift back. Don't reel in till it's level with us though.'

Paulo looked back over his shoulder. 'How am I going to get close without getting caught on this bush?'

Hugo smiled. 'Trust your skill and hope for the best? Just keep everything smooth. Swing your arm out clear of the bush and focus on the spot you're aiming at.'

Paulo allowed himself the briefest of smiles. 'I feel like Darth Vader in Star Wars.' He put on a deep voice. '*Stay on the leader.*'

Everything seemed to happen in slow motion. The rod whipped up, the line sailed through the air and fluttered down onto the surface of the water, landing three feet past the rock. Paulo cursed under his breath. There was no movement up ahead, and the line began drifting back for a second time. Then a ripple swept the surface of the water followed by a loud splash. The line went taut and the rod was almost ripped from Paulo's grasp. He snatched it back and juggled it with both hands.

Hugo was close behind. 'Okay, keep it really steady. Play

him like you did with that one yesterday. He's just going to fight harder, he's even bigger.'

Paulo reeled, let the line out, coaxed it back in, kept it still. If anything, the fish seemed to be gathering energy. Twice, the line went slack and Paulo's jaw dropped, only for another snatch to let him know, the struggle was still on. He wrenched himself sideways and dragged the tight line in a perfect arc through the water.

When the fish appeared just below the surface Paulo was almost losing his grip on the rod. Mud splattered around in the air and, off-balance, he slid one foot behind him, lengthening his arms to release the strain on the line.

He twisted round, veins standing up along the length of his neck.

'It's going to snap!'

Hugo fastened both arms around Paulo's shoulders and yelled from behind. 'Hold it steady, the line should take the strain.' Paulo let out more line, but right away the fish took up all the slack. This time, when he reeled in again, the fish broke the surface of the water and Hugo couldn't tell whether Paulo was scrambling down the bank or whether he was about to fall. Either way, he managed to stay upright.

'Can you get a firm stance and grab him with your hand?'

Paulo dropped into the water, on one knee. His other leg was stretched out on the shale as he heaved backwards. Amidst a fine silvery spray, the fish seemed to stand up vertically and launch into the air as Paulo, clutching the rod in one hand now, edged up to it and pulled it towards him.

The barbel was at least a foot and a half long and its underside, the colour of ripe mango, glistened in the afternoon sun, which was now breaking through the clouds. Half falling, half running, Hugo scrambled down the bank, but by the time he reached Paulo he'd already eased out the hook.

Hugo shouted above the din. 'Do you want to have a go at weighing him?'

'No,' Paulo shot back. 'Just take a photo and let's get him back in.'

Moments later, with both hands cupped around the fish, Paulo eased forward and held it out into the flowing water. The fish had stopped fighting, as though accepting its fate.

Hugo watched on, his face flushed. 'Turn him upriver so he can get some oxygen through his gills. Poor thing's exhausted.' Brushing himself down, he watched as Paulo waited a few seconds before opening his hands to allow the fish to kick gracefully and gratefully, away into the safety of the river.

When Paulo stood up, his face was beetroot red. He slithered up towards Hugo and clapped his arms around him. Then two people from lives that could scarcely be further apart whooped together in delight.

22

'Salvador asked me if I'd help him in your garden.' Paulo was gazing out through the side window at the cave houses nestled in the rocky hills. 'He said he'd teach me all about flowers, and plants.'

'Really? What did you say?'

'I said sure, no problem. I'm going to help him do the digging though. He didn't ask me, but I've watched him when he does it. He needs to keep sitting down all the time.'

'I know he'll appreciate it even if he won't admit it.'

Paulo turned back from the window. 'Can I ask you something? I never know what to call you. Would it be okay for me to call you *Avô*? Like, grandad?'

Hugo paused for a moment. 'Is that what it feels like? I mean me, with you?'

'Kind of. That's how I think of it, I guess.'

'You could just call me Hugo if it's easier, but if that's what you want to call me, it's fine.' Hugo made a clumsy attempt to pronounce the Portuguese word and, punctuated by fits of laughing, Paulo corrected him three times.

Hugo was glad to be forced to keep his eyes on the road

so Paulo couldn't see the sadness when he added, 'It's odd, nobody ever called me dad, yet here I am now, a grandad'.

Early morning light strained to get in around the curtains as Hugo lay awake, trying to decide whether to get up.

He thought about the day ahead. For two years he'd gone about his life, day by day, a small part of a small Spanish community. Fishing, at least during the summer, sharing a drink and a chat with Toni and the regulars at the bar, stopping for coffee in the town. Writing his book.

Paulo's arrival had changed all that, and he was having to admit he was enjoying the boy's company, getting used to him being around. How long had it been since he himself battled with gypsy barbel in the rushing rivers of southern Andalucía? Or just simply stretched out on a rug listening to the tinkling water of the stream, sipping cold beer, chattering away about everything and nothing? Now, too, he was being asked to pass on his knowledge and experience. Gathered over nearly forty years and, until now, pretty much wasted.

But Paulo was not going to be around forever. There was little for him here and he was intelligent and thirsty for knowledge. Once he'd drained every ounce of wisdom from Hugo, he'd return to Brazil.

The feeling would not go away that he had let this boy get under his skin, and after all that had happened in his own life he couldn't trust himself to give love again. Yet how does a person avoid loving someone?

What was it Marietta had so often said about love? The greatest of all emotions, the one that could overcome

197

everything. How could he deny his affection for this kid, who'd spent his every last penny finding him? Who'd experienced pain, sadness and despair on a similar scale to his own? Maybe even more so.

When he went downstairs there was no sign of Paulo. No doubt he'd emerge at midday then complain he didn't have enough time to keep up with his coursework. Hugo put a pot of coffee on and pushed the window open.

He was surprised to hear voices. He craned his neck to look along the path and saw Paulo with Salvador. The old man was pointing to a plant and Paulo was crouching to see. Hugo watched Salvador take hold of the stem of a flower between his fingers and make a circular motion with his free hand. He looked up at Paulo and the two of them burst out laughing.

Hugo thought about taking coffee out to them, but something held him back. He didn't want to disturb this moment. He went out into the garden by the conservatory door at the side, keeping out of sight.

He heard the old man and the teenage boy conversing in three different languages and smiled. Paulo's Spanish was passable, but no more. Salvador understood some Portuguese but couldn't speak it. Paulo's English was good and getting better by the day, while Salvador's was patchy at best.

'... I'm going to dig out the area round those brick columns.' Paulo's higher pitched voice. 'Then we can get those *madressilva* in.'

'Eh,' Salvador replied, 'is almost same word in Brazilian too?'

'Portuguese, Salvador.' Paulo again. 'There is no language Brazilian. *Avô* calls it honey plant or something like that.'

'Honey *suck*,' Salvador corrected him. Round the corner, sipping at his coffee, Hugo narrowly avoided spitting it out. 'Anyway, what does *Avô* mean?'

'*Avô* is like grandpa. Like the father of my father, what he is to me.'

'You mean like *abuelo*?'

'*Abuelo*? Well, I don't know what that means, so how can I tell you if it's like that? Anyway, it sounds like *Avô*. So how come you didn't know the word?'

There was no chatter for a while and Hugo assumed Paulo must have gone off somewhere. Then he heard a metallic scraping and guessed he'd started digging out, ready for the *honey suck*. He went back inside the kitchen and minutes later came back out again, this time through the main door, carrying a tray loaded with a pot of steaming coffee, cups, milk and sugar.

Hugo's voice was jaunty. 'Good morning. What time did you two start work then?' He set the tray down on the garden table.

Paulo turned round as he spoke, a look of surprise crossing his face. 'Oh, hi *Avô*.' He glanced across at Salvador. 'I think it was about seven. I couldn't sleep because of the rain, but when it stopped I got up to open the window and saw Salvador walking across the field. I thought I'd come and help him.'

He sat down at the table and moments later the old man joined them, bending to open the bag he always carried with him. He pulled out a flask of water. 'This boy good help, *Señor*. He happy to dig ground but he full of questions.' He looked at Paulo. 'Did you have lots of flowers where you grow up?'

Paulo laughed.

'What so funny?' the old man asked.

'Flowers don't grow too good in rubble, Salva!'

Hugo noticed Paulo's use of the shortened name, something he himself had never done in all the time he'd known the old man.

'What you mean, rubble?' Salvador asked, a deep frown lining his face. 'Who live in rubble?'

Hugo touched Salvador's sleeve and pointed at Paulo. 'Paulo lived on the streets when he was a kid. He didn't have a home. Well, not a house anyway.'

The old man shook his head and stared at the boy. 'Why you live on street?'

'Because I didn't have a choice,' Paulo replied. 'My family lived in a *favela*.'

Hugo saw Salvador's puzzled look. 'In English, we call it a slum. Lots of people packed in old houses.' He squeezed the palms of his hands together. 'Like *sardinas*.'

Salvador lifted a finger. 'Ah, *un barrio bajo*.' He nodded slowly, chewing on his bottom lip. Paulo slid his hand across the table and rested it on the old man's wrist.

'It's okay, Salva. There were millions of people living like that, still are. It's nothing unusual in Brazil.'

'Nobody should have to live like that,' Salvador replied. 'Even when my country was bad, when Franco here, we had land. People have farms, animals, things grow in

200

garden. We no have to live on streets.' He gestured towards the garden. 'At least now, you have all this. Is much better for you.'

Paulo nodded. 'Only because of *Avô's* son and his wife. People who cared enough to help me, and others too, so I survived.'

The old man tilted his head, his eyes narrowing as he seemed to be searching something in his memory. Then he held up his index finger. '*Ella no sabia llorar por eso no lloraba.*'

'What's that, Salvador?' Hugo wrinkled his forehead.

'Is Neruda, poet from Chile.'

Hugo knew Salvador would almost certainly not be able to explain the words in English and was about to change the subject, but Paulo was ahead of him. 'It's almost the same in Portuguese, *Avô. Ela não sabia chorar, por isso não chorei.* She didn't know how to cry, so she didn't cry".

The old man's eyes stared into the distance. 'I see those kids on news. Children who have no food, they not cry.'

Paulo drew in a deep breath. 'I never used to cry, not once. I saw too much of what happened to other kids to cry for myself.' He stood up. 'Hey, Salva, we don't have time to talk poetry right now, we have work to do.'

In the mornings, Paulo worked alongside Salvador, but as the days passed by, both began to surrender to the heat. By late morning Paulo was normally immersed in his university work and Salvador had strolled back to the coolness of his house. Later, as the sun nestled down into the mountains, they would meet up with Hugo round the garden table to chatter over cold drinks.

It was a time Hugo looked forward to. Paulo and Salvador reminded him of the regulars at the angling club back in Britain, except they were comparing their horticultural achievements instead of boasting about the size of the fish they'd caught. *We were right to put that bush over there*, Salvador would say and Paulo would respond with, *Look, those bulbs would never have come up where we were going to plant them to start with.*

Another thought had drifted into Hugo's mind: until recently he'd believed that the flow of knowledge between himself and the boy was one way. He, the older man, the teacher, Paulo with everything to learn. Now, he was beginning to realize he was learning as much about life from Paulo as he himself was passing on.

It was becoming clear to him, too, just how little time he'd spent with Salvador before Paulo had arrived, how seldom he'd made the effort to encourage the old man to sit down and talk. Without doubt Salvador's life had been filled with just as much richness and colour as this garden he'd created with his young apprentice's help.

Salvador was staying much longer at the house than he'd ever done before. One early evening, as he got up to go home, he clapped his hand to his forehead. '*No me diga!* I nearly forget again.' He bent down to pull his bag from under the table, cursing under his breath. 'I have it yesterday too but I no give it to you.' He shoved the bag on the table and tugged a large book from it. His hand quivered with the weight. 'How I manage to forget something that heavy, I no know.' He pointed at Paulo. 'Is in Spanish, but your Spanish good now.'

Paulo took the book in both hands and studied the cover, then set it down and opened it, his eyes fixed on the pages as he turned them. 'This is incredible, Salva. Can I borrow it?'

'No borrow,' the old man exclaimed. 'Is yours. To keep, for always.' He rested a finger on the open page. 'Everything about garden in there. Bush, trees, flowers. Where they like to be, how you care for, how much water. You can plant things so when one stop flowering, other one start. That way you have colour all year, different colour, different place. I have the book for years, teach me everything I know. You no have garden when you were kid. Now you can make best garden in world.'

Paulo looked up at him. 'But Salva, it's yours, it's precious…'

'No,' the old man interrupted, 'you have now, no good to me anymore.' He tapped the side of his head with a crooked finger and laughed. 'Everything in book, in here anyway.' His face lengthened. '*Sí*, but also, I forget it all again. But now I give book to you, you keep safe. You are old Salvador's *heredero*.'

Hugo gave the old man a quizzical look and Paulo flushed.

'That's the same in Portuguese. Salvador says I am his heir, *Avô*.'

Late one afternoon they dumped the fishing gear in the porch and pulled off their boots. Paulo looked up at Hugo.

'Can we go down to Toni's? Maybe eat there?'

'I thought you'd have had enough of Toni's. You've been in there almost every day this week.'

'I wanted to let you get on with your book.'

'I have, I've written six new chapters.'

'That's great. I didn't tell you, Salva's been teaching me to play chess.'

'He's pretty good. At least he used to be.' Hugo flopped down into an armchair. 'I keep meaning to ask you, isn't your pal in Brazil expecting to hear from you soon?'

'My pal in Brazil…?'

Hugo frowned. 'The one who wants you to go into business.'

Paulo shrugged. 'I guess so. But I think he'll keep the offer open.'

'Aren't you worried he might start thinking you're not interested?'

'Nah, it's no problem,' Paulo replied. 'He knew I was coming here to talk to you. I told him I'd be away a while.' He was heading towards the kitchen door, but stopped and turned round. 'Do you want me to go?'

Hugo flashed him a look of surprise. 'Go from here? No, of course not. That's not what I meant. It's just that I think maybe you should at least give him a call, let him know you're still thinking about it.'

Hugo heard Paulo open the fridge and wriggled into the reassuring comfort of the old chair. He closed his eyes. *No problem*, Paulo says. Strange, he comes almost five thousand miles here to ask advice about him, now he can't even be bothered to ring the guy.

23

One shoulder rose as the other dropped. Then in reverse, like a see-saw. Arms crossing in front before dropping, elegant fingers plunging down long thighs, balling up the silk of the dress, lifted to reveal the flesh below. A crash, heel on floor, a whirl of colour rotating in a fusion of movement and shiny hair, fanned out like a jet-black mane. Eyes to match, deep pools, staring at some distant, secret place, the *drishti*.

The old man's eyes followed the dancer, transfixed.

It had been Paulo's idea to come to Granada, so Salvador could indulge his passion for poetry with a visit to the Lorca museum. But it had been the old man himself who'd suggested the *tablao*, the flamenco restaurant where they sat now.

Behind the woman, the singer's voice reached a seemingly impossible high note and the heavily lined face of the guitarist contorted as he matched the lyrics, stroke for stroke, hardened fingers crashing across the strings. The rhythm quickened and hands clapped together, driving the intensity to a new level.

Shouts. *¡Jaleo!* Belting fists on drum skin. The crescendo, the arm raised in triumph. People jump to their feet in a spontaneous roar of applause. She bows, smiles. Looking at everyone, seeing nobody. *Duende*, that indefinable quality of ecstatic joy, does not recognize ordinary lives.

Through the euphoria Hugo noticed the woman who passed by their table and glanced over without stopping. Moments later, returning in the opposite direction, she approached their table.

'Salvador?'

The old man looked up. For several seconds, he studied her face. Then, slowly, the corners of his thin lips lifted into a smile. 'Carmen, *Cariño. Quetal?*'

The old man's eyes glistened as he moved to embrace the woman and the two began chattering in a language that was not Spanish. Salvador turned round. '*Señor* Hugo, Paulo, this is Carmen. Her mother own this restaurant long time ago. I come here when I young boy.'

The woman extended her hand towards Hugo and Paulo. She did not speak English well, she told them. Would the *señores* mind if she talked to Salvador in *Andalú*?

Hugo glanced at Paulo and nodded in the direction of the door, registering the puzzled look on his face. 'Let's give them a chance to talk together. I don't understand a word of their dialect anyway.'

'Did it make you think of *Vovó* when you watched the dancing?' Paulo asked, as they sat, side-by-side, on bar stools.

Hugo's features crumpled into a puzzled look. 'Why do you ask that? Marietta and I never watched flamenco together.'

'You had tears in your eyes.'

'You weren't supposed to notice in the dark.' He smiled. 'No, it's just the emotion of it all. I'd love to have been able to bring Marietta here, she'd have really understood it. It wasn't to be, but she left me a gift, showed me a way to look at my life differently. I'd started to feel like mine was a pretty useless life, but somehow it doesn't feel like that anymore.'

The sound of clapping and the strains of a guitar had started up again in the restaurant.

As they passed through the door and began making their way back towards the stage, Hugo's jaw dropped and he ushered Paulo over to the side of the room.

In the centre of the stage, Salvador and Carmen were facing each other. The stage lights were still brightly illuminated and the guitarist was strumming a slow melody. The other members of the troupe were sitting round the edge.

In the shadows, Hugo and Paulo watched as the woman held out a hand and Salvador touched it before stepping back, until their fingertips could hold onto each other no longer. Carmen moved in a slow circle before stamping on the wooden floor and closing the gap again. Together they swayed as the rhythm increased, until finally they parted, re-joined, swivelled, steadied, then with a muffled clatter of his shoes the old man bowed and reached to kiss the woman's hand.

Around the now-empty restaurant, the waiters, who had stopped clearing tables, broke out into spontaneous applause and Hugo and Paulo stepped out from their darkened viewing point. Hugo noticed how Salvador's chest heaved as he stepped down from the stage.

But there was something else he saw: the look that lit up an old man's face for one tiny, joyous moment.

24

By mid-June, as the days became unbearably hot, Paulo had still given no indication he'd taken Hugo's advice about telephoning Brazil. Hugo thought he'd heard him upstairs, speaking on his mobile phone, but if it had been his friend in Brasilia he hadn't let on.

Almost every day, Paulo pored over the book Salvador had given him, opening it up on the kitchen table or perching it on his lap outside in the garden. He was spending as much time with Salvador as the relentless sun would allow and when the heat became fiercer by late morning, they'd leave Hugo to his writing and escape down to the bar to play chess. The atmosphere there seemed to be benefiting from the Paulo factor too. From just a few gnarled old regulars drinking coffee and talking, it now seemed to have become a hive of activity. Several of them had played chess with Paulo and beaten him, but Paulo was a gracious loser and a keen learner, popular with everyone. Hugo too had rediscovered his energy and was hammering on with his writing, though in the evenings he looked forward to cooking for the two of them or strolling down to Toni's for dinner.

Late one morning, Hugo was sitting at his desk when Paulo popped his head round the door.

'I called him.'

Hugo took off his spectacles and rotated his chair to face him. 'Called who?'

'Douglas.'

Hugo held his chin and frowned. He was about to ask Paulo to give him the tiniest of clues when it dawned on him. He marvelled at Paulo's habit of continuing, without preamble, conversations which had started days or even weeks earlier. 'Oh, you mean the guy in Brazil? Is that his name, Douglas?'

'Yeah. He says the offer's still open. He's on holiday with his family at the moment, somewhere in the States. He's due back in Brazil in a couple of weeks, but he won't be over in Rio for another two weeks after that. I think he wants to know what I'm going to do by then. He was talking about New York again, he's got this friend there, says there's a chance they can do something together. He wants to move into commodities, says if things go well maybe at some point I could work in that.'

Hugo smiled broadly. 'That's great. You must be very excited.'

'I guess I'm very lucky.'

Hugo glanced at the clock. 'You know what, I'm getting nowhere with this writing today. Let's go over to Toni's for lunch. Maybe we should have a bottle of something to celebrate your new career.'

Paulo needed no second invitation. He suggested they cut through the garden and go out by the back gate, but before they got that far Hugo stopped, inhaling deeply. He scanned the bushes and shrubs around them. 'What's that sweet smell?'

'That's why I wanted you to come this way, I was hoping you'd notice. Look, over there.' He pointed. 'It's a lemon tree. We put it in the other day. It flowers all year round. And there are some scented herbs too, I forgot to show you. I'll give you a little tour when we get back.'

The beginning of an embarrassed smile flickered on Hugo's face. How often had he ever bothered to explore beyond the patio at the rear of his own house? 'That would be wonderful, Paulo, thank you. You're going to give me a tour round my own garden. Will your mate Salvador be here to help, selling tickets at the gate?'

They ambled their way through the scent of warm grass in the fields. The unrelenting heat of the Granada summer was creating a shimmer in the air and an eerie silence was descending all around as the locals retreated to the coolness of their homes for lunch and a siesta.

When they entered the restaurant's garden by the back gate, Paulo pointed to several rows of neatly-raked soil, along which tall canes stood like little watchtowers. 'Salva and me are doing a colour scheme for Toni. We're putting green things over there, spinach and broad beans and cabbages. Red tomatoes and peppers on the other side. Then there are going to be potatoes on the far side but it's too late to put them in now.' He crouched down to take hold of the tiny green stem of a newly-sprouting plant between his fingers. 'This one's called *Col China*, you call it *Bok Choy* in England.'

211

Hugo smiled, shaking his head. 'How on earth do you know that?' As Paulo opened his mouth to reply, he held up a hand. 'Hold on, don't tell me, the book...'

Inside the restaurant it was cooler, though, despite the time of year, the smell of chickens roasting in the oven wafted through to the bar. Hugo and Paulo greeted the regulars already congregated in there and sat down at a table in the corner. A couple of minutes later Toni sauntered through from the back room.

'You eating?'

Hugo nodded. 'Yeah, but just a few *tapas* for me, Toni. Unless Paulo wants something else.'

Paulo shook his head and scanned the room. 'Where's Salvador today?'

'He not been in,' Toni replied. He looked over to a table where some of the regulars were huddled around a chess board. '*Thiago, dónd'está Salvador hoy?*'

One of the men glanced up. '*En casa. Hace demasiado calor.*' Too hot for him. The man glanced towards Paulo. '*Paulito*, you play when we finish?' He pointed in front of him. 'Miguel's king is trapped in corner.'

'Maybe later,' Paulo shouted back, 'when Hugo goes back.'

'Better be quick.' The man pointed at his opponent. 'He not last long.' There was a cackle of laughter from the others.

Another game was well under way by the time they'd finished eating. Hugo downed the last of a cold beer and stood up, raising his arms and clasping his hands together above his head like an athlete who'd just won the mara-

212

thon. 'I'm off back for a *siesta*, Paulo. Stay and have a game of chess. I'll call in on Salvador on the way. He hates it when it gets this hot. He whinges like crazy when he's confined to barracks.'

Seeing the puzzled look on Paulo's face, he added, 'I'll explain that one some other time.'

Salvador's front door appeared to have expanded during the rains of a few weeks earlier. When Hugo pushed it, it sprang back with equal force, jarring his shoulder. He winced, and shoved it harder, this time using his foot on the bottom edge. Reluctantly, it juddered open. Making a mental note to come and fix it, he poked his head round the door.

He kept his voice soft. 'Salvador, can I come in?' Hugo knew he didn't need to ask the old man's permission, but didn't want to startle him if he was asleep.

'Salva?' There was no answer, but even in the gloominess of the shuttered room he could see there was no one around.

He went back outside and peered over the gate, frowning. Where was he? Had he gone up to Hugo's house after all? Mopping his brow, he went back in, and again felt the instant shift in temperature. The ancient walls of Salvador's house were three feet thick and, whatever the weather, it had always felt cool in this room. He noticed the velvety cushion of white ash in the fireplace and shivered involuntarily, remembering the day he'd come here to find Paulo. It was cool in here that day too. Hugo rolled his eyes; the old skinflint had enough money stashed away to afford to use more logs than he did.

Hugo couldn't remember having previously noticed the ornate clock standing in the corner, which was beating out the time with a deep, hollow tock. Someone had once told him the ticking of case clocks soothes people because the rhythm is similar to that of the human heart. He'd never checked if it was true.

Above the fireplace, groups of people from the past and the present stood watching him. Salvador's wife, now dead these twenty years. His sons, one tall for a Spaniard, the other smaller, rounder, standing proudly, holding some kind of trophy. Young children. Hugo realized again how little he knew of Salvador's family.

The door to the kitchen was open and Hugo leaned in, keeping his hand on the door knob. He rolled his eyes. It was siesta time and here the old bugger was, in a rail-backed chair, eyes closed, legs lazily extended out in front of him. On the small table beside him, a battered box that may once have held someone's beautiful new shoes, but which now contained photographs. Resting on his lap, fingers that had long since gone cold, the same yellowy colour as the faded menu they held between them.

Hugo closed his eyes too, allowing the images to play through his head. The three of them in Granada, at the fla-menco *tablao*. The vibrancy of colour. The driving of the guitar. The gravelly voice, soulful, weeping. Salvador's hand, outstretched, drawing the woman in towards him. The clapping, the shouts of *¡Jaleo!* The joy radiating out from eyes that were now pale and unfocused.

The music had stopped and the dancers had gone home.

It must be the end of the show.

Hugo trailed the tips of his fingers across the old man's shoulder and returned to the sitting room. The telephone was behind the curtain.

He made two calls. The second one was to Toni.

25

'Check!'

Paulo used the palm of his hand to knock down the button on the clock. The wiry man in the plaid shirt rubbed his eyes, before glancing up him, then returning his gaze to the board in front of them. He picked up a rook and shifted it two spaces to the left, and then, without hurrying, tapped the button on his own clock.

Paulo paused but didn't look up. He held out his hand, hesitated, then took the tiny mitre at the top of the bishop between the ends of his finger and thumb and eased it along a diagonal row, across four squares.

Check. Click.

His opponent shook his head, and a wry smile crossed his face as he leaned back and exchanged looks with the two men sitting nearby. Then he lifted his king and gently laid it down. '*Muerto*. The King is dead.' He reached across the table and shook Paulo's hand. Paulo smiled, but kept his eyes lowered towards the board, saying only *gracias*.

'You are too modest, Paulo. You win, first time. Come, I buy you a beer.'

As Paulo lifted himself from his chair, he felt big hands

gripping his shoulders. He turned and looked up to see Toni, who was muttering to the other man in dialect. Toni tilted his head towards the door to the back room, beckoning Paulo to follow.

Locked in Toni's enormous arms, the boy who'd grown up on the streets of a ruthless city and never cried at last allowed his tears to flow, and they were free and unstoppable.

Salvador Jesús Ruben Cortes was laid to rest in the local churchyard, next to his beloved wife, two days after Hugo had entered the old man's kitchen for the last time. Later, Hugo would realize that it was also the first time.

It was another three days before Paulo came out from his bedroom, other than to find something to eat or drink and take it back with him. Hugo had tried to make conversation but had met with little response. On one occasion Hugo had followed a rod of light extending along the floor from the door of Paulo's room and, through the narrow opening, had seen him lying on his back with his eyes closed. To his surprise he'd heard J S Bach, sounding tinny as he boomed out from the boy's headphones.

When Paulo eventually emerged, he made toast and coffee before picking up the gardening book, telling Hugo he was going to do some work outside. It was the beginning of another scorching day, yet he worked until sunset. As the light faded from the day, Hugo took a sweater out for him and saw that Paulo had dug out several shallow furrows in one corner of the garden.

'This is going to be your new vegetable garden, *Avô.*'

'That's wonderful, Paulo, thank you. I'll look forward to eating what comes out of it.' Hugo handed him the sweater and waited till he'd pulled it on before putting his arm around his shoulders. They walked back to the house.

'Can we go fishing tomorrow?' Paulo asked. 'I want to catch the biggest fish in the river and baptise him, *Salvador*.'

26

'Are you okay, pal?'

Paulo was sitting on a foldaway chair watching the river meander by when Hugo's voice broke into his reverie.

Paulo snapped out of his trance. 'Sorry? Oh, yeah, I'm fine thanks.'

'You looked miles away.'

'I was just thinking about Salva. Then this decision I've got to make soon. I'm still not totally sure what you're telling me you think I should do.'

'I thought I'd said?'

'Not really. You told me a lot about your own experience, but you weren't exactly enthusiastic about it all. I started off thinking you'd definitely be for the idea then it sounded like you were saying you weren't.'

Hugo strolled over to the cooler box and pulled out a beer. He stared up at the sky for a moment and when he spoke, his voice was matter-of-fact. 'Okay, I'll tell you how I'm thinking. As far as Douglas is concerned, I honestly can't give you very much advice because I've never met the man. I'm sure you'll understand that. I don't know anything about him except the odd bits you've told me.' He shrugged. 'My gut feeling is you need to be very careful with him. But about a career in finance generally? Well, the first thing I'd ask is how *you* feel now, after you've been here all this time?'

Paulo tilted his head. 'I guess I'm excited by the idea. But also, I've listened to you telling me about your own career. And I listened to Salvador. I'm confused now. I'm really not sure about anything.'

'Did Salvador give you some advice?'

'No, not really. I don't think he understood much about it really. But it was just, well, the life he lived. It was so simple. He had good values.'

Hugo nodded and the sadness in his eyes almost spoke its own story. *Marietta, Salvador. A dying breed, literally.* He wiped his brow with the back of his hand. 'Boy, it's hot again today.' Wandering back towards the edge of the water he sat down on the bank and dangled his bare feet in the water. Paulo's eyes followed him all the way, frustration filling his young features.

Suddenly, Hugo leaned forward and plunged his hand into the water, swishing it around below the surface. When he withdrew it again he was holding a pebble between his finger and thumb. As Paulo, a puzzled look on his face, watched on, Hugo stared at the little stone. 'I wonder how many of these there are in this river?'

Paulo wrinkled his brow. 'No idea, why do you ask?'

'It's just, *we're* kind of like that aren't we, little pebbles in a very long river? One day those pebbles won't exist. The longer time goes on the smaller they'll become until eventually they'll have been worn down into sand by the water.'

Paulo groaned. 'This is all a bit heavy for a hot day, *Avô*. What's this got to do with Douglas and my career?'

Hugo laughed. 'Yes, you're right. But eternity's full of people like us. Just passing through.' He tossed the pebble to Paulo. 'But we all play a part. We try to use our short little existence the best way we can. At least, we should do.'

Paulo nodded his head, saying nothing.

'Okay, I think what I'm saying is, if I were as young as you are and I knew what I know now, maybe I'd be trying to do a bit more to help other people than I have done. Your *Vovó* Marietta's eyes used to sparkle when she talked about her work in Rio. In spite of everything that happened to her, she loved her life. I never got any of that kind of joy doing what I did. So, yes, I admit, when I was with her, I was a bit envious. She made me realize there's another definition of wealth.' Hugo smiled, but there was no brightness in his eyes. 'You know, people talk about a person's "net worth" and they always mean money. So, what does that say? Mother Teresa was worth nothing, because she didn't *have* any money?'

Hugo stood up and picked his way through the rocks, back to the grassy bank. 'Look, that's only my personal opinion. That's the only thing in all of this I can give you with any certainty. This thing with Douglas, like I said, just think very carefully. Do your research on him. Is what he's offering truly what you want? You wouldn't be normal if you didn't get excited about the thought of making a lot of money, driving around in expensive cars, eating in nice restaurants, all of that. Especially you, with the life you've had. I was like that once. I used to put money before everything, probably even before my own marriage sometimes.'

Paulo opened his arms. 'But I've never *had* any money.'

Hugo nodded. 'I understand that, Paulo, honestly I do. So I suppose it's just me getting philosophical, but I wonder whether there's any room in whatever you've got planned for helping some of those kids on the streets back in Rio? It doesn't mean you can't make money, I just wonder whether you couldn't achieve both?'

Paulo raised his eyebrows. 'Shit, I didn't have all these decisions until Douglas came on the scene. I wonder sometimes whether it's easier just working in a bar. That way, you don't have too many choices to make.'

Hugo smiled. 'I'm not trying to put you off, Paulo, that's the last thing I want to do. You grew up in a very poor world. I didn't, I was privileged. But like I said, Marietta changed my outlook. She opened up a new world for me. So these days I'm comparing two things, and from where I am now one of them looks a lot better than the other. But listen, if you feel that going into the financial world is the right thing for you to do, do it. Just make sure you put everything into it. I can't tell you any more than that, Paulo. It has to be your decision. Whatever you decide to do, you have my blessing, for what it's worth, and I'll do my best to support you.'

Paulo smiled, looking down at his feet. 'Thanks, *Avô*.'

Hugo clapped him on the shoulder. 'You know what, Paulo?'

The boy looked up. 'Yeah?'

'If it wasn't for this fellow Douglas coming into your life, you might not have come into mine. Think about that.'

The tiny fish lay still in Paulo's cupped hands.

Hugo stared at it. What it lacked in size it made up for with its rich tones: old polished brass, a palette of halo-ringed spots melting into creamy-orange on its lower body. Small, but full of colour. A fitting description of the man it was about to be named after, Hugo thought.

Like a priest, Paulo made the sign of the cross over the little creature, no easy task as he was trying to keep hold of it with his free hand. '*Eu batizar-te, Salvador…*

He looked up at Hugo. 'It means…'

Hugo nodded. 'I think I can work that out, Paulo.'

Paulo turned his attention back to the little fish. 'And now, I let you go. Good luck, my dear, fishy friend. Have a good, long life, and may you never be caught again.'

Convinced this baptism of a trout in old Salvador's memory was intended to be serious, Hugo resisted the urge to chuckle. But he couldn't hold it back any longer when Paulo lifted the fish to his lips and kissed it, before easing it back into the water and opening his hands. The fish was clearly more than happy to escape this bizarre little situation.

Paulo watched the newly-named fish disappear below the surface, then looked up at Hugo.

'And it's time for me to go too, *Avô.*'

Hugo had known this moment would come, but he hadn't been sure how he'd feel. Now he knew. It was as if an unseen hand had squeezed something inside his ribcage.

Ever so gently, just enough to cause a small ache.

He'd been there enough. He nodded and turned away.

27

'Have I helped?' Hugo asked, as they walked back to the house.

Paulo breathed in deeply. 'I think so. I guess I was asking a lot from you. I know you can't make the decision for me.'

'What do you think you'll do?'

'I still don't know for sure, I'll see how I feel when I get back to Rio. But Douglas will be back soon so I need to be there, one way or another.'

Hugo smiled and cocked his head to one side. 'I'm curious to know what Salvador did say to you about your plans.'

'He told me about New York.'

Hugo waited for more, sensing it was a moment he should not interfere with.

Paulo screwed up his eyes and began to recite. '*The light's buried under chains and noises.*' He opened his eyes again and wafted his hand. 'I can't remember the rest, except the pigeons paddle in dirty water.'

Hugo rubbed his chin. 'Salvador said that? I didn't think he ever went to New York.'

'No, it was in this poem he showed me. By Lorca.'

'Lorca? He died donkey's years ago, before the second

World War wasn't it? New York wasn't like that when I was last there. It was pretty clean.'

As they climbed the path, Hugo stopped and turned to face Paulo. 'You know, I don't know anything about Brasilia, but if you do end up going to New York you're going to find life massively expensive. I've been doing a lot of thinking about things.' He held up his hand. 'Just hear me out on this, okay? I don't like saying bad things about my own mother and father, but what they did, with Marietta, was not good. If they'd behaved in the right way, half of their money when they died would have come to me, and when I died it would have gone to Erik. Now Erik's gone and he was practically your father for a long time. I want you to have some of that money.'

'*Avô*, honestly. That's not why I came here.'

'Paulo, I don't *need* that money and I've got no one else to pass it on to when I die. My sister and her husband are well off and the last thing I want is for their son to get his hands on it. I want *you* to have some of it, it'd give you a great start in your career, whatever you decide to do.'

As he was speaking, he felt a tiny speck on his hand and looked up. After another wave of hot weather, rain was beginning to fall again. They started walking, but neither spoke, and Hugo could almost reach out and touch an awkwardness he was sensing. Out of the corner of his eye, he saw Paulo shaking his head.

'Paulo? Have I said something to upset you?'

Paulo glanced over. 'You know, it took a long time for you to accept me coming here, but I thought we understood each other better now.' He looked out over the field and seemed to exaggerate a sigh.

Hugo kept his voice level. 'I'm not with you.'

Paulo turned his eyes back. 'I thought I was honest with you about why I came? I told you I needed advice. I told you I didn't have any family any more. You were going to be *Vovó's* husband.'

'I know all that…'

'Right, so why do you start offering me money all of a sudden? I didn't come for that. I never asked for a cent from you. So why make out I did? It makes me feel like I'm some kind of…' He threw his hands up. 'I don't know the word in English. *Charlatão*…'

Hugo held up the palm of his hand. 'Hey, mate, stop right there. I never said anything about you wanting money from me. I was the one who brought up the subject, because I wanted you to have choices. If I've upset you I'm sorry, I didn't mean to.'

Paulo held his gaze for a moment, then sat down on the low stone wall at the side of the path. They'd arrived at the very same place where Hugo and Salvador had been standing all that time ago, when Paulo had come up the pathway. Salvador had sensed the tension and decided to go back home and Hugo had closed the door in Paulo's face. The face the boy was now cupping in his hands.

Drops of water began to settle on them both as Hugo waited, telling himself he would stay there getting soaked if necessary until Paulo replied, no matter how long the silence lasted. After a few moments, Paulo lifted his head, and the beginning of a weak smile forced its way outwards from the corners of his lips. '*Avô,* I don't want you to think I'm not grateful. I'm grateful for everything you've given me. Taking me into your home, teaching me things. But if I'm going to do this, I have to do it myself, through my own efforts. I'll be okay, I'll try and get my job back at the bar, or somewhere else. And Douglas promised to pay the college fees if I decide to join him. Then if I go and work for him later he'll be paying me a salary.'

Hugo raised his eyebrows for a moment, then nodded. He tightened his lips to return the smile, but it could easily have been mistaken for a grimace.

Outside the house Hugo unlocked the door and stepped inside, but Paulo stayed under the porch. The porch where it had all started for the two of them. And, just as on that first night, Paulo's eyes flickered nervously as he spoke. 'I think I'll go down to Toni's. Some of the guys might be down there, playing chess.'

Hugo nodded. 'Sure, whatever you want. See you for dinner later?'

The corners of Paulo's lips flickered upwards momentarily but no smile followed before he turned away and set off towards the field.

Standing at the door, Hugo watched him follow the track where the grass had been flattened, the same pathway they'd taken to the restaurant on the day Salvador died. Was Paulo thinking about that too? Something was obviously still upsetting him, judging by the way he was trudging along, head down, hands stuffed in the pockets of his shorts. Or was it the little exchange they'd just had, further down the path?

He wondered if he'd ever fathom this kid out.

BOOK THREE

Book Three

28

Paulo dumped his bag on the bed.

The house was deserted. He was exhausted from the long flight and could smell his own body. He headed for the bathroom.

The shower hose hung like a snake down the tiles. As he bent to replace it in its holder, he saw that the drain was clogged up with hair from goodness knows how many heads and bodies. He ripped off a length of toilet tissue and screwed up his face as he cleared it, gathering up a sliver of soap for good measure and stuffing it all into the overflowing bin. He searched for a fresh bar of soap in the cupboard, but, finding nothing, was forced to retrieve the old one, which now also had tissue stuck to it.

After he'd showered he returned to the bedroom and put on a fresh tee-shirt and jeans. He sat down on the edge of the bed and pulled his mobile phone from his bag.

The voice at the other end boomed. 'Hey Paulo! You back home? I'm still in Florida.' Paulo mouthed a silent curse. 'I stayed on a bit longer, be back next week. The week after, I'll come over to Rio. Did you think about what I said?'

'Not much else,' Paulo lied.

'Did you speak to your uncle?'

Paulo rolled his eyes. 'Grandfather.'

'Yeah, right. Anyway, what did he say?'

'Well, he said a lot of things, but in the end he said it was down to me.' Paulo heard clattering in the background on the other end of the line and the muffled sound of Douglas shouting to someone.

'Sorry, pal. The kids are being a pain. Anyway, we can talk when I get over there. Hey, I gotta tell you, this buddy of mine in New York came down here last week. He's into futures, coffee, zinc, all sorts of commodities. You wouldn't believe how much money he's making. But he needs someone back in Brazil, 'specially with coffee trades. We could be very useful to him. It would also mean I'd be able to get something started in New York by next year at the latest. So we'd need you trained up quick.'

The shuffling started up again and Paulo could hear children's voices.

'Listen, kid, I've got to go. Let me give you a call next week and we'll fix up dinner or something.'

Paulo snapped the phone shut and went downstairs. He opened the fridge and found only the remains of a jar of sweet pickle and a bowl of something that might once have been spaghetti sauce but which was now flecked with white and blue mould. He grabbed his jacket and searched through the pockets. Enough to buy a burger and fries. He headed for the door.

On the main street, he dodged in and out of the wave of students returning from classes, nodding when he spotted someone he recognised. Music blared from an upstairs window and he heard a woman screaming curses at an errant husband, or maybe a child. Against a wall lay a completely zipped-up sleeping bag which appeared to contain a human being, though Paulo had no idea if it was a man or a woman, worse still, whether he or she was still alive. Alongside the bag stood a plastic cup. Paulo dipped in his pocket and did a quick calculation before dropping some coins into it.

Ten yards further on, as though to remind visitors that Rio was a place of extremes, a young woman with bright red-dyed hair played Marcello's Oboe Concerto on a violin. Paulo sighed, remembering the haunting music that drifted out from the calm of Hugo's study when he was writing his book.

As he walked, he replayed his conversation with Douglas through his mind. 'Next year at the latest,' he'd said. So how would he, Paulo, be able to carry on at uni, which is what he'd thought Douglas wanted him to do? He couldn't do that if he was in New York, or even Brasilia. And if he stayed in Rio, he'd have precious little time to learn the business and finish his degree.

But if Hugo had taught him anything, it was that you had to grab your chances while you can. It was going to be incredibly hard, but it just might be possible. He would talk to Douglas and try to get a better idea of things.

Even as he analysed the scenario, his heart jumped when he realized there was a more immediate situation to sort out. He was fast running out of money. The first thing he'd have to do was try to get his job back at the bar.

Outside the burger shop, three kids, all about seven or eight, ran up to him, pushing and shoving each other, pulling at his trousers, hands held out, eyes dancing up at him. He knew exactly how much remained inside his pocket and raised his eyebrows as the thought jumped into his head. *Shit, I can manage without the fries.*

Rafa's voice assaulted him. '*Paulinho!*'

A Lanterna's owner swivelled towards a corner table where a group of men were playing cards. 'Guys, look who's back!'

Rafa was a well upholstered man in his mid-forties. His moustache, coaxed upwards at either side, reminded Paulo of a character he'd seen in one of Hugo's collections of British comedies, *'Allo, 'Allo* or something like that. He came out from behind the bar and hugged Paulo, holding him out again to look him up and down. 'When did you get back?'

'This morning.' Paulo glanced around the bar. It was busier than he'd have expected at this time of day.

Rafa patted one of the high bar stools. 'Hey, let me get you a beer, man. On the house. We missed you.'

Paulo pulled the stool towards him. 'Listen, Rafa, I'm going back to college next week. I could do with my job back.'

Rafa pulled a face. 'Shit, man, that's not going to be easy.' He waved his arm vaguely towards the people in the bar. 'You can see how busy we are. After you went, your pal quit too. I was run off my feet. Then, this *gatinha* comes in one day asking for a job. I had to give her a chance.' He grinned. 'She's a real looker, goes down a bomb with the guys in here. You should see her, she'll be in tonight.'

'But that's only one person, Rafa. There used to be two of us.'

'Yeah, well, after your pal went me and my wife had a chat about things. She's the one who does the books and she reckons we can only afford one person. So she says I've got to run the bar during the day, then this chick comes in at six and takes over. My wife comes at eight and works in the bar as well. She says that'll give me time to admire *her* instead of female members of the staff. Man, my sex life's not been as good for years!'

Paulo forced a smile. 'No, that's good, Rafa. I'm pleased for you. Sounds like your wife's got you in line again.'

Rafa caught Paulo's eye. 'Hey, *parceiro*, don't be sad. It'll be okay, something will come up. All the guys along the main street know you did a good job here. Get them to call me.' He held up a finger. 'And wait, I've got something for you.' He rummaged around at the side of the till and pulled a small piece of paper from an untidy pile. 'Yeah, here it is. The night before you went away, you did a shift but I wasn't in that day, remember? I paid you up to the Friday but you worked until the Tuesday after. You've got your wages for the extra days owing, plus your share of the tips.' He hit one of the keys on the ancient metal till and pulled out some notes.

Along the main street, Paulo called in at all of the bars, but the story was the same everywhere. There was lots of life around the college, but not much money. Bar owners couldn't afford to sit around with a couple of regulars all day long while some kid did all the work and then came asking for their pay, even if it was for less than the minimum wage.

In *Palmeira*, where Paulo had so often met with his friends after work, there was a glimmer of hope. The owner greeted him warmly. 'I've had this guy working here at night, you might have seen him. A real *sangue*, very honest. But he's got this uncle in London who owns a restaurant. The kid's not doing too well in college and if he can get a work permit he'll be off in a flash. He's still waiting to find out, but if he goes, you can come here, I'll give you a few hours a week. You remember Bete? She's still working here in the evenings.' He nudged Paulo. 'Wow, what a piece of meat! *Que figura!*'

It was a different type of figure Paulo had in mind as he headed back home. Rafa had just given him about fifty dollars in *reals* and he might have another hundred in his account which he'd left there to keep him going when he got back from Spain. But that wouldn't last more than a couple of weeks and his share of the rent was due soon.

He started thinking about Douglas's offer again. He'd thought Douglas had wanted him to finish his economics course and that he'd pay him for some part-time work while he was learning the trade. Not much, he'd said, but it would have been enough to buy food and cover his share of the rent, and he could work some shifts in the bar. It would have been hard, but worth it in the end.

Now, everything seemed to be changing. There was no work at the bars and on top of that Douglas seemed to be suggesting he'd want him to leave Rio soon anyway.

Paulo's head was spinning. Already, he wished he had Hugo to talk to.

As he turned his pillow over again, the options continued to rattle around Paulo's head. The only thing he knew for certain was that this was not how he had planned things.

The choice was supposed to have been simple. One: carry on at uni, get the degree. Decide. Or two: accept what he thought Douglas had been offering and become part of the financial wheeler-dealering that was the guy's world.

Now though, he was being pressed into a corner by things outside his control. He'd spent almost all the money he'd been left. And why? Because he'd needed Hugo's advice that badly?

A couple of years ago, someone had lent him a book. All about living 'in the now', some European guy, or was he from Canada? Forget the past, forget the future, you're here now. That's what counts.

In the *right now*, he could probably afford to buy something to eat during the day ahead.

But what about tomorrow, what about after that? When it's not *right now* anymore?

He thought about what Hugo had said, the offer he'd made. How ironic that had been. Just as being poor can force you into choices, so too can being wealthy. If he'd agreed to accept Hugo's money, would that have tempted him to say yes to Douglas, get himself a place in Brasilia? Or even New York?

He had no idea how much money Hugo had been

talking about, but did it matter? It still seemed that some unseen hand of fate was propelling him towards Douglas and his offer, whatever that offer turned out to be.

He had to forget what might have been and get on with his life.

In the now.

29

The letter arrived a week later.

Douglas had still not called and Paulo was back in college, struggling to get fired up again.

The *sangue*, the 'reliable boy' at *Palmeira*, had decided he needed time off to do some cramming. Paulo had been promised a weekend's work and he needed the money badly.

He was getting ready for a mid-morning lecture when he heard banging on the door downstairs.

The postman was red in the face as he thrust the envelopes towards Paulo. Now, with his hands free again, he stabbed a finger in the direction of the letter box.

'You need to get that thing fixed!' His voice was high pitched. 'I've already told your friends, that spring is too fierce. One of these days I'm going to get my hand stuck in it and you'll have blood all over your floor. Not to mention, you won't be getting your letters any more. Except one from my lawyer.'

Paulo fanned the letters out in his hand. There were two official looking envelopes for one of his housemates and a smarter, white one which bore his own name.

The postman was still waving his arms around. 'I don't do this job because it pays good. But it does pay something, and it was supposed to be easy enough. *Just go up to the door with the letters*, they told me, *push them through the flap.*' He made a duck's beak with his fingers and thumb and jerked them forwards and backwards to illustrate. 'Easy, eh? But no. Last month I call at this one house and when I *push* the letters through,' he jabbed his hand forward again for emphasis, 'something inside grabs my hand. When I pull it out, it looks like a fresh steak from the butcher's window. Then a woman snatches the door open and asks me what I'm doing, upsetting her dog. She shows me the letters I've just put through the door. *There's blood all over them*, she says. There was too, *my* blood! *How am I going to read these now?* the silly bitch is going on. *Why didn't you knock?* Well, why would I knock? How am *I* supposed to know there's a great big fucking dog behind the door, waiting to eat some poor bastard who's just trying to do his job?'

'Is your hand okay now?' Paulo's attempt at sympathy only provoked another tirade.

'Yes, thanks only to the good grace of the *Virgem Maria* herself,' he replied, crossing himself. He turned to descend the steps, then swung round again. 'You remember, young man! Get that flap fixed or there'll only be one more envelope coming through *your* door. And it won't be a birthday card from your auntie!'

Paulo glanced at the time on his phone. He was running late. He dropped the two manila envelopes on the hall table and stuffed the one addressed to himself into the zip pocket on his backpack. He headed out, making a mental note to tell his pals they were going to need to club together for a new letter box.

More money, he thought, as he pulled the door closed behind him.

Douglas Pereira finally arrived in Rio de Janeiro the following week. He had been delayed in São Paulo, he explained, due to a 'necessary business reconstruction'.

Now he sat opposite Paulo and wiped his fat lips with his serviette. 'This guy in New York is awesome. He went to America with almost nothing, but he's as quick as a cat. Thinks fast, acts fast. Makes lightning decisions that pull in big money, but he's as cool as they come.'

Paulo attempted to look impressed. 'What does he do, exactly?'

'Deals in futures. Like, say a farmer grows corn. It takes ages to grow, and the problem is when it's finished growing, the price of corn might have gone down. So the farmer can take out a futures contract. What he's really doing is betting. If the price of corn goes down, he gets a fixed price. But if it goes up, he only gets what it says in the contract.'

'Who does he take out the contract with?'

'Well, there are two parties to the contract. A hedger and a speculator. In my example, the farmer is the hedger. On the other side of the deal is a speculator.'

'So not another farmer?'

Douglas laughed. 'No, no way. Almost all the deals involve speculators. You can make a fortune if you get it

243

right. But most of the people doing it wouldn't be able to tell a tractor from a donkey!' He picked up his wine glass. 'You have a lot to learn, kid. But listen, if you stick with me you'll get to know all the tricks. I can see you're bright, that's why I'm giving you this chance. What a story that would be.' He pawed the air with two fingers of each hand. '*Street kid from Rio makes first million in futures*. What a headline. Wasn't there a film about something like that?'

The waiter arrived with *feijoada*, the traditional dish of black beans and rice with fish. Douglas stuffed his serviette back inside the open neck of his shirt and began shovelling food into his mouth. Paulo watched, his mind wandering back to the days when he was with his pals on the street and they would forage round for leftover hamburgers in bins. He wished his mother was here to see him now.

No, he just wished his mother was here. Full stop.

Douglas was speaking again and his words cut into Paulo's thoughts. '... what I had in mind was, there's this course. It takes about a year on day release, two evenings a week. You'd learn all about those things.' He cackled. 'You'll end up knowing more than I do, you can teach me all about it afterwards. Anyway, we'd put you on a starter salary. It wouldn't be a fortune, but it'd get you by for a year. You'd have to come and live in Brasilia, of course. I've got a couple of apartments there, so you could use one of those. After that, we can decide whether we open a new office in Rio or whether you want to keep working from Brasilia. The real money will come after that, when you start trading.'

'So I don't finish my degree course?'

Douglas frowned. 'Well, no, but you'll be a hell of a lot richer than those impoverished bastards you hang out with.' He leaned across the table. 'Hey, did you hear this one? What do you say to a kid with a first-class degree in economics? A Big Mac and chips please!' He roared laughing and almost choked on his food as he straightened back up. He drank more wine and set the glass back down on the table. 'No, son, you'll be well out of all that. Money's the object now. Lots of it.' He wiped his mouth a last time, balled up the serviette and threw it onto the plate in front of him.

'So when do I get started?'

'That's the spirit.' Douglas stood up. 'Very soon. I just need to sort out a few things in Brasilia first. Are you ready to move over there?'

'Can't see why not.' A smile broke through on Paulo's face at last. 'Just my packing to do, so it shouldn't take me more than five or six minutes.'

As quickly, or slowly, as Douglas had appeared in Rio, so too did he disappear out of contact again.

Paulo attended all his lectures and spent his free time calling into different bars on the off-chance of some work. The unexpected bonus of working one weekend had helped, but he'd had to pay his rent and his funds were low again.

On a Saturday morning he sat in *A Lanterna* nursing a coffee and reading a newspaper someone had left behind. Rafa was leaning on the bar doing a crossword, glasses perched on the end of his nose. Every now and then he got up to smoke a cigarette out in the street. 'Fucking politicians,' he complained. 'I pay rent here, tax on every penny I make, yet I can't even smoke in my own bar. What will it be next, I can't screw my wife upstairs in case we make too much noise and the customers get over-excited? Bad for their health, give 'em a heart attack?'

Paulo chuckled and folded the newspaper closed. He leaned back in his chair, shutting his eyes. What had he gone and done? He'd spent all his money trying to find someone he'd thought was close to being family, only for Hugo to send him away. Twice. If it hadn't been for an old man he'd only just met, the whole lot would have been wasted. Salvador, who had confided in him that he thought Hugo was doing the wrong thing. Yet who'd also explained that Hugo probably had good cause to think twice, after everything that had happened in his life. *Un hombre quebrantado*, he'd called Hugo, a broken man.

But what about himself? What was he? Hadn't he been *quebrantado* too? He'd felt angry with Hugo for sending him away. Salvador had asked him to think about what it must have looked like to Hugo. A boy he never even knew existed, coming out of nowhere. The old man had surprised Paulo by talking about an American TV series in the eighties which was popular in Spain. There were always people suddenly reappearing from the past, out of nowhere, Salva had said. Lovers who'd died years ago would turn up alive. Young men would arrive at the ranch claiming to be the illegitimate son of somebody or other in the family.

All for the sake of money, and inheritance.

Salvador had said Hugo once used an English expression, *where there's a will, there's a relative*. It seemed to amuse the old man, but Paulo had tried translating it on Google and it didn't make sense. At any rate, he couldn't understand what was so funny about it.

Now, Salvador was dead too.

Shit, Paulo hissed under his breath. All he'd asked Hugo for was his advice. No, that wasn't true. He'd also wanted to find someone he could call family, a kindred spirit.

Out of the corner of his eye, he saw Rafa toss his cigarette end onto the pavement and wander back into the bar. He was closely followed by one of the regulars. Paulo called over to him. 'Hey, Juquinha, *tudo bem*, everything okay? What you up to, *amigo*?'

The man dropped a plastic bag down onto a bar stool. 'I pulled a shelf down at home, reaching up for a glass so I could have a drink. The whole fucking lot fell down on top of me.'

'Wow, bad luck man,' Rafa said, pulling a beer for him. He nodded at the bag, which had the name of a local DIY store on it. 'You been buying stuff to fix it then?'

'Nah,' the man replied, wafting a hand. 'That was three weeks ago. Those are new glasses in there. Why do you think I've been coming in here so much? We've got nothing to fucking drink out of at home.'

Paulo and Rafa burst out laughing. Then Paulo stood up, shaking his head. 'I've got to go.'

'Hey, Paulinho, don't forget to come back tonight. You haven't seen the lovely Gabriela yet.'

Paola turned to wave, and the carrier bag from the hard-

247

ware shop caught his eye again.

The image of the broken letter box flashed into his mind and that reminded him.

The letter.

He almost forgot again when he got back to the house.

Hungry, he popped some bread in the toaster while he heated up some spiced beans. He thought about all the junk food he was eating these days, recalling Hugo's love of cooking and the dinners they'd eaten with friends at Toni's. He thought too about his dwindling funds and his heart jumped as he remembered the letter. Was that what it was about, to tell him he'd gone overdrawn at the bank? He tutted. Why was he fussing around? There was no point avoiding things, the letter wasn't going to go away.

He sat down at the kitchen table with the plate in front of him, and opened up the envelope. The letter inside was written on some kind of expensive paper which made a firm, flapping noise when he unfolded it. Propping it up against the coffee pot, he saw the date on it and glanced up at the calendar on the kitchen wall. The letter was dated over a month earlier. He shook his head.

To my dear Paulo,

You took some finding!

Ever since you left here, the days have been quiet again, but at least I've had a bit of free time to do some searching. And fishing. The brown trout miss you. The other day I pulled out two on the same morning. I named one of them Marietta and the other one Erik. I don't know whether they were male or female, so I hope I got it the right way round. The next one will be Paulo.

Quite possibly you're going to be angry with me, but I hope you will eventually see my point and forgive me. I am old enough, I think, to indulge a little.

I thought long and hard about what I told you that day, about what I believe are your rights as the adopted son of my own son. Now, even my son, the man you called your father, has disappeared. By the way, I want to talk to you about that sometime, I've been doing some research through a company in Mexico – I'll tell you more when I hear back from them.

Anyway, one way or another, I have not been lucky enough to have children, so I have no family now except my sister, who as I've told you is comfortably well off. As the song goes, there's only you and me.

When I was very young, my parents taught me the difference between good and bad. Yet, when I wasn't there to argue, they tried to persuade your vovó, when she was about the same age as you are now, to destroy the baby inside her body. My son, their grandson. Vovó Marietta was stronger than that, even at that young age. Sometimes, I think about what I might have done if I'd arrived back earlier and learned about what was happening. Would I ever have been persuaded by my parents? Who knows, it was a long time ago. But your Vovó Marietta spared me from having to make that choice.

Now, you too have choices and I am genuinely pleased for you. You see, Marietta came back into my life and opened my eyes. Then, she left as quickly as she had come, and I went back into my own shell. Only for you to come along, out of the blue as it were. You asked for nothing but my friendship and advice (although you did eat quite a lot!)

So what options are left for me now, Paulo? Since I have no intention of leaving my money to my sister (or more likely to her spendthrift – google it – son), then all I can think of is that I would have to leave it in my will to charity. But then, I wouldn't have the pleasure of seeing if any good came of it.

Or, I could give it to you. That way you might have even more choices. You could use it to help with your new career, fly back to see me when you're a rich businessman and you've got a gap in your schedule! Alternatively, you could deal with it some other way, as best you see fit, possibly for the good of the kids who are suffering now, like you once did. Or, as I suggested, do both.

So, after you left here, I got in touch with my solicitor in

250

London, and he in turn has been in touch with a firm of lawyers in Rio (details are enclosed). The long and short of it is that I have set up a trust fund for you and it will be available to you when you're twenty-one. If at that time you still don't want it, you can choose which charity it goes to.

I also recognise that you might have more pressing financial needs, and I've put a small amount of money into your private bank account. In this respect, I have to confess to being a bit naughty, since I was passing your bedroom one day and you'd left the door open. I saw your bank card lying on the dressing table and I thought it might help to have the details one day. This, I am afraid, is something else you will have to forgive me for.

Perhaps another way of looking at all this is that if I'd left this money to you when I died, it would be difficult for you to argue with me, so you'd get it anyway. But that way I wouldn't have had the joy of seeing it help you in your life.

I hope you have settled into Rio again and that your treasured gardening book arrived safely with you. We had a small church service the other evening, a memorial for your great friend Salvador. Then we all headed back to Toni's to drink to his memory, which we did quite a lot of on the grounds that there were lots of memories!

I hope you'll understand what I have chosen to do and that you won't be too cross! Think of it this way, at least you will have no excuse now for not coming back here one day to see the grandfather you have adopted. I will look forward to that day very much, and in the meantime you know I am as near to you as the closest telephone.

Affectionately,

Your Avô Hugo

30

Paulo's pocket vibrated and he glanced towards the front of the class, where the lecturer was in full flow. He wriggled around in his chair, struggling to prise the phone far enough out to read the name on the screen.

Douglas.

Half an hour later, when the bell sounded, it was almost drowned out by the clattering of chairs. Students rushed for the door as though they had another class half a mile away in five minutes, rather than, more likely, a free period. Paulo made his way to the door, but before he reached the corridor he heard a shout from behind him.

'Paulo? Do me a favour will you?' du Pont called over. 'Turn your phone off when you come into class, please.'

Paulo made an attempt to sink his head between his shoulders. 'Sorry, Prof.' He walked back towards the desk. 'Listen, I wanted to say thanks for covering for me while I was away. I was going to come and tell you about it, but I haven't had a chance.'

'Next week, maybe?' the professor replied. 'There'll be a few people on placement at the stock exchange so I've got some free periods. Come and find me.' He stood up, gathering his papers together. 'By the way, I've talked to some of my colleagues. They're pleased with what you've done while you were away, looking after your, um, sick relative.'

Paulo grinned and flicked his hand as he headed out. He saw there was an empty classroom and stepped into it. There was no message on his phone so he tapped into the directory, and after what seemed like an eternity, Douglas answered. 'Hey, kid, it's like trying to ring the Pope getting hold of you.'

'Sorry, Douglas, I was in class…'

'… well can't you get out of fucking class? Tell them you're going for a leak or something? Anyway, I've sorted things out now. I'm ready for you to move over here.'

Paulo felt as though all the blood had been drained out of his body. His throat went dry and he grunted before speaking. 'That's great, Douglas…'

'You don't exactly *sound* over the moon.'

'No, I'm okay. I've just got a bit of a cold,' he lied.

'Right. Anyway, next month, the first Monday,' Douglas said. 'I need to get the apartment cleared out. You could move in the weekend before. I've got to go to São Paulo that week, but I'll make sure one of my people gets you settled in and I'll see you at the end of the week. I'll have a contract for you to sign when I get back.'

There was a shuffling noise in the background. Paulo thought he heard a woman's voice, but Douglas was quickly back on the line. 'Listen, kid, I need to go… I'll get my secretary to text you the address of the apartment. See you soon. *Ciao.*'

The phone went dead and Paulo stared at it. *Well, thanks*

for all the information to help me plan this massive change in my life. He shook his head

But at least he now knew what the other option was.

It was early evening, and there were only a couple of people in *A Lanterna*, though Paulo knew it would get a lot busier as people finished college and work for the weekend. Rafa was standing behind the bar, polishing bottles on the back shelf. Paulo wandered up behind him and put his hand on his shoulder.

'Hi, Rafa.'

Rafa swung round, almost dropping a full bottle of vodka on the floor. 'Shit man, you scared the life out of me!' He put the bottle down and leaned on the bar, patting his chest. 'Don't *do* that...'

Paulo grinned and rubbed Rafa's back.

'Hey listen,' Rafa said. 'Despite the fact you clearly want to kill me, I'm glad to see you. Can you work tonight?'

Paulo stared at him. 'Where? Here?'

'What do you mean, where, here? Where else would I want you to fucking work?'

Paulo shrugged. 'Sure, but what happened to, whatever she was called...?'

'Gabriela?' Rafa mimed a spit. '*Bagulho!*'

So the 'eye candy' of a few days ago was apparently now a dishonest slut.

Rafa's voice had risen to the higher octaves. 'We were eighty *reals* short in the till the other night so I asked her about it the next day. So she says, how could that have happened while you were here, Rafa? You must be getting careless in your old age. Cheeky bitch! She says the till must have been short when she came on duty.'

Paulo grimaced. 'That doesn't sound like you, Rafa...'

The big man's eyebrows almost reached the top of his head. 'Fucking right it doesn't. Anyway, listen, so the little cow tries to make out I've taken my own money and then blamed her. Next thing my wife kicks off, tells me to check the money in the safe, where's the rest of it gone? I knew I wouldn't make a mistake like that. Next night we check the till together and we agree, we'll do that every night before she comes on duty. Didn't need to wait very long. Two nights later she clears out the whole fucking till. Casually serves a couple of guys, saunters out for a cigarette, never comes back!'

'Tough luck, man.' Thinking it better to change the subject before Rafa had an apoplectic fit, Paulo affected a look of concern. 'What time do you want me to start?'

Rafa glanced at his watch. 'Like, five minutes ago?' He winked. 'I'm due upstairs.' He lifted the flap at the end of the bar and squeezed his bulky frame through. 'You got your job back if you want it, *gato*. Same rate as before.'

Paulo followed him as he headed towards the stairs. 'You must be joking, Rafa. I know you were paying the *bagulho* more than you paid me.'

Rafa turned round. 'Yeah, but she brought more customers in.'

'And took the takings out.' Paulo reached out for his coat, draped on a bar stool. 'I can go now if you're not happy to pay me the same.'

'Bastard!' Rafa carried on up the stairs. 'Had to pay her

more, didn't I? She might have been a thieving little whore but she had a great ass. Just you make sure we keep those new customers.'

Paulo turned round and waggled his rear end. He heard Rafa laughing as he disappeared upstairs.

Behind the bar, Paulo began tidying up, ready for the evening rush. Rafa had called him a *gato*, a cat. But to a Brazilian, a hot boy. He smiled. He was going to prove Rafa right. Suddenly, the game of chess he seemed to be playing had developed, and another uncertainty had turned into an opening. He had his job back and it was as though he had unexpectedly acquired an extra piece.

It was almost three before Paulo tumbled into bed, falling asleep right away.

He woke again at around five. He'd been dreaming about chess. He was competing in a big international tournament, against a Russian grandmaster, a woman. Every time he moved one of his pieces, it was as though he was in some kind of paralysis, and when he went to position his piece on the square, he couldn't get it down on the board. It was as if there were a magnetic field pushing it back up again. When he did finally succeed in making his move, this woman, who looked like something out of an old James Bond movie, would respond within seconds, slamming her piece down, hitting the button on her clock and crashing back triumphantly into her chair, arms folded in challenge.

Then something strange happened. Earlier in the game he'd sacrificed his Queen in a stupid move. Suddenly it was back on the board again and everything had changed.

Lying awake now in the darkness, his mind was calm and clear. Everything had changed here too.

He hadn't touched any of the money Hugo had put into his bank account. He was aware too that he hadn't even acknowledged Hugo's letter, and resolved to do that as soon as he got up. There were over thirty thousand *reals* in his account, something like ten thousand US dollars. He'd almost given in to temptation and taken some of it out. But what kind of principles would he have had to do that? If he was going to take out a hundred *reals*, what difference would it make if he took out a thousand? He knew that once he helped himself to some of the money he'd be tempted to take more and more of it.

Choices. That was what Hugo had talked about in his letter. The freedom that choices bring. Was last night some sort of omen? Someone had stolen money from Rafa's till, so Paulo had got his job back. Now, if he wanted to, he could go back to doing what he did before, studying for his degree. He could turn down the offer from Douglas and manage fine.

And what about the trust fund Hugo had set up? That was going to be available to him when he was twenty-one. In a couple of years or so he'd have all that too. Yet he still didn't know how much 'all that' was. He'd phoned the lawyer whose name was on the piece of paper enclosed with Hugo's letter. The man had been in a meeting and the receptionist had said he would call back, but although Paulo left his mobile number, he didn't get a call until two days later, and even then it was only the secretary. She'd told him he needed to make an appointment to come into the office, but when he'd asked her how much money was in the trust she told him she couldn't give out that kind of information. He'd have to bring his passport and ID card, and something else showing his address. When he'd put the phone down, his heart had jumped as he remembered that the utilities at the house were not in his name. He didn't know if he had anything that would prove where he lived.

If he did use the money though, and finished his economics degree, what guarantee was there he'd get a job at the end of it? Douglas had sneered about people with first class degrees, working in burger bars. What he was offering was a chance to make huge amounts of money.

Paulo remembered a scene in one of Hugo's favourite films they'd watched together on DVD. *Mr Corleone never asks a second favour once he's been refused the first*, something like that. Maybe men like Douglas were the same when they made offers, they never make them again.

No, Douglas still might have a role in this, but it was he, Paulo, who needed to be calling the shots. Sure, Douglas was a powerful character, but Paulo himself had come up the hard way. He knew how to hide from the police when they came looking. Like a cat, the *gato* as Rafa had called him, he knew how to find food when there was none. Where had his instincts gone? He knew well enough how to outwit people. He had become weak.

It was time to start playing a bigger game.

He drifted back into a deep and satisfying sleep, and when he woke up later, it was as though a stiff breeze had blown away all the clouds cluttering the blue sky hiding behind them. Everything became gloriously bright and clear.

And a very different idea, perhaps, more accurately, lots of ideas rolled together into one, had implanted itself firmly in his mind.

31

By the time the offices, shops and businesses of downtown Rio began opening their doors on Monday morning, Paulo was already making telephone calls.

The secretary at the lawyers' office sympathised with his need to leave Rio earlier than expected but the partner concerned was busy and couldn't see him any quicker.

'Listen,' Paulo said. 'I'm sorry, but my grandfather has set up a trust in my name and he's put a lot of money into it. I'm entitled to have the details. I've waited a long time for an appointment and I need to get my affairs in order before I leave Rio. All I need is some basic information. I don't need to take up much of his time.'

The woman bristled and told him to stay on the line. For almost five minutes her voice was replaced by a synthesiser destroying *Stairway to Heaven* and he was just about to hang up and re-dial when she was back again. Senhor Guest's assistant had 'a cancellation in her schedule' if Paulo was able to come in at eleven thirty.

His next call, to the university, proved to be easier.

He snapped his phone shut and bounded down to the kitchen, where one of his housemates was sitting with a cup of coffee and reading the morning newspaper.

'Ciao, João. No lectures this morning?'

The boy turned over a page without looking up. 'Not till ten.'

Paulo sat down opposite him. 'Listen, I need to ask you something.'

By nine thirty Paulo was in *A Lanterna* with Rafa, stuffing down a doughnut with a large coffee.

At just after eleven, with a folder of documents inside the zip pocket of his backpack and his heart beating just a little quicker than usual, he was walking towards a building with black plate-glass doors in Rio de Janeiro's business quarter.

32

Paulo checked the brass plate. Seeing the name *Adelina Douglas and Co* he breathed a sigh of relief that he'd finally found the place. Brasilia was not as small as people in Rio said it was.

The outside of the building reminded him of a Chicken Shack, only with flakier paint. He checked the company's website on his phone. He hadn't got it wrong, the office was supposed to open at eight thirty. It was now after nine, the door was locked and there was no sign of lights or people inside.

Just as Paulo was about to head off to try and find a coffee shop and decide what to do, a small, overweight man, wearing a shirt that hung outside his trousers, came ambling across the road. A bunch of keys was dangling from his hand. He glanced at Paulo, but when Paulo explained who he was the man nodded and unlocked the door.

Two days earlier, Paulo had picked up a different set of keys and made his way to an apartment on a housing development in one of the suburbs. Inside, the stench of damp assaulted him and he'd forced open the newly-painted windows to let in some air. The taps in the bathroom were so loose he'd had to hold the pipe behind the sink to be able to turn them on and off. The water flow in the shower was weak and he knew he'd need to press himself against the wall to get under it. He didn't investigate too closely the tiny mounds on the floor.

He'd found a hardware store and bought a brush and pan, detergents, insecticides, air fresheners, rubbish sacks and a scrubbing brush. After several hours getting the place into a habitable condition, he'd collapsed onto the sofa and stabbed at the remote control for the television, only to find it didn't work. Sighing, he'd begun making up the bed while waiting for a pizza to be delivered.

Now, he found himself in a client room, watching through the frosted window as several other employees drifted in. One of them was Douglas's secretary, who arrived almost an hour after he had. Her name was Beatriz, she told him. 'Douglas hasn't said much about what he wants you to do. I suppose the best thing is for you to spend some time with the people in the office. Douglas won't be back from São Paulo till Friday, but if he calls in I'll ask him to speak to you. It's better for him to tell you what he wants you to do.'

'He's got business in São Paulo then?'

Beatriz nodded, but Paulo thought there was something odd about the way she looked away. She smiled. 'I'll introduce you to the others. You'll soon get used to how things work round here.'

Paulo spent the morning moving from one desk to another. He'd already made a mental note of who looked the friendliest, and at the first opportunity wheeled his chair across to sit next to a raven-haired girl who introduced herself as Silvia. She passed him a headset and he listened while she made phone calls, telling people about 'new investment opportunities', 'exciting details' of which were written with a thick felt tip pen on a sheet of A4 paper in front of her.

At just before one, people began heading off again. Beatriz reappeared in the main office and asked him if he was planning to go out. When he said no, she glanced towards the pile of brochures Paulo had collected during the morning.

'Would you like me to bring you back a sandwich?'

Paulo gave her some money and picked up the brochures.

By the Friday, Paulo had learned about everyone in the office and what jobs they did. He'd studied the systems and read through client files. Every lunchtime, he'd stayed in the office while the others went out.

At just before eleven, Beatriz appeared, covering the mouthpiece of a phone she held in her hand. Mouthing the word 'Douglas' she passed him the phone.

'Hey, Paulo.' That booming voice again. 'How's it going? I hear you're keeping yourself busy.'

'Yeah, pretty much.'

'Listen, kid, I'm not going to be able to get in today, but I'll see you on Monday, okay? How's the apartment?'

'Yeah, fine. But listen, Douglas, do you have any time free this weekend? Maybe we could go out and get something to eat? My treat. I wanted to talk to you about a few ideas, just you and me.'

'Your treat, eh?' Douglas chortled. 'You come into money?'

Paulo managed to keep the sigh out of his voice. 'I wish. Just got paid at the bar before I came over here.'

'Look, pal, I've been away all week, so I'll get it in the ear from my wife if I go off eating out. I'll tell you what though, why don't you come over to the house on Sunday for lunch? Say about one. Beatriz will give you the address. Don't be late though, my wife makes the best soufflés this side of Rio. She'll be mad if they go soggy.' The line went dead.

Paulo found Beatriz in her office and handed the phone back to her. As he was turning to leave, she called after him. 'Would you like to see a bit of the town tonight? Since it's your first proper weekend? Maybe I could show you some of the places worth going to.'

Paulo felt himself blush as he opened his mouth to answer.

Beatriz lowered her eyes. 'Sorry, I guess you're busy. I'm forgetting you've only just moved into your apartment...'

'No, no I'm not busy,' Paulo interrupted. 'And the last place I want to be on a Friday evening is stuck inside that apartment. I'd love to come with you.'

Brasilia's Friday nightlife spilled out onto the streets in front of salubrious and not-so-salubrious restaurants and nightclubs. Teenagers in Levi's and trainers mixed with business people in suits who hadn't gone home after a day in the office and they in turn were joined by the obviously-wealthy, out on the town in their elegant outfits.

'Is it like this in Rio?' Beatriz asked.

Paulo gazed up at the surrounding buildings. 'Rio's a lot bigger, but it's not as nice. This is really, I dunno, sophist-icated.'

'My dad was a civil servant when they moved the gov-ernment here. They used to be in São Paulo, but I've only ever been there once.'

Paulo laughed. 'Couple of international jet-setters, aren't we?'

They ate pizza and moved on to a bar where they found a table in a corner. Both of them had been drinking Coronas and Paulo was beginning to slur his words.

'What's São Paulo like?' he asked.

Beatriz giggled. 'I told you, I've only been there once.'

'But don't you still have relatives there?'

'Not now,' she said. 'The only time I went was with Douglas.'

Paulo turned towards her. 'With Douglas?' He couldn't disguise the surprise in his voice.

She tapped his arm. 'Nothing like that. He had this idea about opening an office there, but it never came off.'

'So why did he want you there?'

She smiled. 'I do have some uses you know. He wanted me to go and look at some empty offices, give him an opinion. If he'd taken one he'd have wanted me to go back there to set it up.'

'How come he didn't go ahead with it then?'

She shrugged. 'Dunno, he just uses hotels when he goes

there now.'

'Why does he still go there anyway, São Paulo? He doesn't have any clients there as far as I can see.'

'I don't know.'

'But you're his secretary…'

She laughed. 'You ask an awful lot of questions, Rio boy. I might be his secretary, but he doesn't tell me everything.'

The taxi came to a halt outside Beatriz's parents' home in the suburbs. Paulo leaned over and kissed her on the cheek. 'Thanks for that, it was brilliant.'

'No problem, I enjoyed it.' She appeared to be about to ask him something, but checked herself.

Paulo affected a deep, jaunty voice. 'If there was any chance you were going to ask me if I'd like to do it again, the answer is yes, definitely.' He breathed a silent sigh of relief when she returned his grin.

As she opened the door to get out, Paulo rested his hand on her arm. 'Sorry, I nearly forgot to ask you. Is there any way I can get into the office tomorrow? I've been studying those manuals you gave me, but I need to use one of the computers to cross-check a few things. There's no internet at the apartment.'

She pressed her lips together in apology. 'I have got a key, but I'm not sure Douglas would want me to…'

Paulo nodded firmly. 'No, I understand, you're right. Maybe… I know it's Saturday, but perhaps we could go for a coffee or something, in town? All I'd need is to pop into the office for five minutes. You could stay there with me.'

She chuckled. 'That's the last place I'd want to be sitting

on a Saturday morning. But look, you are an employee of the company and I'd like to have a coffee with you tomorrow. I'll tell you what, if you meet me there at ten, I'll let you in. I've got some shopping I can do in the mall. You can call me when you're ready and maybe we can grab a drink and a sandwich afterwards?'

'You're a star, Beatriz.'

In the back of the cab, he turned and waved as the driver pulled away. Then he sat back and smiled.

He would get the opportunity he was looking for in the morning, and he wouldn't be interrupted.

33

Douglas's wife Maria didn't make soufflé, but she turned out to be every bit as good a cook as Paulo had been led to expect. Not that Douglas seemed to be noticing today as he shovelled the food down and emptied most of a bottle of white wine before they'd finished the first course.

'So how did your first week go? Did you set that lazy crew to rights?'

Paulo smiled. 'I don't think that's for me to do, Douglas, I'm the new boy. They seem to know what they're doing well enough.'

'Yeah, well,' Douglas mumbled, 'but just watch them, they're a cute load of bastards.'

'*Da*-ad!' The reproach came from Douglas's young daughter, who carried on tapping into her phone while shovelling egg into her mouth.

'She's quite right, Douglas,' his wife joined in.

The arrival of the main course between Maria's oversized oven gloves encouraged Douglas to uncork a second bottle of wine, this time red.

Maria was clearly pleased to have someone more appreciative to cook for. She beamed as she set the terracotta pot down, glancing at Paulo. '*Tambaqui*. It tastes like veal but it's fish. It's something you mainly get in the north of Brazil.'

When the plates had been cleared after lunch, Douglas ushered Paulo into an enormous conservatory which overlooked the garden. Potted palm trees and other exotic plants lined up along the low wall under the windows and Douglas cackled. 'It's okay, kid, there are no wild animals in here. Couple of tame snakes somewhere... hey, relax, I'm only joking.'

Douglas went to an ornate white table and poured two large glasses of brandy from a cut-glass decanter, passing one of them to Paulo. 'French, you can't get this in Brasilia. Can you believe that? This is supposed to be the fucking capital city and I have to go to São Paulo to buy it.' He held up his glass to the light. 'Look at the colour of this stuff. Never mind amber nectar, this is *gold* nectar!' He gestured towards a cushioned wicker chair and Paulo sat down. Douglas settled into the chair opposite and sipped from his glass before fixing his eyes on him. 'Now, you were keen to take me out to feed me, but I've fed you instead and it didn't cost you a cent. So tell me what's on your mind, *amigo*.'

In south Granada it was early evening and Hugo was also drinking brandy after a long Sunday lunch with the regulars, the last of whom were getting up to go home.

Tony came over to sit down at Hugo's table. 'How's Paulo doing? You heard anything from him?'

'I've no idea how he's doing, Toni.' He frowned. 'All I've had is a text. At least I know he's had my letter.'

'So he no say what he want to do?'

'Not yet. Says he's got some things to sort out and he'll let me know in a week or two. I tell you what, Toni. Letters might be slow, but at least you get more information. Not just a few strange words and a smiley face that tell you nothing.'

The big man laughed heartily. 'That boy, he good one. He not let you down, *Señor*, whatever he choose.'

Hugo drained the remaining brandy from his glass and stood up.

'I only hope you're right, my friend.'

Douglas was standing with his back turned, staring out into his garden.

Paulo gripped the stem of his glass, watching the man's shoulders heaving up and down, in time with what he thought were exaggerated deep breaths. He sipped the brandy to calm his nerves. It was the first time he'd ever drunk brandy and he was struggling to avoid coughing and making it obvious.

As the muted sound of children's voices and clattering drifted in from somewhere in the big, rambling house, Douglas swung round and jabbed his finger at Paulo.

'You have got… one… fucking… nerve.' He lowered his voice to a theatrical whisper. 'I'm trying to stay calm, like my doctor told me. *Inhale through the nose. Deeply. Let the breath out through your mouth.*' He glanced over his shoulder and found a spot where he could sit on the window ledge next to a potted orange tree. From Paulo's viewpoint it looked as though one of the oranges was sitting on top of his head and he fought to keep back a nervous giggle.

'Tell me. Are you being serious or is this just a wind-up?'

Paulo grunted and tried to keep his voice steady, which seemed to irritate Douglas even more. 'It makes sense, Douglas. You win, and everybody else wins too.'

Douglas placed his hands behind him on the ledge and shoved himself up. 'You absolute, fucking, double-crossing little shit…' His voice rose with every word. 'You come here, eat my food, drink my wine, then you…' He looked at the glass in Paulo's hand and stabbed his finger. '*And* my best cognac…'

Paulo quickly put the glass down.

Douglas was off pacing, but turned back and raised his eyebrows into his rapidly reddening brow. 'And, to cap it all off, you set this up on *my time*, while you were supposed to be working for *me*!'

'You don't have to pay me for last week,' Paulo said, levelly. He began to fear Douglas was going to have a seizure on the spot.

'You're *damned right* I don't have to fucking pay you,' he yelled. 'I don't care if you starve, you can forget all about that, you little piece of…'

The clack of the conservatory door cut his sentence short and Maria poked her head inside. 'Douglas, the kids can hear all this shouting and swearing. What's going on?'

'*What's going on?*' Douglas repeated, his voice now at least a couple of octaves higher than his wife's, like an opera singer rehearsing. 'You would not believe me if I told you what's going on…' He pointed at Paulo. 'By which I mean what this little son of… this little guest of ours has just said to me. Never believe it! I can't even bring *myself* to repeat the words, I'd have an apoplectic fit just telling you.'

He wheeled away, shaking his head.

Maria tutted. 'Well, whatever it is, you can't stand there yelling and cursing like that.'

'*Yelling?*' Douglas whipped back round, eyes bulging. 'He's lucky I don't just go and get my hunting rifle and shoot him on the spot.'

Maria raised a finger towards him. 'Now that's enough, Douglas! Just calm yourself down. You'll make yourself ill, and you'll upset the children.'

'Me shouting won't upset them!' he called out to the door as she closed it behind her. 'They'd be more fucking upset if they understood what this ungrateful little creep is asking their father to do!'

Paulo left Brasilia the following morning, pushing the key to the apartment through the door after he'd locked up.

After the scene in Douglas's conservatory, Maria had telephoned for a taxi, worried that her husband might cause Paulo, or himself, an injury.

'Don't worry,' she'd whispered to Paulo as she ushered him to the front door. 'His bite isn't as bad as his bark.'

She hadn't whispered quietly enough because the sound of Douglas's voice had travelled above and around her towards the door. 'He'd *better* worry. Because I'm going to kill him. And very soon!'

Maria's bulk had stood between the two men, so Douglas couldn't get past her and he'd had to stretch his arm out over her shoulder to thrust his finger towards Paulo's retreating form. 'You worry a lot, son. My bite isn't as bad as my bark, eh? Woof woof!' He'd pointed to his mouth. 'Take a look at my teeth.'

Paulo had thanked Maria for lunch and pecked her on the cheek, seeing the confusion on her face as he pulled away from her.

Douglas's voice had followed after him. '*Try to tear a man's heart and soul out then kiss his bloody wife…! You fucking…*'

The taxi driver, hearing the commotion, had thrown the car into gear and the rear wheels sprayed up gravel as they accelerated towards the open gates.

34

Dear Avô,

I'm really sorry I did not send you a letter in good time as you sent me but I hope you got my SMS. I'm not good at writing with a pen anyway, or spelling English words, but I wanted to get this message to you as soon as possible. I had to use the translator on my computer so I hope this does not come out sounding stupid!

I'm not mad at you for sending money or to create a trust for me when I'm older. What you said in your letter about the money (not the bit where you say that it is rightfully mine, but about how I could use it) made a lot of sense. I want to thank you for all you did for me.

I have done a lot since you wrote to me (also I have got my job back at the bar) but I still have a lot of arrangements to make so I can't tell you yet what I'm going to do because I don't know. I would really like to talk to you more about it. Also I miss seeing you. Would you be able to come to Rio to visit me soon? Can you call me some time so we can see if this will be OK?

In the meantime I have a stone that I always have in my pocket wherever I go.

With love, Paulo

35

Douglas's language hadn't improved. 'Listen you *filho da puta!* Don't start thinking you've got one over on me. I ought to come over there and blow out your brains.'

On the other end of the line, Paulo pulled his face, silently mocking his erstwhile boss. 'Good morning to you too.'

'I'm not promising you anything, *bastardo*, so don't start thinking I'm going soft in the head. You'd better be right about this crazy idea or I *will* shoot you, don't think for a moment I won't. All I'll say is I'm going to try to stay calm and listen while you tell me again how this thing works. Slowly, step by step.'

As Paulo finished laying out his plan, the faintest harsh laughter cut into Douglas's voice.

'You're a cunning son of a bitch, I'll give you that. I'm glad you're not on the other side.' Paulo could hear Douglas breathing. 'I'm not promising anything. I'll think about it. That's the best you deserve.'

Paulo took a deep breath. 'Douglas, listen. I haven't got time for you to fuck around thinking about it. If Hugo agrees to come, he could be here soon. I have to get his signature on those papers. And he's clever. Very clever. We have to be mega-careful how we play this. If he starts getting suspicious, that'll be the end of it. I've given you the deal on a plate, now it's up to you. Take it or leave it. But if you're going to take it, you'd better say so, and fast. I've got other options.'

To his own satisfaction, it was Paulo who broke off the call. He'd called Douglas's bluff. Now he could only wait.

36

Toni rested his big fist on the table as he stood behind Hugo and leaned over to read.

'So what he going to do then?'

Hugo's reply came over his shoulder as he stared at the screen. 'Your guess is as good as mine, Toni. I've read the email three times already and I still can't work out what he's up to.'

'Sound like he going to become big finance guy.'

Hugo nodded. 'Maybe. But why does he have to make all these arrangements he's talking about? I sent him enough money for him to get by for a while and then he's got more to come. And he's got his job back in the bar. So it's a straight choice, either go with the guy in Brasilia or carry on with his university course. I don't know why he wants me to go all the way to Brazil to discuss that. But I guess it'll be good to see him again.'

Toni straightened up and stretched his back. 'Whatever he do, that boy make a good job of it. He one smart kid, that one.'

37

Paulo finished his evening shift and waited till he got home to make the call.

The phone rang several times before he heard shuffling and then Douglas's voice, thick with sleep.

'What time of night do you call this…?'

'Yeah well, I'm in college all day tomorrow. I thought you'd want to know what's happening.'

'So, tell me. And it'd better be good.'

'He's coming over. Early next week.'

'Right, and…?'

'Right and what? You know what the situation is. Everything's tied up for two years. Do I have to keep repeating that? Either we get him to sign those papers or from your point of view there's no deal. End of. So either you're in, or you're out. I can't wait any longer.' He paused to gauge Douglas's reaction, but detected none, so he continued. 'I've told you, you won't regret it.'

Paulo could hear Maria's voice in the background and the scraping sound as Douglas covered the phone with his hand. Moments later, he was back.

'All right, here's my answer. Do it. But listen to me kid,

and listen very, very carefully. You let me down on this, double cross me, so help me God, *seu merda…*'

'Douglas…' Paulo sighed. He spoke softly and slowly. 'As soon as he's here, and I've spoken to him, I'll call you. Okay? Just relax. You know your wife hates you swearing.'

'Just *relax*? Look, you little…'

Paulo raised his voice. 'I can hardly hear you, Douglas, you're breaking up…'

He ended the call, before he got another taste of Douglas's version of relaxing.

38

There it was, below. The towering edifice, arms out-stretched, alone on that mountain top, looking down as He might have done, but from a much smaller hill, so many centuries ago.

Hugo wondered about that. What would the real Christ the Redeemer have thought of that sprawling, seething metropolis below, and everything that went on within it? He remembered a film he'd seen once, Michael Caine wasn't it, what was it he'd said? Something like, *São Paulo is where all the work gets done; Rio is where all the fun gets done.*

Hugo thought about Marietta, making a similar trip, all those decades ago. To another country, further north from here. An inexperienced teenager, running away from a nightmare. Her journey had been nothing like this one. No business class. No reclining seat, extra legroom, DVDs and games console, three-course meal and wine.

He couldn't imagine what that journey must have been like for her.

He didn't want to.

As the taxi driver threaded the air-conditioned Mercedes through the line of traffic on the *Linha Vermelha* bridge which would take them towards the city, Hugo reflected on Paulo's email. The heavy feeling returned. There was something not quite right, and he couldn't put his finger on it. Why was Paulo's email so woolly? All the pressure had been taken off him, hadn't it?

Then there was the phone call. Paulo had sounded... what? Evasive? A little too happy-go-lucky, while Hugo's instincts were telling him the kid seemed tense. Fair enough, he'd answered the questions Hugo had asked. He'd given perfectly good reasons for wanting Hugo to fly to Brazil.

So why did he still feel so uneasy?

When he checked in at his hotel, he tried Paulo's phone, but it was constantly engaged. He called room service and after he'd eaten he flopped into bed, exhausted.

Paulo finally called halfway through the following morning and arranged to pick him up later in the day.

As arranged, Hugo was standing on the steps at half past six. At ten past seven, after he'd twice gone back into the foyer to try to ring Paulo, the doorman called over to him.

'I think this is the gentleman, sir.'

Hugo went back out again, where the doorman was staring across the wide expanse of driveway at a battered yellow hatchback belching out a cloud of black smoke. Hugo winced, glancing at the doorman, who, he was certain, had tilted his head back to view the scene down his nose.

Moments later Paulo was hurrying across. '*Avô*,' he called out. 'It's great to see you.' He threw his arms round Hugo and stepped back again. 'Hey, you look great!' He gestured towards the car. 'Are you ready? Let's go over to my place. I've really been looking forward to you coming.'

Paulo chattered away as he cut in and out of traffic. 'It's brilliant you could come over here, *Avô*. How long can you stay? I wanted you to see the uni. I'm going to try and introduce you to my professor if he's around, you'd like him. And maybe you can come over to the bar. I have to work, but you could sit and have a drink and we could go somewhere else when I'm finished.'

Hugo glanced at him. 'You seem very excited, Paulo. I'm glad you're so pleased to see me. How is college, anyway?'

'Great. I'll tell you all about it later. Listen, I've got a little surprise for you tomorrow morning, if you're up for an early start?'

'A mystery tour, eh?' Hugo replied.

'Something like that.' He pointed to the traffic lights ahead of them. 'That's the road I live on. We just hang a left here. It's really cool you coming over here, *Avô*.'

Hugo shifted a pile of papers and magazines onto the floor and cleared a place to sit down on the settee. The house smelled of cooking. He heard the fridge door slamming closed, and a moment later Paulo came back into the living room, shaking his head.

'I went out specially last night after work. There's a late-night store owned by this Indian guy and I bought curry, rice, poppadums, everything, bottle of red wine.

285

Someone's gone and helped himself to it. I thought I could smell curry when we came in.' He rolled his eyes. 'At least the wine's still there.'

Hugo laughed. 'Bad luck. Why don't we go out and get something? My treat.'

Paulo pulled a face. 'Thanks, but if it's okay with you could we get a takeaway? I was up late last night and then we've got this early start tomorrow. If I go now, I can be back in a few minutes. Help yourself to the wine. The bottle's on the table in the kitchen. It should be a good one, the Indian guy said it was.' He grabbed his jacket from the back of the chair.

Hugo pulled his wallet from his inside pocket and took out some money. 'No arguments, it's on me. Is that enough? I don't know what anything costs here, let alone how much that is.'

'Thanks, *Avô*.' Paulo frowned. 'I hate you having to pay for this when I've invited you here, but to be honest I'm a bit short at the moment.' He held up his hands. 'And I know you're going to tell me about that money in the bank, but I haven't drawn a cent of it yet.' He opened the door. 'I'll be back in twenty minutes. There's a corkscrew somewhere, it's in the top drawer I think.'

Hugo wandered into the kitchen. He opened one cupboard door after another, and eventually found an assortment of odd glasses, all of which looked as though they'd been washed in goose fat. He pulled down two glasses and ran the tap until the water came out warm, searching underneath the sink for washing up liquid. The bottle was virtually empty, so he ran water into it and managed to get enough soap out to wash the glasses. After he'd dried them they sparkled again. He poured himself a glass of wine and took it back to the living room.

A few photos hung on the walls, but none of them seemed to include Paulo. Three cheap pictures, the type sold in souvenir shops with imitation brass frames made of plastic, completed the display. A desk in one corner was remarkably tidy, considering the chaos that appeared to exist everywhere else. On its surface stood four neat piles of paper, each one weighed down with a small object of some description or other.

Hugo lifted one of the paperweights and browsed the bits of paper at the top, turning them over to look at the other side. An old shopping list, notes made on cardboard torn from cereal boxes, a post-it note with the details of an appointment scribbled on it with a felt tipped pen. He put them back on the pile and replaced the weight. He knew there were four housemates and guessed that each stack of papers corresponded to one of them.

The third pile was obviously Paulo's. Hugo recognised his handwriting. Some ideas for projects, some indecipherable scribblings surrounded by doodles. A pink post-it note, similar to the kind he'd seen in the first pile. It reminded him of Laura and how she'd always used them to leave messages for him, despite her reservations. He picked it up and skim read it.

Paulinho, teu amigo Douglas telefonou... peça
ignorante de merda... o teu avô a assinar os papéis
rapidamente... Ele diz... a próxima semana, caso

contrário o negócio está fechado... Soa um bastardo
assustador... Eu não gostaria de antagonizar ele. Ciao.
João.

Hugo sensed that whoever had written this note had not been entirely happy about something. He knew the word *avô*, of course; how could he not by now? Douglas's name was there too, plus a couple of profanities he recognized as similar to the Spanish. He had no idea what it was in this formation of words, most of which he didn't understand, that made him feel uneasy. He studied the message again and flapped it around as he struggled to make sense of it.

He remembered spotting Paulo's heavily scratched laptop charging on the kitchen top and went and opened it up. Silently, he prayed it wouldn't need a password, and he let out a sigh of relief when the welcome page appeared. When he clicked on the translation app he saw it was already set to translate from Portuguese into English, and he remembered Paulo saying he'd used it when he'd written the email to him.

Hugo held the pink note in one hand and typed with the other. As he entered words into the box on the left side of the screen, other words began filling the one on the right.

Paulinho, your friend Douglas called. Ignorant piece of
shit. He said to make sure you get your grandfather to
sign the papers quickly. He says to tell you that you have
until next week otherwise the deal is off and you better
keep looking over your shoulder. Sounds a scary bastard.
I would not want to cross him. Ciao. João

Hugo could almost hear his own heart. He felt his mouth go dry. He read the message a second time.

What did this all mean, these words in front of him? What was Paulo up to? Hugo had read about people travelling to exotic foreign countries and getting themselves caught up in impossibly stupid situations. This place was not Britain. It wasn't even Europe. Paulo himself had spoken about how the police were part of the crimes, how they took bribes. This man Douglas was not only rich, but sounded unscrupulous too. What was Paulo mixed up in, and what did he have to gain?

Hugo closed his eyes and breathed deeply, letting the air out of his lungs slowly. He cursed himself for not having done some checking. That long name in the passport, none of which he recognised; he could so easily have got the solicitor in Rio to check the name of Erik's wife, to see if what Paulo had told him was true. Why had he just taken it all on trust? And now Paulo was talking about some sort of mystery trip tomorrow. What was that all about?

No, he thought, *I must have this wrong*. Paulo had become the nearest thing he had to family. He'd thought Paulo felt the same. *God, please don't let this all be happening again.*

He heard the thud of a door closing and had time only to slap the lid of the laptop down and hurry to return the pink post-it sticker to its little stack before Paulo came in.

Hugo sat in the darkness of the taxi on the way back to the hotel, staring out at the bright lights of suburban Rio.

Once more in his life he was grateful for jet lag. Paulo

had brought back a Chinese takeaway and had laid out all the cardboard cartons on the coffee table. The conversation had been stilted, and Hugo had hardly eaten anything. Several times he'd sensed Paulo glancing over at him.

'You're quiet tonight, *Avô*. You tired?'

Hugo had snapped out of his deepest thoughts. 'Sorry? Oh, yeah, it's just the long flight catching up on me.' He'd set his plate down on the table. 'Aren't you going to give me any clue where we're going tomorrow morning?'

Paulo had smiled. 'It will spoil the surprise.'

The hotel bar was deserted apart from a couple in one corner who looked like they were having an affair. Once they'd glanced over to ensure it wasn't one of their spouses coming through the door they went back to whispering in each other's ears.

The barman brought him a large single malt.

'Have you been to Brazil before? Are you staying long?'

Uncomplicated conversation. Normality. Hugo began to feel calmness coursing through his veins, dissolved in whisky.

He tossed around in his head what he knew, analysing every angle. What was the worst that could happen? The note had talked about getting him to sign some sort of papers. Well, any papers anyone forced him to sign would have to be witnessed by someone else. And where were the papers? His heart accelerated for a moment when it occurred to him that Douglas might be bringing them. But Paulo hadn't mentioned anything about Douglas even being in Rio.

Maybe he could call the lawyer in the morning and ask him if he'd been instructed to draw up any documents. Hugo grimaced, making a hissing noise. That wouldn't work; he was meeting Paulo at eight. He was sure the office wouldn't be open by then.

He called the barman over and ordered another large Scotch. The thought passed through his head that this man serving him drinks looked like the kind he'd met in hotels all round the world. They could get you any information you wanted, at a price. Would this barman know someone who could get him a handgun, at short notice? Hugo almost snorted into his drink. Marietta had once said something about him riding into town with his family, like someone in a cowboy film. Well, he wasn't about to start charging around with a pistol in his hand, with or without a horse.

What the hell could they do anyway? Was Douglas really going to show up and hold him at gunpoint? Make him speak to the lawyer on the phone? What did it matter anyway? He'd already given the money away. What else did they think they could get from him?

Should he just try to call Paulo and demand to know what was happening? He glanced at his watch; no, it was too late now. In the morning maybe? But Paulo was coming at eight.

Hugo sighed as the reality hit him. It wasn't the money that bothered him. Nor was this feeling in the pit of his stomach fear.

It was the loss of something, some*one*. A person he'd allowed into his life, who he'd thought had been dear to his

291

heart. The same heart he'd once decided he'd never let anyone get near to again.

When would he ever learn?

39

For the first time Hugo could remember, Paulo arrived on time, pulling up in the old Nissan under the nose of the doorman.

Now Hugo stared out of the side window at the decrepit houses as they flashed by. He patted his jacket pocket, feeling the paper knife he'd taken from his hotel room. It was the best he could do at short notice. He raised his eyebrows. What good would that do, if someone pulled a gun on him?

And what of Paulo this morning? He was quieter than usual, none of the incessant chatter of the previous day when he'd driven him to his house. Hugo swept his gaze in an arc, pretending to be studying the shops and local office buildings, but trying to assess the look on Paulo's face. He seemed... what? Older than usual? Maybe, Hugo thought, but also nervous. Tapping his fingers on the steering wheel as though to a rock song, but the radio was silent. Well, pal, Hugo mused, whatever you've got in mind, it's not going to pan out the way you think. The note he'd given the doorman as he passed through the foyer would see to that. They could do what they wanted here, wherever it was they were heading to. He wasn't going to resist. If Paulo had betrayed him then fine, okay. What did he have left anyway? Why bother harming him if he cooperated? And if he did cooperate, Jeremy Guest would contact the police when he received the note, and make sure everything was voided. A note that would be transported to him by courier if Hugo didn't get back to the hotel by nightfall.

Paulo swung the Nissan from the road into a potholed track and as it rattled and bumped along Hugo stared out at the unruly bushes lining the sides, behind which enormous trees drooped their branches like tentacles. He remembered Marietta comparing his late wife Sarah to Rebecca, and pondered how this place would fit the bill as her Manderley; dark, claustrophobic, foreboding. If anything sinister was going to happen, this would be an ideal setting.

As the vision of Marietta came into his mind he suddenly felt a wave of determination pass through his entire body. They were obviously near to where they were going, wherever that was, but this was his opportunity. He took a deep breath and looked over at Paulo.

'Listen, I need to ask you something...'

Paulo glanced at Hugo out of the corner of his eye and at that moment wrenched the steering wheel over to one side. The rear wheels threw up chunks of mud as the car skidded and he hauled in the opposite direction as the track curved round to the left. Hugo's shoulder thumped against the door and images flashed through his head of that day on the motorway in Italy.

'*Merda*!' Paulo yelled out. 'I didn't see that pothole, it wasn't here last time I drove down here.'

Hugo began rubbing his shoulder as they emerged from the bend, and in a second spotted the first signs of some sort of structure ahead. The wheels were now flinging up clouds of dust, but as they approached he could just make out a run-down wooden building with a large porch. As they emerged from the density, the early sunlight of a new day lit the whole area and he could see that two flights of steps climbed the right-hand elevation.

In front of them now was a circular area of sand and grit. Hugo waited for his eyes to adjust to the brighter light and then tried to get a better view of the building. The grey stone Georgian mansion of the Daphne du Maurier story it certainly was not.

Paulo drew the car up in the partial shade of a hedge. Hugo's senses seemed to have become acute and he heard the rattle of the handbrake and clenched his teeth, feeling around for the door handle. He stepped out into the early morning air, which reeked of dry cement, pausing and listening. So far as he could make out, there was no one else around.

From across the litter-strewn expanse in front of him, Hugo could see there was some kind of sign creaking from chains above the front entrance to the building. Perhaps that might give him a clue, though he doubted it. He took a deep breath, filling his lungs and holding the air. Without waiting for Paulo, he crunched towards it.

40

Jeremy Guest was still taking off his jacket after bidding goodbye to a client when his office door opened again. He looked up and saw his elegantly-dressed secretary, who had worked for him for over twenty years since fleeing the conflict in Bosnia.

'I'm sorry to bother you, Jeremy, but that dreadful man from Adelina Douglas has been on the phone again. That's the third time this week. I keep telling him we can't supply information relating to client matters, but he says all he wants to know is if we've been given any instructions to draw up some papers. It's to do with that trust fund the gentleman in Spain set up for his relative here.'

'Yes, I remember the one,' the solicitor replied. 'Difficult to forget a settlement as generous as that for someone so young. The boy was in here a couple of weeks ago, wasn't he?'

'Yes, Júlia saw him,' the woman answered. 'Anyway, I've told the man you can't speak to him. He's not a client. I did look up his company's name and they're a securities firm up in Brasilia. I'm amazed he doesn't seem to know about client confidentiality.'

Guest pulled out his chair and settled into it. He rubbed his chin thoughtfully. 'Is he likely to ring again, do you think?'

'I doubt it.' The woman smiled. 'People from my part of the world have a reputation for speaking bluntly.'

Guest returned the smile. 'Good. But just to be on the safe side, can you see if we've got a phone number on file for the English fellow in Spain? I think maybe we should let him know somebody's taking an unwelcome interest in something that doesn't concern them. Out of interest, *have* we been given any instructions to draw up documents?'

'The young man rang about another appointment last week,' the woman replied. 'But I seem to recall he was more interested in bringing *in* some papers that have already been drawn up. He wanted us to look through them.'

41

Hugo narrowed his eyes and stared up at the neatly-painted sign.

The copperplate letters were painted in orange, against a dark brown background.

THE MARIETTA FORSBERG CENTER

He could just about make out some smaller words underneath. *A project proudly sponsored by Adelina Douglas & Co.*

'Those were *Vovô*'s favourite colours. She used to say orange and brown were the colours of a South American sunset. Sorry about the American spelling.'

For a moment, Hugo had forgotten that Paulo was standing right behind him. He glanced over his shoulder and saw that his face was filled with a grin. 'I know you told me people shouldn't feel proud of themselves, *Avô*. But maybe I can feel a bit pleased?'

Hugo took a deep breath and noticed how it shuddered in his chest. He let his eyes travel the length of the front of the building then turned round. 'Where's Douglas?'

'Douglas?' Paulo's grin disappeared. He cocked his head to one side, his brow furrowed. 'Why would he be here?'

Hugo was unable to prevent himself frowning. What in the name of God was going on?

The sign above his head came to his rescue. He pointed. 'Isn't that his name? Up there?'

Paulo's happy demeanour returned. 'Yeah, well, that's another story.' He tapped Hugo's arm. 'Come and have a look inside.'

Hugo hesitated, but followed Paulo up the steps. There was no door and they passed straight into the front room. Chalk hung in the air, hovering over the walk boards and cardboard sheets lining the floor.

Paulo turned round. 'Some of the guys will be along soon. They're good workers but they hate getting up early.' He pointed up at the ceiling. 'They've just finished fixing all the leaks. It was throwing it down last week but no water got in. All the kids working here are from the streets, but they learn quickly.' He glanced outside. 'Oh, wait, I've got something else to show you. I've left it in the car.' He hurried back through the hole in the wall.

Hugo wandered around the room, peering through the various openings. All around were signs of activity. Exposed pipes crossed the floors like circuit boards and, overhead, cables with bared ends waited to be connected to something. White rubble lay everywhere and dust puffed up in miniature clouds as he picked his way to the far side.

He was filled with an emotion he couldn't identify. A feeling that something else, something more than a mere building project, lay within these walls. This was an enterprise that was not standing still. People, lots of them, for the moment unseen, were fusing energies together for a cause that mattered to them. Some special force was driving it all forward.

The hollow sound of approaching footsteps pulled him out of his reverie. Seeing the papers in Paulo's hand, Hugo tensed. This was what he'd been expecting. But what the hell was all this?

'Have a look at these.' Paulo gestured for Hugo to follow him through one of the openings. In a smaller room, a trestle table leaned upright against a wall, and Paulo dragged it into the rectangle of light beneath what was obviously going to become a window. He stood the table on its legs and dusted the surface with his hand before rolling out the paper, weighing down the four corners with lumps of rubble from the floor.

Paulo tapped on the expanse of paper, which Hugo could now see was a plan of the building. 'This is where we are now.' He ran his finger to one side. 'This is going to be a games room. These other rooms will be a dining room, a community room and a medical area. Upstairs, five bedrooms, two bathrooms.'

Hugo pointed to an area at the top of the drawing. 'What's that, is that an annex?'

Paulo knitted his brow. 'Ah, *anexo*, yes. I mean, no, it's not an annex. That's *Vovó*'s old office.'

Hugo attempted to smile. 'Has that all been gutted out then?'

Paulo shook his head. 'It's not going to be gutted out, *Avô*. We left it like it was. I knew you'd want to see where

300

she worked. Maybe one day we'll turn it into an office for the centre, but not yet. I wanted to keep her bedroom the same too, at least till you'd seen it, but it would have held the work back. We wouldn't have been able to start doing anything upstairs and we need to keep going. But I did take some photos.'

Paulo led the way back out and underneath the metal staircase outside, towards an expanse of red-brown earth encircled by a chain-link fence. Hugo saw that the ground had been turned over and raked. In the centre, a brick wall had been built to form a smaller circle.

If the flatness of the compound itself created a stark contrast to the rough land surrounding it, the rich earth piled into this central structure stood out even more, like black cobalt inside a giant terracotta pot. Hugo followed Paulo through a gate in the fence. As they approached the brick construction in the middle, his eyes were drawn towards two upright stakes about three feet apart, driven into the soil and rising up like watch towers.

Paulo swept his arm in an arc. 'This whole area's going to be a garden. It's not very big at the moment, but when we get some more money we'll take it right out to the edge of that land over there.' He pointed. 'That belongs to us too. The most important thing is to grow vegetables and fruit right now. This bit in the middle's just going to have scented flowers in it, like the ones Salvador and me put in your garden.'

Hugo waggled his finger at the vertical posts. 'What are those for?'

Paulo pulled a face. 'I was hoping we'd have had that finished for you to see today but the kid who does the painting hasn't been in for a couple of days. He lives on the street like the others, but someone said his mum's ill, so he's had to go and look after her. He's doing a sign to hang between them. We're calling this part *Os Jardins do Salvador.*'

Hugo smiled. 'You're going to name this garden after your old pal.'

'Yes, but it has a double meaning,' Paulo replied. 'Salvador is Saviour in Portuguese as well as in Spanish. So it's also the Gardens of the Saviour. It's going to be our little version of the big monument above Rio.' He chuckled. 'Maybe we'll get a plastic miniature of it from a souvenir shop and stand it next to the sign!'

Paulo led the way through the rear of the compound. Now Hugo could see the wooden entrance porch he'd taken to be an annex on the plans, but, unlike the drawings, the real-life version exuded warmth and vitality. It snuggled inside a blanket of begonia and bougainvillea, deep purple flowers melting into a wall of white jasmine like a beacon, standing imperiously amid the rubble all around. Hugo knew instinctively that this arrangement of nature had to have been planted years ago, and for the first time sensed the real presence of Marietta in this house.

'Wanna go in?'

Hugo swallowed hard as Paulo's voice intruded into his private thoughts. He sighed, and turned to face the boy. When he spoke, it was little more than a whisper.

'Not yet, Paulo. I will do, just give me a little more time.'

Hugo pressed up against the car door as they clattered over the potholes again, reasoning it was better than being thrown against it when Paulo negotiated the bends.

'I'm bursting to know how you've managed to do all that? I thought you said you hadn't touched the money I sent you?'

'I haven't.' Paulo laughed. 'But I did have a little help from a friend, kind of.'

Hugo furrowed his brow. 'Which friend?'

'Douglas Pereira. He took a bit of persuading.'

'He's called Pereira then? So who's Adelina?'

'That's his wife's middle name. That was the minimum he wanted, his firm's name on the sign.'

'Wanted in return for what?'

'It's kind of a long story.'

'I've nowhere else to go, Paulo.'

'Well, like I told you, I didn't want to use the money you sent me, and the trust fund is locked away until I'm twenty-one, right?'

'Right, so…?'.

'So, it'd be good if I could introduce you to Douglas before you go back. He's a bit flash and he likes to tell people how good he is at making money. But to be fair, he is. He makes lots of money for his clients. I had a week working for him. I went through almost all the client port-folios. Most of them are well in profit, way above average. I rang round a few of the investment companies to double-check the figures, and they were all kosher.'

Hugo lifted his eyebrows at this latest example of Paulo's ever-expanding colloquial English.

'There's no evidence of anything funny going on,' Paulo continued. 'So I rang Mr Guest's office and spoke to one of his people. I asked whether there'd be any chance the trustees would consider letting Douglas's company be the investment managers for the trust.' Keeping his hands locked on the steering wheel, he glanced at Hugo. 'I hope you don't mind, *Avô*. Mr Guest's assistant said he'd ring me back after he'd checked them out. Then he called and said he couldn't see why they wouldn't. In principle, provided you agreed. He said you weren't a trustee because you don't live in Brazil, but you're something called a protector.'

Hugo nodded.

'So, if you were okay with the idea, he'd want you to go to their offices while you're over here to sign the authorization. Then the trustees will pay Adelina Douglas an annual management fee for investing the money. He doesn't come cheap, but like I said, he's good.'

Hugo mumbled under his breath. 'So those were the documents...'

'What was that, *Avô*?'

Hugo shook his head, as if in doing so he could empty it of the mistrust and suspicion that seemed to follow him around. 'Nothing. Ignore me.' He looked back at Paulo. 'I'm puzzled, though. If Douglas manages the trust funds, he gets a fee for it. So, how come he gets his name over the door of the Centre too?'

'Because he's going to pay towards the reconstruction of the Centre.'

'What, Douglas is going to put money into it?' Hugo's eyes widened.

'Yes. And it gets better.'

Hugo rotated his finger in a circle, encouraging Paulo to carry on.

'Well, all the guys on the building are doing it for nothing. It keeps them off the streets...' He began laughing.

Hugo nodded and smiled. 'Oh, very funny, Paulo.'

'Yeah, I thought you'd like that. Anyway, they're happy to do the work because they know they'll benefit from it some day. But we also need materials and equipment. And we had to sort things out with the charity because the building belonged to them.'

'Belonged?'

'Yeah, remember, *Vovó* left it to them in her will. But they didn't have the money to renovate it. They were happy to sell it to me though, and they gave me a good price. That way, they get the problem off their hands, and we can get on with the work knowing it's our own building.'

'Right, but how does Douglas come into this? Did he put up the money to buy it?'

'No chance!' Paulo almost coughed the words out. 'He wouldn't go that far. But he did organize a loan through one of his contacts. So now I own the building, and as soon as the charity got paid they gave me a grant to buy materials. Plus, we need money to feed the guys. They might work for free but they still have to eat.'

'But now you've got interest to pay on the loan,' Hugo pointed out.

Though he tried hard, Paulo failed to conceal the smile that spread across his face. 'I did tell you it gets better.'

'I can't wait.'

'Well, he pays the interest.'

'Who pays the interest?'

'Douglas pays the interest.'

'Douglas pays the interest?'

'We're sounding like parrots, *Avô*.'

'Douglas pays the interest but it's *your* loan?'

'Yes, because he sponsors the project and he gets the fees for the investment management. It's kind of a commission for me. He took some persuading.'

'I'll bet he did,' Hugo replied. 'So far as I can see, all he ends up with is his company's name above the door in tiny letters, and nobody can see that sign anyway unless they go to the place. It's half a mile off the main road.'

'I know, but I persuaded Douglas he ought to become a phil... anthropist. Is that the right word?'

'It is if you mean you told him he should be giving his money away, yes.'

'You remember that movie, the one where the guy persuades the concentration camp chief to understand what true power is, the power to be merciful?'

'*Schindler's List*, yes.'

'Well, I did something like that. I told Douglas he needed to use his money to help people less well off. It was about time he did something good for someone else instead of keeping it all for himself.'

'I'll bet that went down well.'

The grin had not left Paulo's face all the time they'd been talking. 'Well, I had to do some research first. But Douglas is his own worst enemy. He was happy for me to use his computer because he was too mean to buy me one of my own. But then I noticed how many things he had that were password-protected, and I wondered why. Even simple things like his emails. He's so predictable, though. You know what Latin people are like, boys are always the most important. So I put in his son's name. Wrong. Then his daughter's. Wrong again. Then I tried his dog's name. You'll never believe it...'

'Bingo!'

The smile left Paulo's face. 'No, his dog's called Caesar, that was the password. Don't get me wrong, Douglas is very bright. If there's one thing he knows how to do it's make money. But most of the people working for him are taking the piss.'

Paulo glanced in the wing mirror and swung the car out into the adjoining lane, ignoring the horn from the car behind. 'When he isn't there, which is most of the time, those people come and go when they want to. They go drinking in a bar at lunchtime and then they're half asleep for most of the afternoon. They don't record things properly, so Douglas is in danger of getting into trouble with the financial authorities without even knowing it. I told him most of that. And I told him I'd sort the whole thing out for him, really get the place in top-class order. It will save him a fortune.'

Hugo nodded. 'You told him *most* of that? What didn't you tell him?'

'About hacking into his computer. He was mad enough with me anyway.'

'Why? It's all for his benefit, isn't it?'

'Yeah, but I told him once I'd done all that, I wouldn't work for him anymore. I told him about the plan for the Centre and that I wanted him to sponsor it. It was a gamble anyway. If it all worked out, he was going to get the fees for the investment work. It was just when I said I wanted him to pay the interest on the loan he started getting antsy. He was ranting on about doing up the apartment for me to live in, said it had cost him a fortune. I said, no way, it's a shit-hole. It was worse than *Casa Marietta* was before we started the work. There was water coming in through the ceilings, plaster falling off the walls. It was more comfortable when I used to sleep on the street. At least you can find a dry place under a bridge or something.'

'How did he react when you said that?'

'He threatened to shoot me at one point.'

Hugo shook his head, his eyebrows raised. 'Seems a bit of a nutter to me. So he spends a bit of money on his own property. If he does that, he improves the place doesn't he?'

Paulo laughed.

Hugo glanced at him. 'What's so funny?'

'I'm not quite sure how to put this. He wasn't mad, I mean really mad, at that point. Let's just say he didn't buy into the idea right away. He wouldn't admit it at the time, but he knew I was offering him a good deal. Even after paying the interest on the loan, he'd still get all those investment fees. Plus, his company would be even more profitable once I'd restructured it.'

'Okay, but you didn't answer my question. What was so funny?'

'Well, I got friendly with his secretary. She's lovely. She

308

told me Douglas made frequent trips to São Paulo, but I couldn't figure out why. He didn't seem to have any clients there. Then, like I said, I got into his emails and it seems he has another kind of interest there.'

Hugo nodded his head. 'Ah, you mean the type his wife might not be too pleased to hear about?'

'Right first time. His wife's really nice too. On his computer, though, he's got this photo of Miss Brazil.' He glanced at Hugo. 'Well, she certainly could be. And you'll never guess what her name is...'

Like the two speakers in a stereo system, they exclaimed the name together: 'Maria!'

'Same as his wife's,' Paulo added. 'Comes in handy if you slip up now and again!'

Hugo laughed. 'So you let him know you knew about this other Maria?'

'I didn't plan to. I didn't want to. It was, how do you say in English, the card up my sleeve?'

'Something like that.'

'Well, he forced me to play it. That's when he threatened to go and get the gun!'

They'd reached the hotel and Paulo drew the Nissan into a vacant space opposite the entrance. He wrenched the handbrake on and Hugo winced again.

'Whatever I did, it worked. He was on the phone to me a couple of days later.' Paulo put his fist to his ear, thumb and little finger extended. '*Run that by me again.*' He grinned, reaching for the door handle, then turned back to face Hugo. 'What was that you were saying earlier about those being the documents, *Avô*?'

309

Hugo felt a lump rising up in his throat and tried to concentrate on the grinding and cracking noises as the engine began to cool down. Then he forced a weak smile.

'Nothing, forget it. I was just a bit confused. Old men like me shouldn't be jetting across the world and then trying to get up early in the mornings. And then, when I saw what you'd done at *Casa Marietta*, it just left me feeling emotional.' He smiled. 'I'm truly proud of you, Paulo. What you've done is amazing. I couldn't have wished for a better grandson.'

As he got out of the car, Hugo turned and waved. Then he felt something digging uncomfortably into his shirt, and remembered the paperknife he was carrying in his jacket. When he walked inside the hotel, he nodded to the doorman, who followed him and, without a word, pulled an envelope from his pocket.

42

Hugo called Paulo after breakfast the following morning.

'I don't need a lift, just the address of the Centre and someone to let me in. I'm ready now, I'd like to go and see Marietta's office.'

'Sure, I'll text it to you. I have to go and see my tutor in a few minutes, but I'll make sure one of the boys is there to let you in.'

"One of the boys" turned out to be Alanza, a girl who couldn't have been more than fifteen and who introduced herself as the site foreman.

As they picked a path around the side of the building, Alanza cursed as she bent to retrieve a spade which was lying on the ground, propping it against the wall. 'Watch you don't trip over this shit,' she warned Hugo. 'I keep telling them, someone's going to break their neck one day.'

This tiny girl reminded Hugo of the Artful Dodger in the Oliver Twist films he'd watched as a kid. His thoughts were transported back to San Francisco and the movie star. She'd mentioned the word *gamines* and he'd looked it up afterwards. Boyish looking girls preyed upon by men who afterwards would go home to their wives and kids. Hugo glanced sideways at her. 'How come your English is so good?'

Alanza shrugged. 'Yeah, well, we get all these tourists in Rio. Americans, Australians from London, all that stuff. If you don't speak English they don't give you any money.' She fiddled around in the deep front pocket of her canvas dungarees, which were at least two sizes too big for her, and as if in triumph held up a large, ornate key, which she manoeuvred into the door lock. She pushed the door open and stepped aside for Hugo to go in.

'Give me a shout if you need anything,' she called out as she made her way back to her important, site foreman's, duties.

Hugo stood in the tiny entrance porch, savouring the sudden coolness. Though he could just about hear the sound of the work going on around the building, it seemed strangely distant and muffled. He reached for the round knob of the inner door and eased it open, noticing the tiny squeak of the hinges.

When he'd stepped out of the taxi, he'd felt the heat in the air, even though it was still only mid-morning. The noises of a busy day of work were gathering force.

Yet everything in this room was a contrast to the outside world. It was maybe even a little cold. He took time to look around him, letting his eyes wander over the different corners, taking measured breaths in the peace and stillness. Nothing appeared to have been disturbed. He closed his eyes and tried to identify the different smells, imagining

Marietta sitting at the desk underneath the window.

What would she have done there, at that desk? He tried to build up a picture in his mind. Did she write letters with a fountain pen? Had there been a small vase of fresh flowers, gathered from the garden outside, reflecting their bright colours into the polished surface? Filling the room with the scent of lavender and roses?

He knew too: all this was probably just a romantic image, far from reality and the practical person he knew Marietta to have been. Other than the one that had changed the course of his life all those years ago and the one she'd written to her friend Rosa from Italy, there was very little evidence she was any great writer of letters. He smiled. He could almost see Marietta now, in fits of laughter, looking down on him in this, her room, watching him trying to create imaginary scenes. What would she be saying to him? *Hugo, it was more likely I'd be yelling at someone on the phone because they hadn't turned up with some medication they'd promised. And by the way, I used email and texts, not posh writing paper!*

For no particular reason he could understand, that name came back into his head like an echoed whisper. *Rosa.* Strange, he thought. When words, rather than images, come into your mind, how do they do that? Are those words spoken by your own voice? This word, Rosa, seemed as if it were being spoken in a woman's voice. Was it Marietta's? He tried to remember Marietta's voice, but realized to his dismay that he couldn't. It was only a year ago, but he was unable to bring back the sound of her. What words did she use, what things did she say when they were together, in Italy? How could he recreate her now?

He knew he was becoming too sentimental, too emotional. Because he was here, in this room. Marietta's room, the closest he'd been to her since that day. There was nothing mysterious about Rosa's name coming into his mind like that. Hadn't he just been thinking about Marietta's letter to that very same person?

He had come here for a purpose, and it would be his own wit, not some ghostly voice in his head, that would resolve that. The answer lay in his own hands, no one else's.

On the desk stood the ubiquitous green shaded lamp; he had one himself. He located the switch on the cable, relieved that the power to this room had not been turned off. A circle of gentle amber light served only to emphasize the warmth of the mahogany.

A small ledger lay on the desk. He picked it up and flipped through the pages: only numbers in columns, a standard accounting journal. As he laid it back down, he noticed there was no shiny rectangle underneath where it had sat. Someone had polished this desk and judging by the amount of dust swirling around outside it must have been recently.

He opened the top drawer. Nothing but the normal stationery items to be expected in an office. The lower drawer slid open to reveal an unopened packet of copy paper; a pad of yellow post-it notes, none with anything written on it. Further back, a leather-bound book, with the tail of a red silk ribbon trailing from the bottom edge. He picked it up and opened it. Illegible words, doodles, little sketches of buildings. Quotations, some of which he recognised, presumably copied from other books.

Just before the last written page he saw it. The letter H, and alongside it, his old telephone number in London. Jotted down a long time ago by Marietta, who would have had no idea at the time what the impact would be one day.

He replaced the book and wandered across to the mantelpiece. An old clock, nineteen fifties he guessed, had stopped at just after quarter to twelve. There were no photographs.

In the far corner was an armchair: the type younger people might describe simply as 'old' or 'worn', but which those from an earlier generation would cherish as 'comfortable' or 'cosy'. Next to it, an occasional table with another reading lamp. Along the wall, books of all shapes, sizes and descriptions: travellers' tales, a full set of Dickens. Marquez's epic, the one with possibly the greatest hook of an opening sentence ever written, but a book which he himself had found impossible to finish reading. He ran the tip of his finger along the top. Not a speck of dust here either.

He was certain Paulo would not have allowed anyone inside Marietta's room. Why would he need to anyway, given they were not going to do any work in it for the moment? So was it Paulo himself who'd been preserving this room? He had needed to come here at least once, to find something, anything, that might give him a clue where to find Hugo. But that was months ago. With all the work going on outside the building and people banging around upstairs, even with the doors and windows closed it would have been impossible for it to have stayed like this without someone caring for it.

So what was the sequence of events? Marietta had told Paulo about Hugo after she'd arrived back from San Francisco. Almost certainly, she'd said she'd called him in London, and that they were going to meet in Italy. And after she'd gone there Paulo had never seen her again. But he'd remembered: *Vovó's* friend had been in the financial world and he might be the best person to talk to when Douglas Pereira had come calling. Maybe the only one.

Just the previous evening, after Paulo had dropped him off at the hotel, it had finally dawned on Hugo what it was about Marietta's letter to Rosa that didn't quite fit. *Here we go again*, he'd thought.

And that was one of the reasons he'd wanted to come here today.

Hugo sighed. Whatever it was he was seeking, it was not in here. Marietta's soul had flown and only this deserted room was left behind.

He headed back to the door and stood still, surveying the room one last time. And at that moment, it was as though the clouds in a grey sky had suddenly parted and the sun had pushed its way through. He clapped his hand to his forehead. How could he have been such an idiot? True, he knew now what it was about the letter that was odd, but it was more than that: if Marietta wrote the letter to her friend Rosa, how come Paulo found it here, in this room? How was it the letter wasn't at Rosa's home, wherever it was she lived?

He knew too that all this wasn't desperately important in

the end. It was just a missing piece in the tapestry of their brief time together. 'No big deal' as Paulo might have put it.

But it was important to himself. He would ask Paulo where he could find Rosa.

As he opened the door, it seemed as though the room was pulling him back, desperate for him not to go, not to leave it for someone to come and strip it of its furnishings and its wall coverings and its memories and its life. To stop them carrying away its possessions, Marietta's possessions, and with them any remaining trace of her spirit. He felt the familiar lump in his throat.

Outside, he screwed his eyes up against the brightness of the morning.

He had come here to find Marietta again. In that respect he had failed.

But not completely failed, because there was still Paulo, and there was still him.

43

Hugo's forehead was practically resting on the bars of the gate. At the far end of the gravel driveway, which was lined along both sides with exotic bushes, the walls of a white stuccoed building were doing their best to hide between the trees.

He stood back to survey the black iron gates, which looked as though they had long been crying out for a coat of paint. A small, grey stone plaque, partly obscured by overgrown foliage, peeked out, high up on one of the gateposts. He walked over and stood beneath it, studying the brief inscription. *Nossa Senhora da Piedade.*

He tried to relate the Portuguese words to the Spanish. Lady of something? He knew *piedra* meant stone in Spanish, although *pied* was the French for a foot, wasn't it? Was this woman in some kind of business? Had the taxi even dropped him off at the right place? It was too late now, it was gone.

Underneath the sign was an electric bell push. He held the button down. It struck him as being out of context with the building he could just about see in the distance. A heavy iron bell and a chain would surely have been more fitting, though he realized no one would hear it from the far end of the drive.

A full minute passed, and Hugo was about to push the bell again when he heard hurrying footsteps crunching on the gravel. Moments later, a tiny figure scuttled from the cover of the trees and Hugo decided there must be at least one smaller path merging into the main driveway.

The woman who was approaching the gate now was dressed in a brown and black habit and Hugo's body sagged. He was almost overcome with dismay.

Rosa was in nursing care.

The woman was busy fishing around in her pocket. She produced several keys on a ring, quickly found the right one and inserted it into the lock.

'*Bom Dia*,' she greeted him.

'Good morning, Sister,' he called to her, hoping that was the correct form of address. 'I've come to see Rosa Serafim.'

'Yes, yes, of course.' The frail old woman began tugging the gate and Hugo grabbed hold of one of the bars to push from the outside. 'She is expecting you.' She ushered him in and with both hands and one foot forced the gate closed again.

The closer they got to the front entrance of the house, the stronger was the fragrance drifting through the warm air. Hugo could now see the exotic bushes close up. The spiked leaves of some of the bigger plants looked lethal.

'You were Miss Forsberg's fiancé, were you not? We miss her so much.'

Crackly as the old woman's voice was, its warmth

wrapped itself around him. She clapped her hand to her mouth. 'Dear me, you must forgive me,' she said. 'I haven't introduced myself. My name is Sister Beatrice.' She did not offer her hand as she carried on hobbling in the direction of the door.

The front porch into which they stepped did not lead to the inside of the building as Hugo had expected, but opened out into a glass-covered circular courtyard. He looked around. The place was like a grander version of the terrariums he'd seen in people's houses. Out of the corner of his eye he spotted movement and rushed to catch up with the scurrying figure, heading through a second door.

Now they found themselves inside a brightly-lit atrium, around the walls of which were four doors, all of them closed. In the middle of this room was a simple fountain. The silvery cascade sounded like a musical instrument, beginning its journey as a trickle down from the top, before gathering pace until finally splashing into the waiting depths of the pool below.

'The water is pure,' Sister Beatrice said. 'It runs down through the hills around us.' She waved him towards a lime-green wicker armchair. 'Please, sit. I'll bring you some water.' She giggled as she headed towards one of the rear doors. 'We don't expect our guests to drink from the fountain. I'll let Sister Rosa know you're here.'

'*Sister* Rosa?'

The nun turned and studied the creases in his face. 'You didn't know Rosa is with our Order?'

'No,' he replied. 'Marietta, I mean Miss Forsberg, she never mentioned...'

The woman's voice was as squeaky as the gate. 'We are a Carmelite Order. Our Lady of Mercy.'

Hugo pictured the plaque outside. *Mercy*. That was the word, that was what he'd been searching for.

He crossed to the opposite side of the room. In spite of the greenery surrounding the atrium, he could see that the low brickwork and the wooden frames above it were decaying. At this hour of the morning the room was cool, but it would be too hot to sit in as the day wore on, now the long shadows of winter were being replaced by the early shoots of a South American spring.

He checked his pocket for the letter, then shook his head. Unless it had managed to climb up the pocket, undo the small button at the top and work its way out of his jacket, it would still be there. He slipped it out anyway. Not for the first time, he saw Marietta's spidery handwriting on the envelope, but this time he realized his error. He had thought the abbreviation before Rosa's name was *Sra*, *Senhora*, the title of a married woman. Now, as he inspected the envelope more closely, he understood where he'd gone wrong. The first letter was not an *S* but an *F*; he had missed the tiny horizontal cross line through the curve of the *S*. He took out his mobile phone but, remembering where he was and hearing footsteps approaching, decided to wait until later to check the meaning.

The door through which Sister Beatrice had left the room a few minutes earlier opened again, and another woman wearing the same colour habit entered. Beatrice followed behind, carrying a small tray.

Hugo slipped the envelope back into his pocket and was surprised to feel the whole of his skin prickle.

In contrast to Sister Beatrice's kind but unassuming presence, the woman who approached him now filled the room with light and radiance. Sister Rosa was meadow-fresh and exuded calm. She was taller than Sister Beatrice, but not by much, slim without being skinny. She offered her hand, and when Hugo took it he thought he detected the faintest scent of sandalwood.

'Mr Whiting, it's such a pleasure to meet you. I'm Rosa Serafim.' She gestured to a small table at the far side of the room. 'Please, let us sit down.'

Hugo pulled back a chair, intending it for Sister Rosa, but she took the other one. Sister Beatrice set the tray between them and turned to leave. As the sound of her footsteps disappeared, Sister Rosa searched Hugo's features.

'So, you came then.' Her soft smile remained on her lips.

Hugo hoped he hadn't shown surprise. Sister Rosa's intonation did not betray whether she had just asked him a question or simply made an observation. He decided to err on the safe side and answer.

'Yes, I very much wanted to meet you. I think you already know Paulo... he told me you were a friend of my late fiancée.'

'Marietta came here often,' the nun replied. 'Many times we would just sit and talk, or walk around the gardens. Occasionally we would do some work outside, looking after the flowers and vegetables. At other times we would just simply pray together. She worked so hard with the young children, and I know she regarded our home here as an escape, somewhere she could find peace and friendship.' Sister Rosa's smile broadened as her voice trilled.

'How did you meet Marietta?' Hugo noticed how gentle his own words had become, his voice quiet and relaxed.

'Many years ago she came here.' Sister Rosa's voice rose and fell, as though she were singing a melody. 'Her son had vanished and his wife had been killed, in Mexico. Marietta was finding it difficult to come to terms with things.'

Hugo's lips widened out. 'It was all so sudden, of course.'

'That is so,' the nun replied, 'and as I suggested, Marietta wanted to understand what had happened in her life, and why.' The last word was emphasised.

'Do you mean what happened to Erik and Maria, or other things too?'

Sister Rosa lifted her glass to her lips and sipped water. Again, Hugo was taken aback by the serenity she radiated, her eyes winking back the light which was now beginning to penetrate through the glass roof as the sun edged round.

'You came to see me because you saw Marietta's letter.' Her words pulled him back into the conversation.

'Yes, there was something odd about it.'

Sister Rosa tilted her head slightly, but didn't speak, so Hugo continued. 'It was as if, I don't know quite how to put it, as if she was telling you some news. But somehow, it sounded as though she'd already told you that news. Or was it simply that she'd phoned you before she sent the letter?'

The nun chuckled. 'We don't have telephones here. At least, not in the sense that Marietta would be able to call me very easily. One telephone is essential, and that is in the Sister Superior's office. As you might imagine, we most certainly don't have mobile telephones.' Sister Rosa's eyes drifted to one side. 'Do you know, the priest in the local church here has put a sign on the door. Translated into English, it says *The Lord calls you everywhere. But he certainly won't call you on your cell phone. Please switch it off before you come in.*' She permitted herself another gentle laugh as she returned her eyes to Hugo. 'As I told you, Marietta came here frequently. But when she was away, she used to write to me.'

Hugo retrieved the envelope and placed it on the table, turning it round so the address was facing the nun. 'In this letter Marietta starts off talking about what she's dreamed about all her life and says it's happening at last. But it's as though she knew you would *understand* what she was talking about. It could have been anything, something to do with her job, the charity. Or just that she'd met me again. She never mentions the word marriage. Why wouldn't the first thing she said in the letter be "Hugo and I are going to be married", or something like that?'

Sister Rosa's smile changed almost imperceptibly. Hugo dismissed the vague feeling that she was being ever so slightly mischievous.

'Your adopted grandson told you where he found the letter.'

The thought crossed Hugo's mind that in an age when so many people turn statements into questions, Sister Rosa was inclined to do the opposite. He would have to learn to detect whether she was asking him something or telling him. Again, he elected to reply.

'Yes, he found it in Marietta's sitting room.'

'And that puzzled you.'

'Not at first, but now I've started wondering how it came to be there.'

The smile again, lingering, inviting him to continue with this conundrum.

Hugo looked off to one side, then directly back at her. Then he nodded slowly.

'You put it there...'

Her eyes widened. 'I put it there because I wanted it to be found.'

'For Paulo's benefit, or mine?'

Her voice tinkled again, as musically as the fountain. 'For both of you!' She slipped back the cuff of her wide sleeve to reveal a small wristwatch. 'Hugo... may I call you Hugo?'

He nodded. 'Of course.'

'Would you join us for lunch? It's only a very simple affair, soup, bread, fruit. We can talk later, but now it's almost midday.'

Sister Rosa said Grace, then lifted the lid from the glazed pot. Fragrant steam drifted into the air.

'The vegetables are all from the garden here and we bake our own bread. We have no animals now, so these days a man comes from the local village with cheese, butter and milk.'

'You live a very peaceful life here,' Hugo replied, picking up Sister Rosa's ambiguous intonation. The nun evidently decided it was a statement, and changed the subject. 'Paulo is a fine boy.'

Sister Rosa's capricious manner of speaking had wrong-footed Hugo again. He opened his mouth, then thought better about responding and cast his eyes around the room. Several of the sisters were having their lunch around a much larger table. Clearly this was by no means a silent Order, but their conversation appeared to rumble like a quiet chant. The effect on him was becoming hypnotic, so much so that he hadn't noticed Sister Rosa had continued speaking.

'... I know that from Marietta. I have met the young man twice. For a boy who lived most of his early years on the streets, he's come through remarkably well.' She chuckled. 'Although, when he's found his confidence, he can be quite excitable and given to making rash choices.'

Hugo rested his arm on the low ledge at the side of him, feeling strangely at home in this place, such a contrast from most of the life he'd led in the hustle and bustle of a major city. However short a time it might last, he began to feel that the true peace he and Marietta had enjoyed in Italy was returning.

Not for the first time, Sister Rosa's voice drew him away from his thoughts, although now it seemed as though she had learned to read them too.

'Marietta spoke many times about you. She told me a little about your career, but more than that she spoke of the type of man you were. When she... when the accident happened, I felt that Paulo would benefit from meeting you, so I wrote to him and asked him to come to see me. I wanted to find out how he was coping. He had been very close to Marietta's son and his wife and had suddenly lost them a few years ago. And of course, he'd always been close to Marietta.'

She paused to sip water, then set the glass down. 'The boy's whole life has been like that, of course. Every time he gets to love someone, they are taken away from him. But he is very resilient. He came to see me, and he talked about getting a place at university. I was thrilled for him. After a while, he came to see me again. He wanted to talk about the house, the one he'd stayed in with Marietta. As I think you know, Marietta left the house in her will to a charity, but I don't believe that will was drawn up particularly well. Our legal experts in Brazil are sometimes, shall I say, wanting. I have always suspected the lawyers were at fault but no one will ever know and it's too late now. At any rate, the boy was effectively left homeless again. Perhaps Marietta believed the charity would let him stay there. They did, of course, for a while, but the house was starting to fall to bits and they had no money to sort it out.'

Hugo narrowed his eyes. 'So was that why you left the letter at the house, because you wanted Paulo to find it?'

Sister Rosa's lips flickered, betraying the briefest hint of irony. 'You are very perceptive, Hugo. I wondered if you would work out that the letter couldn't have been the first one. Of course, there were other letters Marietta and I wrote to each other, but, as you detected, the one Paulo found was the second she'd written from Italy.' She smiled. 'A letter that served a second purpose too.'

'It allowed Paulo to find me?'

327

'That was the first purpose.'

Hugo tilted his head. 'So, the second purpose was to let me know there was an earlier letter?'

Sister Rosa beamed a smile and pressed the palms of her hands together.

'Both you and your newly-found grandson are very astute, Hugo. You are meant for each other.'

'So am I also astute in concluding that it was you who kept Marietta's room so spotless?'

Sister Rosa raised her eyebrows. 'I try to do the Lord's work, Hugo. Although I frequently fail, I am not beyond wielding a duster. I can be a Martha as well as a Mary, if you're familiar with that story. But that was only on the one occasion, and it was some while ago. I doubt it would still be spotless on my account. Unless...' She left the sentence unfinished.

Hugo finished it for her. 'Paulo.' He nodded. 'So if I can ask, what happened to the first letter?'

Sister Rosa took a piece of bread and tore it over her side plate.

'Please, enjoy your soup before it goes cold. Afterwards, we can have a wander round the garden, and I'll bring the letter to you.'

44

Paulo's eyes travelled along the tightly packed book-shelves covering the whole of one wall in du Pont's oak-panelled study.

The air was thick with the aroma of pipe tobacco and Paulo imagined there had to be layer upon layer of ash and dust on those books. He couldn't believe the professor would ever deign to take a duster to anything and as far as he knew the university didn't provide cleaners for the tutors' private collections.

Du Pont stretched out his legs. 'So, when are you coming back?'

Paulo's voice was bursting with excitement. 'Very soon, I hope. And listen, thanks for covering for me. Again.'

The professor grunted and rolled his eyes. 'What did you do about your job, at the bar?'

'I passed it on to my pal João,' Paulo said. 'He was grateful for the extra money for a while.'

Du Pont sucked on his pipe, then removed it from his mouth and studied the tobacco in the bowl before opening a drawer and taking out a box of matches. Paulo was certain the law forbade smoking in places like this, but du

Pont was a law unto himself and Paulo wouldn't have wanted to be the person to challenge him about it.

'So what's the agenda now?' The professor didn't look up from his pipe as he spoke.

'We're ahead of schedule on the house. We've got enough capital to do the repairs and renovations, but we don't have any income yet. Pereira's payments cover the interest on the loans, but there's nothing spare. It's only going to be a problem until I'm twenty-one, though, then there'll be no more interest to pay. I'm hoping Douglas might keep the sponsorship running after that, but we'll have to see.'

Du Pont circled a match over the pipe and plumes rose up like smoke signals. He watched Paulo out of the corner of his eye. 'So, how does that work for you? Aren't you going to need to be there yourself, at the house?'

Paulo shook his head vigorously. 'No, I have a girl there who looks after things, keeps the guys in check. I'll go over now and then to see what's happening, but I'll carry on my course here, with your support.'

Du Pont nodded. 'You'll have that. But what then? Aren't you going to join this man Pereira at some point?'

'I don't know yet.' Paulo pretended to scratch his nose, attempting to fend off the first cloud of pipe smoke that was threatening to engulf him, without making it obvious. 'If I do, it will only be as a partner in the business. There's no way I'd work for him. But I am going to need some income of my own at some point.'

'What are you doing for income now?' the professor asked. 'Even assuming you claim your job back, part-time work in a bar can't pay much.' He held up his fingers and counted the points off one by one. 'You've got your course here, then that ramshackle house to fix, plus you're planning to take in street kids, and that will mean you'll have medical bills, and you have to pay your rent. Now and then, if you get time, you might want to eat. How on earth are you going to keep all those plates spinning?'

Paulo grinned. 'Tell you what, Prof, in my *Avô* Hugo's favourite film, there's a line that keeps coming up: *I don't know, it's a mystery.*'

45

'These were Marietta's favourites.' Sister Rosa turned to look back.

Hugo had stopped following her. He was gazing along the displays of plants, tiny bushes, flowers and goodness knew what other specimens of nature, resting on two levels of white wooden shelves to either side of him. It wasn't difficult to see that there was at least another dozen such rows in parallel lines.

A bumble bee drifted across his vision, ignoring these two humans as it went about its business. Sweetness lay in the warmth, a perfume he recognized, though he couldn't call its name to mind.

Sister Rosa hooked the tip of her index finger behind the stem of a delicate, pale purple-coloured bloom. 'This variety of orchid is comparatively rare. Sadly, it's endangered too. I doubt these flowers would survive out in the open, the way their habitat's changing. Not to mention well-meaning people picking them to take home, so they die even more quickly.'

She gestured towards a small wrought-iron table and they sat down opposite each other.

Hugo's brow was wrinkled. 'You know, I'm puzzled about the timing of events, Sister. You said Marietta first came to see you several years ago, after what happened to Erik and Maria. But you must know of course, she and I only met again about a year ago.'

Once again, the nun seemed to be ahead of his thoughts.

'If you're asking me, did Marietta only start talking to me about you after you met each other again, the answer is that she talked about you from the very first day we met.'

Sister Rosa spotted the surprise that crossed Hugo's face and smiled. 'When she came to see me that first time, after what happened in Mexico, she told me about you, how she'd been forced to give up your relationship when you were both very young. How she'd brought up Erik on her own. By that time, you and she had been separated for maybe thirty years, but I knew she had never stopped loving you.'

Hugo nibbled on his bottom lip. 'You said she talked to you about my career, though. But she and I didn't have any contact during all those years. How could she have known?'

Like the exotic flowers by which they were surrounded, it appeared Sister Rosa's beatific smile had many different varieties. This time it portrayed a sympathy that struck Hugo as clearly coming from her heart. 'My dear, did you not understand what I said a moment ago? Marietta never stopped loving you. Even though you didn't know where she was, she knew where you were. She read everything she could find about you. In the later years, of course, she had the internet. But even before that, she would ask her parents about you, tell them to let her know if they heard any news. She knew about your getting married, and later, about your wife's passing. She also knew you and your wife had no children, and she was sad for you. She knew you'd have been a good father.'

'But was there never a time she felt she could get in touch again? We might at least have had some more time together. Things might have been different.'

Sister Rosa closed her eyes for a brief moment. 'Things will only ever be the way they are planned for us. Marietta watched you from afar. When she believed your life was happy, she was happy for you. When she knew you'd be sad, she was sad too. Always, though, there were obstacles. But Marietta was a strong woman. She came into your life and brought you love and joy. Then she left it again. It may have been for only a short time, but you were blessed and privileged to have known her. How you deal with her memory in the future of course is something only you can decide.'

Hugo opened his mouth to speak, but then stopped himself. By the time he'd worked out what he wanted to ask, Sister Rosa had slipped her hand in her pocket and produced an envelope. She held it out across the table.

Hugo studied the writing on the front. There it was again, clearer this time, not *Sra* but *Fra*. And as with the letter inside his pocket, the address was a mailbox number. Hugo pointed at the envelope.

'Sister Rosa, what is this abbreviation, here?'

'It means *Freira*,' she replied. 'Sister.'

He removed the letter between the tips of two fingers

and the nun clasped her hands together on her lap, surveying them as he read.

After a minute, Hugo folded the letter again, and replaced it in the envelope without looking up. Opposite him, Sister Rosa remained absolutely silent, but Hugo felt her gentle but powerful presence, as though she were reaching across and transmitting strength and energy to him at the moment he needed it most.

Avoiding blinking his eyes, Hugo held the envelope out towards her.

Sister Rosa shook her head. 'No, you must keep it. It was Marietta's gift to me. Now it's my gift to you.'

She stood up. 'Before you leave, you must come to see the rest of the treasures here. Many of them were cultivated with Marietta's help and they brought her a great deal of peace. I should like you to see them.'

At the far end of the greenhouse, a side door led to a pathway, which Hugo could see followed the front of the house to join up with the main driveway. It occurred to him that this must have been the path Sister Beatrice had used to come and let him in earlier.

Sister Rosa smiled. 'I am happy you came, Hugo. You will always be welcome to come to see me here if ever you feel it will help.'

At the back of the greenhouse, a door opened, and, as if summoned by some spiritually-transmitted call, the tiny woman appeared again.

Rosa greeted her. 'Ah, Sister Beatrice. Would you be good enough to show our guest to the gate please?' She

335

turned back to Hugo. 'You'll need transport back to your hotel. When you go out through the gate, turn left and then left again where the little lane starts. About a hundred metres along you'll see a house on the right with a taxi parked outside. The man who lives there goes by the name of Edison.' She glanced at her watch. 'He will be just about finishing his lunch at this time and will be expecting to take his siesta. Tell him Sister Rosa sends her best regards and don't listen to him if he complains he's off duty.'

Hugo offered his hand, but Sister Rosa had raised hers to her lips. 'My goodness, how the years catch up on one. I nearly forgot, I have something else here for you.' She began rooting in her capacious side pocket again. 'It's a photograph you might like to have.' She held out a lilac envelope.

Hugo stared at it.

'Of your son, Erik. With Marietta. Wait till you get back to your hotel. It was the only one I found among Marietta's papers when I went over there but possibly the charity people have some others.'

Hugo's features tightened. 'I'm sorry, I don't quite understand. You left Marietta's letter there for me to find. But you took the photo away?'

Sister Rosa's brief nod of the head appeared reproachful. 'One cannot be too careful. Those boys and girls are learning fast, but they're not professional builders. They're working on the bedrooms, above Marietta's study. If they'd come crashing through the ceiling or caused a water pipe to burst, the photograph might have been lost forever. And for all I know it might be the only one of Erik.'

Hugo frowned. 'But they could easily have damaged the letter too.'

'Of course.' Sister Rosa's eyes sparkled. 'But I could always have told anyone who enquired what was in the letter. The photograph could never have been replaced.'

Hugo put his hand on his furrowed brow and rubbed. 'But Sister, what if the letter *had* been damaged? I might well not have come here today.'

She chuckled. 'What little faith you have, my dear.'

Hugo looked up towards the ceiling and began nodding.

'You're right. I suppose it takes time to recover it. So many times I think about how I'm still here to tell the tale. Marietta isn't.'

Sister Rosa reached out and took Hugo's hands in hers, transferring the envelope into them. 'You know, hundreds of years ago there was a scientist, oddly enough, given what I'm about to tell you, from Marietta's own country. He was also a mystic. He published an enormous opus on the subject of angels. Of course, people today would probably laugh at what he said, that's if they could ever be bothered to read such a large work in the first instance. We live in an age where so many people are unable to accept anything they haven't seen with their own eyes. This man though, his name was Swedenborg, believed that each of us has at least two guardian angels looking after us. Unfortunately, they can't always prevent accidents occurring, though they do frequently succeed.' She looked at him directly. 'Maybe your own guardian angels did succeed, Hugo. The challenge for you now is how do you respond to that?'

Hugo held her gaze, seeking answers in her eyes. 'I'm not

sure I understand what you mean, Sister...'

'What I mean is, do you spend the rest of your life reflecting on what happened? Or do you use it as an energy for good, in the future? Through Marietta, other things, other people, have opened up in your life.' She inclined her head. 'You carry her legacy, Hugo. Whether you like it or not.'

Yet again, Hugo opened his mouth to speak but did not trust himself to do so.

Sister Rosa gave him one more display of her serene smile. 'Goodbye, Hugo, and good luck.' She squeezed his hands and released them before turning away.

46

In the small pool of light cast by the table lamp, Hugo opened the last of the three envelopes that Sister Rosa had gone to such lengths to ensure ended up in his hands. Hands that were beginning to shake now, as he held the photograph by the corner and slipped it out.

There, smiling back at him, was Marietta, dressed in an olive-green tee-shirt and khaki-coloured chinos. Standing beside her, a man Hugo guessed must be almost a foot taller. A man accustomed to being out in the open air, face roughened by the sun, deep and lined. Balding a little at the front, with a short beard, wearing a red checked shirt with sleeves rolled half-way up strong forearms. Blue jeans and a genuine smile, instantly reassuring.

His son, Erik.

Behind the two figures, green and purple hills loomed up into a cornflower sky.

Who had taken this photo? Presumably Maria, Erik's wife.

What had Erik missed, this handsome man in front of him now, with his wide-open smile?

What had Hugo lost? Precisely that.

The father and son who never met.

Make-believe images trailed through his mind like the out-takes at the end of a movie. Watching his son struggling to keep his eyes open as his dad read him a story at bedtime. Teaching him to swim, ride a bike. Running alongside, holding the saddle, then secretly letting go, like he'd seen his pals do with their kids. Or simply giving him a hug when he fell and skinned his knees. And, as he grew older, buying him a pint, or sitting beside him on a river bank as they dangled fishing rods into the river on a summer afternoon, listening to the music of Georges Bizet or George Michael drifting from the radio.

In short, the opportunity to watch him develop into the kind soul Hugo knew his son had grown up to be.

Yet Erik's life would have been all so different anyway. He would never have been in South America. But what if he'd had similar ambitions somewhere else? Would he, Hugo, have tried to change his plans, encourage him into a career in business, instead of working for low pay, for the charity? A dangerous job, the complete opposite of what Hugo had thought Paulo might choose.

He placed the photograph carefully on the desk and picked up the letter again.

My dearest Rosa,

I have the most wonderful news to tell you, so forgive me for bowling in straight away in my excitement. Hugo has proposed to me, and at long, long last we are to be married, as soon as we can arrange it.

We met up as planned in Rome. Strange that I should be telling you that he chose a former monastery. I suppose I might have added 'of all places' but then you would probably have replied 'why not?' But Hugo knows nothing of you yet, so was that not an odd coincidence?

Things were desperate at first. I know now that I was naïve to have expected that the past we shared might have helped overcome the awful news I had to give to him. But our lives have passed along separately, if maybe in parallel, and he has had a wife who as you know died, and we were different people from the ones who were so carefree and in love when we were young.

That love hasn't died though, Rosa. He is every bit the man I knew he would become and I hold the hope that he feels the same way about me. At any rate we overcame our differences before it was too late, I'm glad to report.

The thought of our being married is wonderful enough on its own, my dear, but what has brought me even more joy - if that were possible - is that Hugo wants to come to Brazil and get involved with my work there. Despite his career in the financial world (in fact I think because of it) he feels a deep pity and concern for those poor children. How wonderful it would be for us to spend at least a few months in Rio each year as man and wife, working together to help the children. This is my dearest wish and one which I could never have dared ask for, but I hope I am not being too selfish in saying that I think after all that has happened perhaps I am entitled to a little true happiness in my 'mature years'! Hugo laughs when he says he needs something like that to 'cleanse his soul' but I really think he means it. He will also be able to help Paulo - I haven't told him yet about Erik and Maria adopting him. I want that to be a surprise, because Paulo is his son's adopted son, so what does that make him to Hugo? Adopted grandson? No, I don't think so as Hugo hasn't adopted him! Anyway, whatever he's called I'm sure they'll like each other.

As I am also sure that he will like you, Rosa. I have kept you a secret too, so he will have a second surprise when we come over to Nossa Senhora, which we will do as soon as possible after we get to Rio.

Take care my dear friend, I cannot wait for our arrival in Brazil (Hugo has never been there) after our honeymoon, and as a married woman to introduce my new husband to you. I will tell you everything then. That's if you can bear to listen to me babble on - I'm like an excited teenager again.

How lucky we are to have this second chance, Rosa.
I feel so happy. Every day I am reminded that we
only have one life and it really doesn't last very long.
I intend to use what's left of mine (ours!) to make
up for lost time.

My fondest wishes and affection.

Marietta xx

Hugo picked up the photograph again and kissed the images of his fiancée and their son, before sliding both documents into their separate envelopes. They would travel with him wherever he went in the world.

For now, though, the past was the past. He recalled Sister Rosa's words. *Do you use it as an energy for good, in the future?*

47

Paulo called early the next day.

'It's your birthday on Sunday, *Avô.*'

Hugo paused for a second then stared into space, shaking his head. 'You know, I'd completely forgotten.'

'I got a reminder on Facebook.'

How on earth did I not think of that? Hugo thought, but didn't say.

'I've got a couple of surprises for you. How'd you fancy lunch up in the mountains?'

'Sounds wonderful.'

'I'll pick you up at ten, outside the hotel. Can you make sure you're on time?'

Hugo almost gasped. Mr Last Minute Dot Com was telling him not to be late. He managed to swallow his words before they could come tumbling out.

For once, Paulo was on time, and an hour later they'd climbed up through the mountains in Paulo's protesting motor car.

At the end of another, but this time much wider, pot-holed track, the Nissan came to a halt alongside a corrugated iron hanger. Hugo followed Paulo through a door and his eyes widened as he found himself in the middle of some kind of shop. It was filled with sports clothes of every description and colour, hanging from every wall and on racks.

'Hey, Paulo!' The bellow was followed by an enormous bearded man, dressed in a Hawaiian shirt and baggy shorts, who had emerged from the far end of the shop. The two of them slapped high fives and Paulo rested his hand on Hugo's arm. 'Rikki, this is my grandfather, Hugo.'

'Great to meet you, man!' Rikki roared, slapping Hugo on the back and causing Paulo to turn away in embarrassment. 'Dude, you're in for some fun today! Come on, we're all ready for you.'

Before Hugo had a chance to ask what they were ready for, a dark-haired boy who couldn't have been five feet tall arrived. 'Hello, sir, I'm Jorge, your instructor for today.'

Hugo shook the boy's outstretched hand. 'Instructor for what?'

'Paragliding, sir.'

'*Paragliding?*' Hugo pointed at him. 'And you're the instructor? How old are you?'

Jorge affected a look of much-put-upon patience. 'I'll be seventeen in January, sir.'

It was too late now. Rio de Janeiro was spread out below them and they were stepping into the sky.

One almost imperceptible jolt and the big sail above them settled into position, as did Hugo, despite a brief twinge in his shoulder.

Now, they were gliding like some huge red and white striped bird as, in every direction, the landmarks of Rio de Janeiro revealed themselves. Copacabana, Ipanema, Sugar-loaf Mountain and the cable car that took tourists up to the great statue he'd seen from an aeroplane not that long ago. When Hugo looked up, the white-tipped edges of the sail ruffled back at him.

'Look! Over there!' Jorge was yelling above the roar of the wind, pointing with his gloved hand. 'Guanabara Bay.'

A sudden gust swung them like a pendulum but Jorge steered the glider back on course. Down below, Hugo could see the tops of the skyscrapers bordering the coastal resort. Ahead, the sea rolled towards the golden sand like a pure green silk carpet, white ridges combing its surface.

He remembered the dreams he'd had as a boy. In those dreams, he'd been able to fly, climbing towards the cotton-wool clouds in the sky. Soaring over buildings made tiny by perspective, floating over fields and cars and people reduced to tiny specks. Seeing everyone and everything while he himself remained invisible.

Now here was his dream, come to visit him in real life.

Jorge tapped Hugo on the shoulder and pointed off to the side. Close by, another glider was tracking them. Someone was waving, turning in towards them. Jorge held up a hand in acknowledgement.

Paulo had joined them, riding alone, and Hugo realized he must have been drifting behind them all the way.

Side-by-side, like migrating birds, they swept along on the currents, marvelling in each other's companionship, even at a distance. Now swooping, now steadying, arcing from one direction to the other.

Another memory flashed into Hugo's mind, a passage written by one of his favourite authors. In the book, someone had been doing something just like this. Was it paragliding, hang gliding? He couldn't recall. But he did remember the eagle that appeared, following the glider through every descent, every rise and turn. Climbing away and bidding its farewell only when the craft began its final descent towards the safety of land.

There was no eagle here with them today.

Yet something else, just as marvellous, had come in its place.

And suddenly, as if the Universe had opened up its greatest secrets to him, he saw it all as it was meant to be, as clear as the sky he was racing through and the ocean that awaited him ahead.

That was how it had happened.

Himself and Marietta. Marietta and Erik. Erik and Paulo. Paulo and himself.

The circle was complete, and because it was so, he in turn had opened up to the Universe and whatever it wanted him to be.

48

Paulo had not quite finished with the birthday surprises. Afterwards they returned together to *Casa Marietta*.

Everywhere, the acrid tang of emulsion had driven out the smell of dry chalk. The hole in the wall, which Hugo had passed through on his previous visit, was now hung with a clean, stripped pine door and, behind it, oak stairs, painted white, led the way to a long corridor above.

Paulo waved an outstretched arm. 'This is where the bedrooms will be. We're getting stuff to put on the walls to brighten it all up. Some of the kids do paintings and things.' One by one, he pushed open every door, seven in all, each one revealing newly plastered walls ready for painting. Hugo knew instinctively that Marietta's bedroom had gone forever and had expected that. Paulo had left enough of her spirit elsewhere in the house.

They went back downstairs by a door at the opposite end of the corridor, arriving into another large room which Hugo could see adjoined the main one. This area had been laid out with long tables and chairs.

Hugo stood and stared. 'Where did you get all those from?'

Paulo grinned. 'You'll never guess. From a friend of Douglas. I rang Douglas the other night and told him you were going into the lawyers' offices to sign his investment management contract. He's been getting a bit itchy about it, giving me a lot of hassle. Anyway, he was over the moon when I gave him the news and he told me about this pal of his who owned a restaurant. Apparently, it's gone into liquidation and the bank's foreclosed. The place was stacked up with tables and chairs and Douglas's mate said the bank wouldn't be bothered about them. I got the feeling the guy was so mad with the bank he didn't give two hoots either way.'

Hugo smiled, wondering whether Paulo was picking these expressions up from him. At least they were cleaner than his usual ones.

'We're going to have a ping-pong table over there.' Paulo pointed towards the far end of the room. 'Then behind the building we'll have the football pitch. I'm chasing the uni for some nets and balls and things.'

They headed back across the front room and stepped outside through the main porch. Hugo turned back to gaze up at the building, then looked round at Paulo, shaking his head.

'I hardly know what to say. You've done an incredible job, you and your pals from the street.'

For a moment his face tightened. 'I suppose I'm going to have to face it sometime or other though. What have you done with…?' He lifted his arm and pointed, as if over the roof to the back of the building.

'… *Vovó*'s room? Nothing. For one thing, we haven't had

349

time. But in any case, it needs sorting out properly. I could ask Rosa, but it'd be better if you did it. You could do the design too if you wanted.'

Hugo nodded and tapped Paulo's arm. 'Listen, I've got something else to tell you.' He put his hand in his side pocket and pulled out a key fob. 'Before you start protesting, it's already done, it'll be standing outside the hotel when we get back. Even if you still say you don't need a new car, I'm not going anywhere in that old banger of yours again. Ever.'

Paulo took the fob Hugo was holding towards him and stared at the maker's insignia. He closed his eyes, and when he opened them again he stepped forward and hugged Hugo. 'That's really awesome, *Avô*. Honestly, you didn't need to, I'm fine.' He allowed a smile to break through. 'I am grateful, though, especially as you keep complaining about your shoulder an awful lot. I can't wait to see it.'

Hugo rolled his eyes. 'Think of it as being as much for me as for you.'

As they walked towards the side of the house, Paulo turned to face Hugo. He was still flushed. 'I don't want you to think I'm being ungrateful about the car, *Avô*. You're right, mine is a wreck. I'll give my half to my pal, the one I share it with.'

'Good,' Hugo replied. 'He can join the two halves together again. I'm sure he'll be your friend for life.'

'It's just, I worry about my pals. They've no chance of having anything like that themselves.'

As they reached the low gate to the compound, Hugo stopped and put his hands on Paulo's shoulders. 'Can I just say one thing to you?' He stared straight into Paulo's eyes, then turned him round and pointed at the building they'd just left. 'None of this would have existed if it weren't for you. Don't ever be ashamed of what you have, so long as you acquired it honestly and you don't rub it in other people's faces. If you think about it, without all this you've created, there'd have been nowhere for those kids to come. Nobody to give them food, look after them when they're ill. And you couldn't have done this without all the effort you put in. At the university, working at the bar, all that clever business you did with Douglas – which still makes me laugh every day, by the way. *You* made all this happen. And you've given those kids hope for the future. It's an example for them, of what *they* can achieve. Something "one of their own" managed to do.'

Hugo gestured to the garden gate. 'End of speech. Let's go and see what it is you want to show me.'

Paulo led the way through the archway, now partially covered on both sides with newly-planted jasmine and bougainvillea. Hugo knew that when these plants were in full bloom their flowers would produce a contrast of purple and white, and the jasmine would release its unique, heady perfume. Just as it did in his own garden, back in Spain.

On the other side of the archway, Hugo came to a sudden halt. He stared, mouth open. Right in the middle of the rich, black earth he'd seen on his previous visit, a small sculpted fountain stood resplendent, surrounded by flowers with deep brown and orange blooms. He knew immediately where he'd seen this fountain before, or something remarkably like it.

'I wanted to have the water running before you got here.' Paulo's voice cut into his thoughts. 'Only I couldn't get the guy who does the plumbing over here till next week.'

Hugo's jaw had dropped. 'Isn't this the fountain from the convent?'

Paulo laughed. 'Not that one, but yes, it's exactly the same. Sister Rosa let Alanza sit in there one afternoon and sketch it. She said she got some funny looks from the nuns, sitting there in her ripped jeans and yellow football shirt. I told her not to smoke any spliffs while she was in there!'

Behind the fountain, the wooden stakes Hugo had seen on his earlier visit rose up, but a plaque now hung from chains on each side.

Hugo read the inscription, which looked as though it had been burned into the wood: *Os Jardins do Salvador*. The Gardens of the Saviour.

Or, of a great friend who unfortunately couldn't be here today. Take your pick.

'Now come and have a look at this, *Avô*.' Hugo turned to see Paulo heading back out of the compound and followed him through the low gate.

Minutes earlier, after he'd stepped out the house through the front porch and turned back to admire it, Hugo had half noticed an unpainted door, left standing against the wall to the right of the entrance. He'd thought nothing of it. Now, Paulo was shifting the door to one side, revealing a paint-covered sheet that must once have been white, hanging from two nails driven into the wall.

Like an over-officious wedding photographer positioning an unruly guest for a shot, Paulo placed his hands on Hugo's upper arms and turned him to face the sheet. 'Just stand there, *Avô*.'

Hugo turned his head away to hide the smile that crossed his face as he witnessed the young man's developing confidence.

Paulo stood to one side of the draped sheet and pulled at it. It dropped to the floor.

Underneath was a rectangular plaque which was entirely covered with pebbles of different shapes and sizes, although most were a slate grey colour. A mosaic had been created by working in a number of lighter, sandy-coloured stones to form words.

Hugo read aloud.

Bienvenue Chez Nous
Une Maison Remplie de Vie

Hugo glanced sideways at Paulo. '*Welcome to our house, a house*... my French is a little rusty, what's *remplie*...?'

'Like, full...'

'Ah, so, *a house full of life*. That's nice.'

Paulo held up a finger. Careful not to stand in front of the mosaic, he reached across the plaque and picked at one of the pebbles. Like a magician delivering his final trick, he held his hand up. Hugo saw that between his thumb and forefinger he was holding one of the darker coloured pebbles between which the lettering was worked.

'Look at it again now, *Avô*. Go a bit closer.'

Hugo took a step forward and bent to see the mosaic

better. He could now make out a letter *D*, painted on the surface of the brickwork in the gap where the extracted pebble had been.

Paulo was holding up the pebble in his hand. 'Bet you can't guess which pebble this is.'

Hugo's eyes widened. 'Not...?'

'Right first time, *Avô*. The one you gave me...'

'From the river, in Spain...?'

Paulo turned it round in his fingers and laughed. 'Look, it's got a bit of Blu-tack on it, but we'll fix it properly soon.'

Hugo turned back to the ornate design on the plaque. 'So, by taking that pebble out, you've changed what it says.'

'It wasn't really *my* idea,' Paulo said. 'It was du Pont's, my professor. He's French. *Vie* in French means...'

'... life. I know that much. But now with the D exposed it reads *Vide*.'

'Emptiness.' Paulo emphasised the word with a clenched fist. 'You remember you told me something like, if the river represented eternity, one person's life was about the size of...' He held up the pebble, turning his head to one side and raising his eyebrows as though inviting Hugo to answer a question.

'Right, so once you take that out, instead of saying *A House Full of Life*, it says *A House Full of Emptiness*.'

Paulo nodded. 'Not the best grammar, du Pont says, "full of emptiness", but that's what happens. Without the person, life turns into emptiness. And the pebble represents the person.'

Hugo pointed towards Paulo's hand. 'And that pebble there represents you, because it's the one I gave you.'

'Well, not just me. It could have been any pebble in that river. It can be anyone.'

Hugo had shed many tears in his life. Enough, too, during the last few months. It had taught him that if you keep your eyes wide open, don't blink, the tears don't break loose. Then maybe people don't see that you're crying.

Paulo saw. He turned away and fiddled around much longer than he needed to fix the pebble back in its place, with its little bit of sticky blue putty.

49

Paulo sat at the desk that had once been Marietta's, gazing out at the expanse of grass.

The tournament was in full flow. Spring had arrived, and through the open window Paulo could hear the children's excited shouts.

One of the boys had the ball in his hands and was trying to force it down a few yards from the goal. Another was trying to wrestle it out of his arms. A third, older boy approached and spoke to both of them. Paulo watched him pat downwards in a gesture of calmness, which seemed to succeed in commanding the attention of the other two. Moments later, the first boy handed the ball to the older one and the game was restarted with a bounce-up.

Paulo was startled out of his trance by a knock at the door. A mop of black hair poked round it, and a thin young man entered the room. Roque, one of Paulo's brothers, had turned up in the City Hospital two months earlier, rushed there after an overdose of methamphetamine, crystal meth. Afterwards, he'd been referred for counselling and was living at *Casa Marietta* and being looked after night and day by Paulo and his friends from the street.

'Hey, Pauli. There's a parcel for you.' He held it out and Paulo took it from him.

'*Obrigado, amigo.*'

'*Magina.*' No worries.

'How you feeling, Bro?'

'Man, I'm still getting a lot of headaches, but I don't shake so much anymore. I can light my own cigarette now.'

Paulo grinned and slapped hands with him. His brother would be okay, he'd make sure of it.

When Roque had closed the door behind him, Paulo put the parcel on the desk and sat down. He reached into the side drawer and pulled out the paper knife Marietta had used to open letters. Carefully slitting the tape round the package, he pulled the flaps away to reveal thin, creamy-coloured paper, held together in the middle by a tiny slip of transparent adhesive tape. He reached back into the drawer for a pair of scissors and snipped it.

He knew what he would find inside the package. He lifted out the book, smiling at the image of a cottage under a setting sun. In the background, a calm sea nestled under an orange and brown sky. Tiny white writing along the bottom edge of the cover revealed the book's title: *The Pebble*. Then followed the author's name: the man Paulo had adopted as his grandfather, to replace the one he'd never known.

Paulo pulled away the small envelope taped loosely inside the flap of the packaging. It wasn't sealed. He slid out the letter, which was written in Portuguese.

This is a translation.

My dearest grandson, Paulo,

*Just as you once did, I must apologize that this letter,
originally written by me in English, has had to be
passed through a translator. In this case the task was
carried out by an employee of my publisher in London,
who comes from Lisbon, so it should make some sense!*

*As you can see, I finally finished my novel. This is the
first copy anyone has had, as it doesn't go on sale till next
month. You will remember my attempt at writing a
book started with a story about a lottery winner, and I
still have hopes to write that book one day. The one I
have enclosed, though, is a story about an old man and
a young man who meet by sheer fate. The young man is
a product of the streets of a big city, the old man,
someone who has led a life dominated by material
things. A certain event which took place years before the
story starts has changed the old man's attitude forever,
and, as a result, his life improves beyond recognition.
When he meets the young man, he realizes that here is a
person who is seeking a life similar to the one he himself
lived. He does not want to say as much, but he is
concerned that someone else should end up making the
same mistakes. So, little by little, he tells his own story,
and the young man listens...*

I can't think where I got that idea, but you'll notice each time you lift the book up that a person's life isn't very heavy!

I won't tell you any more than that as it will spoil the story if you have time to read it. Suffice it to say, you might recognize some events in the book. I hope you will enjoy it.

Now I must tell you that I have made a lot of decisions recently, the first of which is that I am going to sell my house in Granada and return to live in London. All good things must come to an end. I will miss the rivers and I will miss Toni and 'the crowd' but I have other things to do in my life, what's left of it – and I'm hoping that's a fair bit yet. My plan is to do some work with two different charities, both of which look after young people who, for one reason or another, are homeless. You see, they may be of a different nature, but Britain has similar problems.

I am also going to come to Rio twice a year and assist you with Casa Marietta, if you'll allow me. I have met someone (more about that another time) who's a retired doctor and who will be very happy to come with me, to help in your medical rooms.

Before then, though, I need to ask you something, and if you don't want to get involved in this I will fully understand. But I was in London recently and I have been talking to a journalist there who has written several books about South American gangs. He has been to Mexico many times and one of his books was about a well-known gang boss. Anyway, the guy knows his stuff alright and has survived a lot of dangerous situations. Now, after making some enquiries, he's discovered that about the time Maria was killed and Erik disappeared in the raid on the Red Cross camp, there was a serious crash involving a truck not far from that area. It went off the road after police officers opened fire on it. It seems there were some survivors but at the moment it's not clear what happened to them. To be straight with you right now, Paulo, I don't want to build your hopes up (mine neither). The odds are overwhelmingly that your adopted father, my son, is dead. However, as long as we both accept that, maybe we have little to lose by following up this lead. Hopefully it will not be a dangerous expedition for us as we'll be going straight to Mexico City and should not have to journey far from there. We will also link up with the journalist and his Mexican contact when we get there. But if nothing else, if we can only find out where Erik is buried, it will be something, and I already know for certain we have Marietta's blessing.

If you feel up to joining me on this quest, let me know and we can discuss the travel details.

On a lighter note, I want to get back to that earlier book, and for many reasons it's easier to do that in

London. I never did sell my home there, as I'd planned. After your Vovó died, I lost the heart to do that, and decided to rent it out. The tenants have just given notice, so now is a good time.

In the meantime, I hope you and Roque and your friends and 'residents' are doing well and that you are keeping that fellow Douglas under control!

We will, I am sure, speak soon.

    Lovingly,

    Your Avô, Hugo

Paulo picked up the book and ran his fingers across the front cover, before opening it. Then, page by page, he scanned the text until he came to one that contained only these lines:

This book is dedicated to Marietta Forsberg, who taught me what life is really for.

And to Paulo, who gave me the courage and determination to pass the lessons on.

Outside, the youngster who'd been demanding the ball earlier had finally succeeded in striking it past the goal-keeper, high into the back of the net, and was performing an elaborate and noisy celebration. Just as he must have seen his heroes do on television.

Paulo smiled and stood to close the window.

Then he picked up the telephone on the desk and began to dial.

ACKNOWLEDGEMENTS

Special thanks to my wonderful editors Claire Wingfield and Philippa Donovan, and to Holly Seddon, who took time away from writing yet another bestseller to provide additional, and valuable, input.

I am indebted to John Bailey, that doyen of the fishing world – or is it the angling world? – for all his detailed and patient explanations on the ins and outs of fly fishing in Spanish rivers. As a very famous actor – coincidentally referred to in this book – claims he didn't really say: 'Not a lot of people know that!'

Incidentally, the bar and restaurant run by Toni in this story exist, very close to one of those rivers, although to the best of my knowledge there is no Toni there.

Thanks to Jacqueline MacDonald-Lowe for medical insights and support and to David Chambers for keeping my description of paragliding on course, just as he does with the real airborne crafts he loves so much.

My gratitude to everyone who supported me through the difficult times when it looked like Marietta and Hugo's love story might not see the light of day. Some of you might detect echoes of yourselves in the book. If we know each other, these are most likely intentional!

I was given willing help by *Task Brasil* and *Streetchildren UK* when the story took us to Rio de Janeiro and also – though I doubt I'll ever be able to let him know – a young man named Hamilton. He appears in *Hamilton's Story* (ticktock Media Ltd, 2005), a short book from which more fortunate pupils of British schools can get an idea of the horrors of life for children living on the streets of major cities all around the world.

With renewed love and gratitude to my wife Ann for her continued patience when the time inevitably arrives for me to put abstract ideas into written form.

Finally, thank you to my agent Tom Cull for all his support and perseverance. We got there in the end!

Philip Platts, July 2022